THE JAGUAR QUEEN

PRAISE FOR BETSEY KULAKOWSKI AND THE VERITAS CODEX SERIES

"Realistic heroes and villains. International intrigue. More plot twists than a cup of nightcrawlers. Betsey has definitely raised the bar [in *The Jaguar Queen*]."

— J. DON WRIGHT, AUTHOR OF *BEHOLD!*

"The Jaguar Queen keeps the momentum going in the Veritas Codex series. I am becoming very invested in the team of Lauren, Rowan, Bahati and Jean-Rene. "

— DONNA KEY

"I couldn't put [*The Veritas Codex*] down! I knew halfway through that it was going to be a late night because I couldn't quit turning the pages. I can't wait for the next book in the series."

— LISA SMALLWOOD

"I enjoyed [*The Veritas Codex*]. The writing is well done. I really liked the characters. It kept me engaged to the point I was speed reading (to find out what was going to happen) and I had to slow myself down!"

— TERRI FOLKS

"Loved it, very engrossing and well written!"

— KRISTY DEWBERRY

THE JAGUAR QUEEN

BETSEY KULAKOWSKI

For Dwayne, Ian and Rachel. Thank you for always supporting me and encouraging me to achieve my dreams.

Some say the world will end in fire,
Some say in ice.

—Robert Frost

PROLOGUE

"Think anyone will miss these?" Matt asked as he came into the lab carrying a crate from the antiquities room.

"What's this?" Dr. Enrique DeLaFuentes glanced up at his research assistant.

"I found some more pieces in the warehouse we can... fence," the assistant said, lowering his voice. "You want to see?"

"I do not," the professor snapped. "I told you. I can't be associated with this little side project you have going."

"And I thought we were a team." Matt smirked.

"You know I can't ..." Dr. DeLaFuentes scowled, sitting back from his work. "And you know why."

"I get it," Matt said, glancing up as there was a shuffle at the door. Voices from the hallway alerted them. The two men exchanged fearful glances and DeLaFuentes nodded at him to move on. Matt quickly retreated to the desk at the back of the lab, trying to melt into the shadows as he booted up the computer and slunk back behind the monitor. The last thing he needed was to get in trouble with the Dean. Dr. DeLaFuentes returned his attention to his work.

"Enrique," Dr. Alvarado said as he came into the lab. "Dr.

DeLaFuentes? You were expected in my office at 10:00. We had a meeting."

The professor looked up from the worktable where he sat hovering over scraps of an ancient document. He seemed surprised to find anyone in the room, much less his boss. The oculus of the jeweler's loupe made his left eye appear grotesquely oversized. He looked lost, oblivious to his surroundings.

"Our meeting isn't until Thursday." Enrique DeLaFuentes grunted.

"Today *is* Thursday," Alvarado snapped.

"Oh," he just shrugged. He returned his attention to his work.

"Excuse me?"

"Huh?" The professor looked up, still oblivious to his boss' anger or the reason for it.

"What are you looking at that is so important that you chose not to show up for a mandatory meeting?"

"The Codex." He grunted, drawn back to the document.

Alvarado's brow lifted. "Which one?"

"Grolier." He answered curtly.

"Bah! Everyone knows, the Grolier Codex is a fake! Some clever forger was trying to intimate something he saw on a Maya calendar somewhere." Suddenly the administrator seemed more interested in the work than some stupid meeting.

DeLaFuentes' head shot up and his eyes narrowed. "I disagree. I don't think it is a fake—and I can prove it." The professor shook his head. If the Dean wanted a fight, he'd give him one. "Look." He slid back off the stool and handed the loupe to his doubting colleague.

The document on the table was in bad shape. Large sections were missing, and the edges where the pages had crumbled away were browned and faded from the intrusion of water. The tallest fragment might have measured 17 centimeters at best, while the width was little more than 12 centimeters. It was no grand grimoire, but the line drawings of Maya gods reflected the art of the ancient era, influenced by the work of the Toltec and other tribes that battled for authority in the region. "It references the *star* of Venus, which would have been visible in the region. Similar references have been found in other murals in the Yucatán. There are deities that are known, such as the Death God you see here, and this…" His hand moved to the other side of the page. "The Jaguar Queen, a goddess who fell from the stars and became one of the greatest Queens of the ancient era." DeLaFuentes pointed. "Before she was sacrificed to the gods."

"Sacrificed?"

"You know about the blood rituals, right?"

"Yes of course. They were intended to give back to the gods what the gods had given."

"Well, when famine and war decimated the region, the Jaguar King realized he had to give her back to the gods," DeLaFuentes said.

Alvarado studied the images amazed they were still legible, considering the thousands of years they had spent lost beneath the consuming jungle, followed by another decade of hanging on the wall in a cantina in a cheap picture frame. The smell of moldering earth and cigarette smoke lingered as they both leaned over and inspected it.

"What is it I am looking at, Enrique?" Alvarado groused, thoroughly inspecting the document with the loupe. "Ink? What's the big deal about the ink?"

"Look past the ink," he said. "That's not the real treasure here. What do you see?"

"I see plaster, what looks like surgically precise cuts … like scalpel marks."

"It's what you can't see that is truly spectacular," Enrique said. "I've conducted a full chemical analysis of the page. It contains only minerals used prior to the European conquest of the Americas. There are no modern inorganic materials.

There's nothing here that would contradict the fact that this codex is authentic."

"But what about these cuts? Looks like modern tooling. The water staining at the edges?"

"Induced degradation. Cracks in the gypsum plaster used to prepare the surface of the document prior to painting." DeLaFuentes growled. "Look, all the figures conform to the use of sketch and gridlines we typically see in Maya murals." There was a long pause as DeLaFuentes sat stewing. "You know if this document had been found in a library or a museum, we wouldn't be having this conversation and I wouldn't have to justify my research to anyone. But just because someone framed it and hung it on the wall in a bar, suddenly *my* credibility comes into question."

"So what does it mean?" Alvarado sat back and waved his hand over the page.

"Radiocarbon dating places the Grolier Codex at approximately 1230."

Alvarado turned and arched a curious brow at the much older scientist. "Did you say 1230? Pre-Columbian?"

"Give or take 110 years, plus or minus."

"No modern pigments are found here. This is the traditional Maya ink seen in other codices. It's exceedingly difficult, if not impossible to reproduce ancient inks using modern ingredients."

"But … if … *if* it's authentic, that would make this one of the oldest Maya codices ever found in Meso-America."

"*The* oldest Maya codex … the *only* pre-Columbian codex discovered in the course of the 20th century." DeLaFuentes corrected him. "And there are no *ifs* about it. It is genuine. And this codex can help prove my theory." Alvarado glanced up at him. "The Maya were not *indigenous* to Meso-America."

"Not indigenous? What do you mean not indigenous? Where did they come from?"

"It's no coincidence that Maya temples are very much like those in Angkor Wat or Egypt."

"Interesting theory, Doctor." His boss sniffed. "But it will have to wait for another day."

DeLaFuentes' heavy brow joined into a unified line of bushy gray over his eyes and nose.

"This so-called Apocalypse is coming," the boss said. "The field research teams have been selected to go to Chichén Itzá and assignments have been made. You missed last week's meeting too. So, you will remain here and help the field research teams on the back end. Dr. Acela will need your help gathering equipment and getting everything ready for the team. Dr. Bechtler and Dr. Haas have teams going to Tikal to examine the structure his team found with the LIDAR. You will also have to fill in and lecture for Dr. Soto's class. Her undergrad students aren't eligible to conduct field research. It's a new cohort and they don't have enough education or experience in the field."

DeLaFuentes was about to protest when the computer beeped, and a shuffling noise followed. Alvarado's eye was drawn to the back of the lab. "Who's back there?"

The assistant popped up, busted. "I'm Matt ... Matt Iago," he said with an awkward wave. "I'm ..." His eyes darted to Professor DeLaFuentes.

"He's my research assistant." DeLaFuentes snapped.

Alvarado fixed his eye on him, sharply. "Aren't you a little old to be a research assistant?" Alvarado took a verbal swipe at him, even though they were about the same age.

"He's a grad student ..." DeLaFuentes defended.

"I'm a late bloomer." Iago added with a wry grin.

Alvarado stood and scowled at the assistant who stood transfixed, looking like a frightened deer in the headlights. Alvarado caught DeLaFuentes by the lapel of his moth-eaten old lab coat and all but drug him out to the doorway. "The reason I wanted you in my office this morning was to speak with you about the artifact log."

"What about it?"

"You've signed out nineteen different artifacts in the past two weeks," he said. "Why do you need so many?"

"I'm a research scientist," DeLaFuentes said, as if that were sufficient.

"You know the rules," Alvarado spat. "One artifact at a time."

DeLaFuentes' eyes shifted side-to-side before he puffed up. His color rose until his cheeks and eyelids were almost purple. "But ... but ..." he sputtered. "I am a tenured professor! I will not be micromanaged like a stupid lab assistant!"

Alvarado held up a finger. "The rules apply to everyone, even tenured professors."

DeLaFuentes' upper lip rolled up and his mustache looked like a writhing wooly caterpillar beneath his wide, flat nose as he sneered. "Fine." He spat, resigning indignantly. "But I expect to be assigned to field work just like all the snot-nosed brats in this department!"

"You'll get field work when I say you get field work," Alvarado stated flatly. He turned and walked away. "And make sure all those artifacts on your work bench are returned to the vault immediately," he called back.

Matt was standing at the work bench with the crate in front of him, waiting for the tirade to end, but DeLaFuentes made a beeline for him. He was furious with the assistant. "Are you trying to get me fired? *You* signed out artifacts under *my* name, didn't you?"

"Not all of them." He held up his hands defensively. "And all the ones I signed out under your name I put back. I might be a lab assistant, but I am not stupid!"

"If you blow this, I will cut your throat myself," DeLaFuentes said.

"But Professor." The student gulped. "I was incredibly

careful. I checked to see what Dr. Soto and Dr. Bechtler's teams were studying. I pulled artifacts related to their work. No one's going to catch us. I told you. We're going to get rich. No one is going to find out. We're smarter than all of them."

DeLaFuentes scowled.

"You know they don't appreciate you." Matt softened his tone. "You've worked your whole life for this University and what have they ever given you? Nothing. They don't pay you a fair wage. They don't respect you. You are the pre-eminent expert on the Maya here, and yet they're not even taking you to Chichén Itzá on the eve of what is being touted as the end of the world—the Maya Apocalypse? They probably won't even give you a lousy gold watch when you retire."

"This is all true." The older man's anger seemed to flame out and he sunk to the stool by the work bench. The chip on his shoulder, however, weighed heavily on him. "I should be leading that team."

"Yes you should. Meanwhile, all that ancient treasure sits down the hall gathering dust. Just imagine how much money one postage-stamp size fragment of that codex would bring. More than this stupid relic." He picked up a ceramic tile with a Maya glyph carved into its surface. "This is your chance to share our Maya culture with the world, and... get what's coming to you. You know you deserve it."

"You're right," DeLaFuentes stood. Resolve spread over his haggard face. "I do deserve it."

"Damned right you do." Matt patted him on the shoulder. *And so do I.*

MATT WAS BROODING WHEN HE RETURNED TO THE ANTIQUITIES room with the crate of pieces he'd planned to abscond with. He sat the crate down on a workbench next to the sign out sheet. He glanced at the log. As he inspected it, he noticed that he wasn't the only one signing out multiple pieces at the same time. He scowled as he debated what he was going to do now. He'd been skimming obscure pieces here and there for the past few months. He knew a guy who'd take them and sell them to collectors for a small commission. Then he'd tell the crusty old professor he'd made half that, and they'd share the rest, fifty-fifty. Of course he was really getting 70 percent. But the way Matt saw it, he was taking all the risk. Why shouldn't he get the lion's share? Besides, he needed the money to finance a bigger project.

This little ruse was all part of his master plan to get back to Chichén Itzá. He hoped this Maya Apocalypse foolishness combined with DeLaFuentes' expertise would be his golden ticket. Alone, he was little more than a tourist. A tourist who had to buy a ticket and stay with a group and a lame tour guide. He needed full access to the site, one without prying eyes or incessant questions.

"Hey!" A voice found him lost in thought. He nearly startled out of his skin.

"Oh, hey, Ria." He picked up the crate.

"You got told to put back all the extra artifacts too?" Ria asked. She was Dr. Soto's lab assistant. She had several items of her own to check in.

"Yeah," Matt said. "Like what difference does it make?"

"Well I heard someone's been stealing and selling artifacts on the black market," she blabbed.

Matt turned sharply. "What?" He drug the word out, trying to come off as completely stunned.

"I know, right?" She bought his act, he was sure.

"How do you know this?"

"I overheard Dr. Alvarado talking to Dr. Soto yesterday."

"Who do they think would do that?" He crossed his arms and ran his thumb over his lower lip as he eyed her. His mind was awash with panic.

Ria hesitated, looking over her shoulder to make sure she

wasn't overheard. "The only name I heard mentioned ... was DeLaFuentes. You know him better than anyone. Do you think he could do something like that?"

Matt looked over the bin in front of him. His eye found the ceremonial dagger he already had a buyer for. "Who would want to take these ... these beautiful pieces? I mean ... this is our history."

Ria leaned in to inspect the tray and a flicker sparked in her eye. Her gaze lifted to match his. Her face went blank as if she were trying to hide the pieces she had just put together. Matt's smile faded just as quickly as her's did. Her finger raised weakly, pointing at him. "You ..." she started, but she didn't finish.

Like a jaguar striking, Matt turned sharply, moving so fast she never saw it coming. The obsidian blade, though ancient, was plenty sharp enough for the job. A thin red line formed across her neck. It seemed to widen. Then, in a gush, the blood poured from her throat. Her eyes went wide, but she remained frozen. She coughed, and the blood sprayed. Matt leapt aside, dodging it. Panic gripped him as he realized what he'd done. He'd had to. He had no choice. She'd caught him at his game, and he couldn't afford to be caught. He'd already escaped from one jail. He would die before he went back.

1

"You want to do a show about what?" Lauren looked up at Rowan sharply. The phone on the table between them was set to speaker mode. Cable television's newest power couple sat on the balcony of their condo, over-looking the harbor and Coronado Island. The show was on hiatus. Rowan and Lauren hadn't expected the call, and they certainly hadn't expected to be called back to work any time soon.

"The Mayan Apocalypse," Jacob enthused. "The end of the Mayan calendar? Maybe you've heard of it?"

Lauren ran her hand over her face in disgust. Her fingers knotted in her hair and tugged tufts of it from the bonds of her braid. "No, I've heard of the *Maya* Apocalypse and the end of the *Maya* calendar," she corrected him curtly.

"Iceberg, Goldberg … what does it matter?"

"The proper expression is—"

"It matters," Rowan cut his wife off before the argument ensued. She glared at him knowing he knew how she felt about it. He gave her a stern expression that said *drop it*.

"Sure we've heard of it, but…that's in just a few weeks," Rowan said. "There isn't time to put everything in place to do a show that quickly."

"Have you lost your ever-lovin' mind?" Lauren groused, unable to keep her ire in check.

"To speak to Rowan's point, I know your team can pull it off," Jacob said. If Lauren knew him, the Network boss was probably sitting in his corner office on the tenth floor overlooking the Gas Light District in downtown San Diego. Lauren could see him with his feet on the desk; his favorite Friday afternoon pose. "You have the Network's full support. Lauren, I understand you won't be able to go, but if you are up to it, you can work here on research and production support."

She narrowed her brows, glaring at her husband, but angry at her boss. "Why now?" Lauren pursed her lips.

"Haven't you heard?" Jacob snorted. "It's the end of the world as we know it."

Rowan rolled his eyes. "We'll think about it." He hit the red button on the screen.

"Bloody hell." Lauren leaned back, her hand going to her protruding belly. "I'm going to kill that little nerd."

WITH SEVERAL HOURS TO CALM HERSELF, LAUREN SAT IN HER favorite wicker chair on the balcony watching the sun set with her new journal in her lap. Mindless of the rocking motion of her chair, that mimicked the pace of the waves on the distant shore, she was no longer brooding. Instead, she was giving serious consideration to this whole idea of a show on the so-called Maya Apocalypse. After a day of reading up on it, she jotted notes in the leather-bound book. She had a dozen more like this one packed in a box on a shelf in her closet. Each one documented her life's work and the mysteries they had explored. She loved the feel of the gel ink pen as it glided across the page in her own personal font; a script she'd been perfecting.

At the end of the 13th b'ak'tun, the ancient Maya predicted the world would end. Or did they? Their stone circle calendars simply stopped. Some read that to mean the end of the world was inevitable. The end had already come for the ancient civilization. Many of their cities had been reclaimed by the jungles. Others had been excavated and stood for tourists to snap selfies in front of. The ruins were also Meccas for scientists to study. Yet Maya people still lived in the Yucatán Peninsula, to this day.

Lauren paused, collecting her thoughts. She'd decided that much of the confusion arose from the various interpretations of how the ancient Maya calculated time. If one method were correct, the world would supposedly end on the 21st of December in 2012. This was the date marking the end of the 5,125-year Maya long-count calendar. This was the commonly accepted date of the prophesied apocalypse. Already in many countries, frightened citizens were storing away food and hoarding – of all things, toilet paper. One group in France assembled on a mountain called *Pic de Bugarach*, to await rescue by aliens, whom they believed would come and spirit them away to the Heavens before the world ended.

Rowan joined her and handed her a bottle of water. He had a beer. "I can see your gears turning," he said as he sat down beside her. "What's on your mind?"

"You know, I think I have it figured out."

"Oh?" His brow arched.

"You know how the Science Channel has been getting slammed over that stupid pseudo-documentary about how the earth's wobble was going to spin the planet out of orbit and we were going to crash into the sun?"

"I think we can both agree," he said. "That was the dumbest thing our sister-station has ever done. I mean, it was only mildly entertaining at best."

"Laughable if you ask me," Lauren said. "I mean the whole mermaid mummy thing they tried to pull off ten years ago should have been a lesson learned. Only *Ripley's Believe it or Not* could get away with something like that."

"I agree, but what's your point?"

"Well, with that whole fiasco, their credibility is wounded. You don't think they're relying on us to pull them out of a jam, do you?"

"I wouldn't put it past them," Rowan said.

"The idea of this being the end of the world is provocative, but hardly anything to get excited about." Lauren continued. "The Exploration Channel clearly wants in on the action. I just don't understand why it has to be us?"

"Who else would they come to for the truth?" Rowan suggested.

Ever since the Bigfoot episode won awards and accolades, Lauren and Rowan were the most popular celebrities on cable television. *The Veritas Codex* was now the #1 rated travel/adventure show on cable.

Lauren was not happy at all with the whole idea. "I was afraid this would happen," she bemoaned.

Rowan shook his head. "We don't have to do it."

Lauren knitted her brows. "As much as I hate the idea, I hate telling the Network no even more. You can lead the team just as easily as I can."

"It's *your* show," Rowan said.

Lauren softened. "It hasn't been *my* show since you joined the team. It's *our* show."

"But I don't want to be away from you now," he protested.

"I'm not due 'til February." She shook her head. "You'll have plenty of time to go and still be home before the baby comes."

"We'll be down there at the exact time the world is supposed to end." Rowan drained his beer.

"You don't believe that. Do you? Really?"

"I believe that if the world ends, *this* is where I want to be." He reached a hand to rest on the swell of her abdomen.

A tiny foot pressed against her stomach. The baby stretched and rolled under his hand. Rowan's whole countenance glowed at the thought of being a father, but Lauren winced. "Surely, it's not getting cramped in there already, is it?"

"This kid is kicking a lot more these days." She leaned back in her chair, stretching her aching back.

"How could I miss all of this?" He stood and paced at the balcony rail. "I'm not going," he said. "We told them when we found out you were pregnant that we didn't plan to do any traveling for a while. Your health comes first. Our family comes first. Besides, we've got a real estate deal to close. We'll want to get started moving as soon as the papers are signed."

That made Lauren smile. They had less than three months left on their lease and she was anxious to get settled into their new home. She'd longed for a house over-looking the beach and that dream was about to come true. "So, how are you going to break it to the Network?"

"Screw the Network." He turned back around, throwing up a hand in disgust. "I'm not leaving and that's final."

It was an argument he would not win.

LAUREN DROPPED HIM OFF AT THE AIRPORT THREE WEEKS later. He leaned in the car window and kissed her. "Call me on the satellite phone if there are any problems." His hand snaked across her stomach. It was a silent farewell to his child.

"Just hurry up and come home," she said. "We'll be fine. You heard what the doctor said this morning. There's nothing to worry about."

"That only helps me feel slightly better about leaving you." He kissed her again. He collected his bags from the back of the SUV before he closed it. He gave the back of the car a hearty slap to let her know it was safe to go. He waved as she did. Jean-René and his small team were waiting for him on the curb with their equipment.

"Come on, guys. Let's go."

～

LAUREN SAT AT HER DESK ON THE SIXTH FLOOR. HER OFFICE overlooked the harbor. In the distance, she could see the Navy Pier, and the USS Midway. Smaller sailboats and yachts lined the harbor. Her thoughts were a million miles away. Her head ached as she tried to wrap her mind around the mystery before her.

Lately, she could barely reach her keyboard. Her abdomen was in the way. It was getting harder and harder to get comfortable. Her feet were starting to swell if she sat too long, and her back ached. She couldn't even put shoes on by herself. She sat now with her bare feet up in a second chair, her keyboard on her legs. The basketball that took up most of her lap made it hard to see the keys. Fortunately she was a competent typist.

She tried to convince herself that keeping busy was the best thing for her while Rowan was gone. Still, it was difficult to keep her mind on her work. "Come on, focus." She scolded. "Let's figure out how to read this Maya calendar." She opened the internet browser. The baby inside her stretched and pushed a foot into her ribs. "Settle down, you." She poked back. "It's your nap time." It didn't help. "Okay. So by the long count, a *kin* is a day, *uinal* equals 20 *kin* or 20 days. A *tun* equals 18 *uinal*, or 360 days. A *katun* equals 20 *tun*, or 7,200 days and a *b'ak'tun* is 20 *katun*, or 400 *tun* or 7,200 *uinal* or 144,000 days. Got it. Easy peasy." Except she didn't have it and she knew it. "Stupid placenta brain." She'd been having a hard time concentrating. She blamed it on being pregnant and sleep deprived. It wasn't getting any better. "Stupid, stupid, stupid ..."

"Lauren?" Bahati poked her head into her office. "Are you okay?"

"I'm fine." She grimaced. "My brain isn't working today."

"Maybe it needs something to eat," Bahati said. "It's almost lunch time."

Lauren glanced up at the clock on the wall. "Where did the morning go?"

"I don't know, but I'm starving," she said. "Do you want me to go get you something?"

Lauren stood, stretching her back as she set the keyboard aside. "I need a break," she said. "A walk in the fresh air might do me good."

"Are you sure?"

"As long as it's a short walk."

It was a beautiful day in San Diego, despite being December. It was one of the reasons Lauren liked living there. After spending several winters roughing it in Yellowstone, she didn't like being cold. She didn't hate it as much as Rowan did though. Today, it was 74 and sunny with a light breeze. Perfect.

"What sounds good?"

"Food," Lauren growled. "Meat."

Bahati mused. "Iron deficient much?"

"Not according to the doctor," she said. "This kid is going to be a carnivore; I can tell you that much. I'm craving meat."

"So Tu Tio's or Zorba's?" They paused at the corner, debating which way to go.

"Zorba's," Lauren said. "I can smell it from here."

"You picked it because it's closer, didn't you?" Bahati asked as they crossed the street and headed towards the Greek Restaurant.

"Of course."

Once they had their food, they found a covered picnic table nearby. "Have you heard from Rowan yet?" Bahati asked.

"No." Lauren glanced at her cell phone on the table. "I figure they got in late last night. If I know Rowan, they found some dinner and hit the sack. I'm sure they got an early start this morning. There's a professor at the University in Mexico City they have to interview before they could head to Chichén Itzá."

"Jean-René told me," Bahati said. "I bet their first stop was for tacos."

"I hope he gets sick on tacos."

"So, you want tacos too, don't you?"

"No, I just want him to hurry home."

"Rolling stone..." Bahati began.

"That's Rowan. Gathering no moss." Lauren sighed wearily. She didn't sleep well when he traveled. It was rare either of them went anywhere without the other. Lauren didn't like being left alone.

"What's the latest on your house?" Bahati asked.

With the query, Lauren deflated. "The whole deal fell through." She looked away.

"What?" Bahati's face twisted in surprise. "What do you mean the deal fell through? I thought it was a done deal."

"We were supposed to have the papers signed before Rowan left, but the sellers got a better offer at the last minute. We scrambled to come up with additional financing. We just couldn't beat it. We're back at square one."

"What are you going to do?"

"Start looking again," she said, taking a bite of her gyro. She chewed thoughtfully for a moment, then swallowed. "I found one in San Clemente that looks promising. It's small, but it's close to the beach."

"That's going to be quite a commute, isn't it?" Bahati's brow narrowed. "What about Chula Vista?"

"Might as well move to Tijuana." She wiped her mouth with a paper napkin, wadding it up and tossing it aside. She sighed. "It's just really a bad time to be buying a house."

"I'd be happy to tag along if you need a second opinion."

Lauren brightened. "I'd enjoy the company."

"So what are you looking for?"

While they ate, Lauren detailed the ideal home she and Rowan wanted to raise their children in. Unfortunately, the market wasn't good. Properties were expensive and there weren't many available single family homes in their price range. Lauren sold her condo when they got married. They were living in Rowan's one-bedroom town house. They needed a place for their family to grow, preferably one with a yard. Something close to the beach. They'd been spending a lot of time at the shore lately. Lauren had the tan to prove it. Her naturally light copper skin had gone russet brown since they weren't traveling all over the world these days. It had been a welcomed break from their normally hectic schedule.

"You may have to look further north," Bahati suggested. "Los Angeles isn't that far away."

"I don't want to live in Los Angeles." Lauren wrinkled her nose.

"If you could live anywhere in the world, where would you live?" Bahati asked.

Lauren lifted a shoulder. "We've been to so many beautiful places. It would be hard to pick one."

"I'd live in the North of France," Bahati said without hesitation. "I lived there for a time when I was a girl. I've always wanted to go back."

"What's it like?"

"We stayed in a little village called *Cappelle-la-Grande*, not too far outside Dunkirk," Bahati said. "The winters were cool, and the summers were warm. The food was good. All French cuisine is, of course. I became quite fond of *poulet à la bière*."

"Really? Chicken in beer? That sounds fancy," Lauren said. "Rowan would like that."

"There were museums and bicycle races. We would take the ferry to London from time to time. Sometimes we took the train down to Paris. Weekend trips to Switzerland weren't uncommon."

"What took you to that part of the world?" Lauren asked.

"My father taught physics. He took a job at the University there."

"Why did I think your dad was an astronomer?" Lauren asked.

"He was. He worked as an astronomer at the University when I was older. Before that, he was a physics teacher."

Lauren gazed out across the ocean. "I think I could be very happy in Hawaii."

"Which island?"

"The Big Island. They call it the land of fire and ice ..."

"Ice?" Bahati recoiled. "You're talking about Hawaii, right?"

"They actually have snow on Mauna Loa and Mauna Kea from time to time," Lauren said. "When Rowan and I were there on our honeymoon, we rented a bungalow outside of Hilo near a little town called *Laupahoehoe*."

"Easy for you to say," Bahati effervesced.

"It means *a leaf of lava*," Lauren said. "The bungalow overlooked the ocean. We drank coffee on the lanai every morning. It was warm and it rained almost every afternoon. We spent much of our time... indoors." She blushed.

"That's what one would expect on a honeymoon." Bahati grinned. "But I thought he took you to some uninhabited island?"

"He did, but our flight from Tahiti took us to Hilo and Rowan arranged for a long layover. We spent a week there before we flew back to the Mainland," she said. "He tricked me into thinking we were going there on an investigation. I got to go to a *luau* and see the volcano. We rented a car and drove all the way around the island. We spent an afternoon on the black-sand beaches. It was lovely."

"You're so lucky." Bahati said. "Rowan is awesome."

"Yes, but he's in trouble with me at the moment." She rose abruptly, pushing away the rest of her food. She walked away. "He should have called by now."

"He's not used to traveling without you," Bahati said. "Why don't you call him on the sat-phone?"

"That's only for emergencies." She wrapped her arms around herself. "I keep telling myself I'm being irrational."

"You're pregnant," Bahati said. "You have every right to be irrational."

"So I am being irrational?" Lauren whipped around.

"I thought irrational and due-any-day were synonymous." Bahati clucked her tongue. "Rowan just left. You're getting ready to give birth. You just lost the house you'd been dreaming of. So you have every reason to be *irrational*." She stood and came over taking her friend by the arms. "Look, Rowan knows what he's doing. I'm sure he's fine."

"I hope you're right," Lauren said, shaking her head.

"Come on," Bahati said. "Let's get back to the office. Rowan needs us to help him with research and script development. I'm sure he'll call soon. What could possibly happen?"

2

R owan sat with his back against the adobe wall, his knees drawn up, his head down on his chest. It had gone from 105 to what seemed like freezing overnight. Now, it was sweltering again. He found himself wondering how he was going to be able to explain all this to Lauren, presuming he lived long enough. Less than twenty-four hours in Mexico, and he was already locked up in a filthy, run-down Mexican jail.

Still, he was optimistic. He hoped two things would happen. First, he hoped Jean-René and the team were working to get him bailed out. He also hoped no one had told Lauren.

This was all a stupid misunderstanding. He'd been filming a couple of introductory shots in one of the markets in a village outside Mexico City. He stopped to try on a sombrero when the shopkeeper took exception to him and the camera crew. He took off the hat and returned it to the owner. The man demanded that he pay for it, but Rowan's Spanish was lacking, and he misunderstood, thinking he wanted him to leave. "Okay, okay, I'll leave," he said, but when he did, the man called over the local *policia*, and the next thing Rowan knew, he was being arrested. He'd been here all night, and half of the day. He had no food or water. He didn't even get a phone call. He was feeling especially sorry for himself. Panic was setting in.

He flinched at the sound of a rattling key in the door against the metal bars of the cell. Before he could gather his wits, he was dragged up and hauled out to the street. The light blinded him. He had barely gotten his feet under him when he was shoved out onto the sidewalk. He landed on his hands and knees. The police officer spat at him in Spanish as he collected himself. He yelled something and threw his hand up before turning around and going back inside, leaving Rowan to wonder what the hell had just happened.

"Rowan!" Jean-René was at his side, helping him to his feet. "Thank God!"

"What the hell was that?"

"We have an hour to get out of town," Jean-René said, his accent more pronounced than usual. "He said if we were still here when the sun set, he'd have all of us arrested."

"How did you …?"

"Don't ask questions, Boss."

"Did you pay …?" Jean-René locked his eyes on him and made a noise that told Rowan to zip it. What he didn't know wouldn't get him in trouble with his wife.

"Oh." Rowan finally steadied. "In that case, let's get out of here."

"I couldn't agree more," Jean-René said. "I've got the team packing everything up. I finally got a hold of the professor from the University of Mexico. He has agreed to meet us at Chichén Itzá." The professor had stood them up for their meeting the day before, which is why they'd ended up in this little town in the first place.

"Well dammit," Rowan pursed his lips, his brow clamping down over his eyes "We could have flown into Mérida, Progresso or heck, even Cozumel." He shook his head. The meeting with the professor in Mexico City had dictated their travel arrangements. It was a much longer drive from Mexico City than it would have been from any of the other cities in the Yucatán.

Jean-René held his hands up in surrender. "We did what we could, Boss."

"Good work," Rowan said as they hurried along. "I can't believe all of this is over a stupid hat."

"He thought you were making fun of him," Jean-René said. "He didn't like being mocked."

"But I wasn't ..." Rowan shook his head.

"It doesn't matter now." Jean-René had him by the arm as they crossed the street.

THE TEAM DROVE FOR HOURS, STOPPING FOR GAS IN Villahermosa. Rowan stayed close to the Spanish-speaking members of the team. Jean-René and Alejandro were his best buddies from then on.

That night, they camped on the beach. The weather was pleasant, and the moon was full. Rowan felt much better after a dinner of fresh-caught fish, cooked over the roaring bonfire. Someone had the foresight to fill a cooler with sliced limes and Mexican beer. The party lasted well into night. Rowan, however, turned in early, and slept through all of it.

ROWAN WAS THE FIRST ONE UP. HE COLLECTED ALL THE BEER bottles and rekindled the fire before he went to the water. He caught some more fish for their breakfast. He had the meal ready when everyone else finally rolled out of their tents. Rowan sat on the beach watching the sunrise, eating fish off a roasting spit, appreciating his freedom.

"Has anyone called Lauren since we got here?" He'd been dreading the thought of having to explain to her what had happened.

"No," Alejandro said. "We didn't think it wise to worry her."

"Before we get too far into the jungle, I should stop and call her."

"Everyone's already been sworn to secrecy about what happened," Jean-René said, pulling Rowan aside. "All the video has been destroyed."

"Thanks, man." He slapped Jean-René on the back. "You are a good friend."

"Lauren would kill me if I let anything happen to you," Jean-René said.

"Kill you? She'd kill me."

"She'd kill us both," Jean-René said. "You getting killed by your wife is one thing. But I didn't do anything wrong. I'm certainly not going to get myself killed." He rose and tossed fish bones back into the water. "Come on, we have a long way to go."

LAUREN SPENT ALL DAY WITH BAHATI, DRIVING AROUND looking at houses. They were no closer to finding the Pierce family a new home. She was tired, but she was also worried about Rowan.

Sitting around with nothing to do would make it worse. With several hours of daylight left, she put on her bikini. She tied her sarong around her expanding waist, slipped into her sandals and headed for the beach. She made a place for herself on the sand, letting it and the sun warm her through and through. The baby stirred. Her belly quivered as it rolled inside her. She sat back on her elbows and watched in awe. She smiled and lay back. She turned her sunglasses towards the sky. Her body turned to putty as the sinking sun warmed her soul. Giving into the sand and salt air would be the healing balm she needed, and she let it work its magic on her.

She had a *banh mi* on a crusty French roll she picked up at the nearby Asian market. She'd become a fan of the popular street food on a trip to Vietnam a few years ago. The pickled daikon radishes and carrots accented the grilled pork and jalapeños, which were cooled by the slices of cucumber. As she sat munching on it, her cell phone rang. She set her sandwich aside and snagged her phone from her bag.

"Hello beautiful." His voice sent a wave of relief through her. "What are you doing?"

"Thank God, Rowan." She sat back on her elbow. A silent prayer joined her relief. "I've been worried sick."

"Sorry, honey," he said. "We had some car trouble outside of Tepito. We got stranded overnight. I couldn't get to a phone. I didn't want to call you on the satellite because I was afraid you might think it was an emergency."

"I would have, too." She sat back up. "Where are you now?"

"We spent the day driving and we just got settled in Mérida. We're headed to Chichén Itzá tomorrow morning. The professor is meeting us at the Maya ruins," he said.

"I thought you were meeting him in Mexico City." She crossed her legs.

"After the car broke down, we missed our appointment," Rowan said.

"Other than car trouble are there any other issues I need to know about?"

"Nope," he said, maybe a bit too fast.

"Really?"

"Jean-René has been suffering from Montezuma's revenge. That's why we're so late getting in. Other than that, everything is okay." She could hear his smile.

"Poor Jean-René."

"What are you doing?"

She smiled to herself. "I'll give you two guesses."

"Oh. So we're playing games?" Rowan asked. "I only need one. It's about 4:30 on a Saturday. You're sitting on the beach, probably having *bahn mi*."

"Correct."

"Any luck with the house hunting?"

"I found a beach-front bungalow for 5.3 million dollars on the Pacific Coast Highway today," she said, picking a carrot off her sandwich, nibbling on it. "It was a fixer-upper, too."

"Ouch."

"Exactly," she said. "Maybe we should consider relocating. The cost of a house here is just ridiculous."

"I'll watch for houses here," he mused.

"Let me know what you find," she retorted.

"We most likely won't have a cell signal, so we'll be out of contact for the next few days. Please don't worry if you don't get a phone call any time soon, okay?"

"No problem." She swallowed hard.

"But if I find a Maya temple with three bedrooms and two baths for under a million, I'll call you," he joked. "I'll charge the sat phone tonight, if you should need to reach me."

"Be safe," she said stoically.

"I promise."

3

Lauren hadn't expected to feel so lonely with Rowan gone. She spent the entire evening scrolling through the real estate listings trying to find a house. The demand for single-family homes in San Diego was so high that it was hard to find one. They sold almost as fast as they went on the market, and the demand ran the prices up. Bidding wars often erupted, which had been the case with the house they lost. She found herself day dreaming about a home on the Big Island.

At three in the morning she was still looking at beach front cottages and mountain-side bungalows from Kona to Hilo. Houses were cheaper on the islands than they were in Southern California, but not by much. She could only imagine the cost of living on a remote island would be much higher, but it didn't hurt to dream.

Rowan was from Colorado, so when she ran out of options in Hawaii, she started searching around Estes Park. The passing thought of spending their summers in the mountains, hanging out with the local Bigfoot population—if they were still there—had a certain appeal.

She wondered about *The People* often. But Tsul'Kalu had been silent for months. She had a nagging feeling that something was wrong. The bond they shared was unique and inexplicable. Normally, she could hear him in her head even when they were hundreds of miles apart. She'd grown accustomed to it. It was a comfort to have his counsel. His abrupt absence made her heart ache.

She never quite figured out how many of the Bigfoot had fled from the volcano's minor eruption. Besides Tsul'Kalu and the white female, she guessed there might have been at least thirty she had seen. *How many others had been living in the lava tubes beneath Mt. St. Helens? Where had they all gone?*

It would help to have someone to talk to. She didn't. She had told Rowan the truth, but Lauren was certain he did not believe her. Some days, she wondered if she'd been hallucinating. Maybe she'd had a mental break. Maybe it was the results of the head injury she had sustained. Still, she was convinced. She knew what she'd seen. She knew the truth. It was a truth she could never tell.

It used to bother her that they rarely found anything. Especially when her brother, Michael, gave her grief about it. But it wasn't like they weren't trying.

In all the years of doing the show, they had made some interesting discoveries. There were the possible Yeti tracks in Nepal. The unidentifiable DNA from the corpse in Peru was provocative even though all the tests had been inconclusive. They'd sent the results back to the government escort and there had been some discussion about having the team return to Peru to do additional research. They'd even nabbed a diamond thief and won praise from the FBI for their role. The US Forestry Department and FBI turned over the evidence against the surviving accomplice, but also recommended the DA dismiss the case, which she did. Instead, they found a nice place for Billy to go live in Tacoma. The half-way house helped him get a good job and last Lauren heard, he was doing quite well without his lousy cousin.

Their episode on Bigfoot left everyone with more questions than answers — well everyone but Lauren. The Bigfoot had spoken to her, and only her. It was a secret she kept close to her heart. She still struggled with how to explain what she knew and her ability to understand the ancient All-language she couldn't possibly know.

The thought sent shivers down her spine, and she glanced up, realizing it was nearly morning. She yawned and put down her iPad. Lauren rose, stretching out her sore back. She walked out onto the balcony and watched the western sky lighten as the pink of dawn stretched to reach the sea. Rowan and his team would be getting up soon and would be on the road to Chichén Itzá. She went back inside and crawled into bed. She was fast asleep before she knew it.

For the first time in months, she dreamt of Tsul'Kalu—finally. The shaman of the Ancient Tribe of Bigfoot had been kind and wise. Old beyond measure, he smelled of wood smoke, and beast, but his presence instilled a sense of peace. He sat across the fire from her, the light of it flickering in his dark eyes. He spoke with his hands, and a voice that filled her head, but not her ears.

"Truth Seeker is troubled," he said in the ancient All-Language. "Tell me, what worries you?"

"You have been gone," she said.

"Only for a time," he said. "I cannot be with you always, but I still watch over you."

"But I have missed you; I tried calling out to you."

"I am here when you need me. Now, tell me the real reason you are troubled, little one."

"The Protector has traveled far without me." She called Rowan by the name Tsul'Kalu had given him. "I am troubled because I miss him, and I wish I could be with him."

"You have a greater purpose here," the old Shaman said.

"I'm carrying his child." Her hand went to her swollen stomach.

"It is good to have children," he said. "It is not wrong to

make a home and keep a hearth for the Protector and his offspring. There will be a day when you can all journey again together."

"I'm not one of these women who are content to bake and sew." She ran a hand over her brow. "I want to see the world and discover its mysteries."

"This is the Truth Seeker I know and care for," he said with a beatific smile. "Enjoy home while you can. Children grow and leave their parents. Mothers miss their sons and daughters, but this... this is a gift you must treasure."

"And I do," she said. There was a long pause between them. "Tell me how it goes with the People?"

"We are well." He seemed to smile. "We think of our friends often and miss you. But now you must rest. There is much work for you to do, and you must do it well."

With a wave of his hand, the scene went dark, and her eyes opened. The sun was shining brightly in her west-facing window. She sat up slowly, glancing at the clock. It was nearly two in the afternoon.

The ever-present urge to pee was the only thing that got her out of bed. She showered and braided her hair before getting dressed. Her stomach growled. She headed to the kitchen to find something to eat. There wasn't much to be had but she made do with what she found, a grilled cheese sandwich and an apple. Sitting at the table, she made her shopping list as she ate. She had nothing planned for the day. A trip to the store and a drive along the coast was the best she could come up with, and that would be enough.

BAHATI WAS ALREADY AT HER DESK WHEN LAUREN ROLLED IN, ten minutes late. Lauren was in a foul mood. "You look exhausted." Bahati got up. She followed the boss into her office. Lauren tossed her purse in the corner. "Are you okay?"

Bahati crossed her arms, tilted her head and furrowed her brow as Lauren sunk into her chair.

"More or less." She took a deep breath. "I didn't sleep very well."

"What? Like a couple of hours?"

"Yeah," Lauren said. "All weekend."

"I guess it's getting harder and harder to get comfortable, huh?"

"Yeah." Lauren took a deep breath, steeling herself. "It doesn't help that Rowan isn't here to snuggle with."

"TMI, Boss," she said. "Can I get you some coffee?"

"No," Lauren said. "I'll get some tea later. I was reading about the Maya's blood sacrifice rituals last night. I want to dig into that some more."

"What'd you find out?" Bahati sat down across from her.

"Well, Maya society was sharply divided between the elite and commoners. As population increased over time, various sectors of society became increasingly specialized. That prompted the political climate to become increasingly complex," Lauren explained. "At the core of Maya religious practice was ancestor worship. They would pray to their lost kin to act as a go-between for their living descendants in dealings with the denizens of the supernatural realm. Blood was viewed as a potent source of nourishment for the Maya deities. The sacrifice of a living creature was a powerful blood offering. By extension, the sacrifice of a human life was the ultimate offering of blood to the gods. You can imagine, one of the most important Maya rituals culminated in human sacrifice."

"Creepy," Bahati said.

"Generally, only high-status prisoners of war were sacrificed. Low-status captives were used for slave labor."

Lauren skimmed the article. "In the early days of their culture, decapitation was the standard method of sacrifice, but later on, the heart was ripped from the victim while still alive."

"Gross," Bahati cringed. "I knew about the beheading but not the heart. I mean that's some serious Indiana Jones stuff right there."

"I don't think I'd care for either." Lauren ignored the reference to Rowan's favorite movie. "Look at some of this artwork." She motioned Bahati over. "The victims were often tortured, beaten, scalped, burnt or disemboweled."

"And I thought William Wallace's execution was gross." Bahati wrinkled up her nose at the graphic display of art available on the World Wide Web. "So, can you explain why everyone thinks they are predicting the world is going to end?"

Lauren tried to explain *kins, uinal, tuns* and *b'ak'tuns*. She tried to explain how the calendars were like circles. Finally, she stopped and shook her head. "I think the neophytes aren't seeing the whole picture. I mean, when my Gregorian calendar comes to an end, what do I do?" She held up her day planner. "I don't go crying the sky is falling, do I? No. I go and I buy a new calendar. There's another calendar out there with the next b'ak'tun on it. We just haven't found it yet. That doesn't mean the apocalypse is coming."

Bahati sat down at her desk across from her, shaking her head. "You've done it. You solved the mystery, Lauren."

"And I didn't have to go to Mexico to do it."

4

The ancient site wasn't exactly what Rowan had expected. The jungle crowded the edges of an expansive field. The grass around the massive structures had been worn thin and was brown from the repeated foot traffic from the scientists and tourists who'd come before. There was a visitors' center at the entrance, and a narrow, shaded footpath led them into the site. Normally, there were tables lining the walkways loaded with merchandise to sell. Descendants of the ancient architects who built this city sold baubles and disks of obsidian glass to the tourists. It was the only way they had to make a living. But with the site closed to the public, they had closed up shop. They knew the scientists weren't about to fall for their screen-printed t-shirts of jaguars or wooden key chains with the Maya calendar carved into them.

They waited all day for the university professor to arrive. Jean-René, who'd coordinated the meeting, used the sat phone to call the University. The University insisted Dr. DeLaFuentes left Mexico City in plenty of time to get there. They could only assume he'd had car trouble. So they had waited, but he hadn't arrived. With or without him, they had a job to do. They couldn't wait any more.

Jean-René spent the day getting their permits coordinated with the curators of the site. While he did that, Rowan made friends with one of the Maya tour guides. Tuuk was on hand to help the visiting scientists answer any questions or find their way around the site.

"Tuuk? Is that your name?" Rowan looked down at the diminutive guide who barely came to his waist.

"Tuuk, is my Maya family name." He spoke with a thick Spanish accent.

"You're Maya?"

"*Si*. Yes." He smiled brightly.

"I thought the Maya would be…" Rowan hesitated.

"Taller?" Tuuk chuckled. "I hear that a lot."

"Are all the Maya…?" Rowan didn't know how to ask.

"Short? Well, there are some that are taller. They've done DNA testing. The scientists found we share the same DNA as the Mongols."

"Mongolian? Like the Mongol hordes?"

"*Si*."

"Fascinating. I've learned something new already." Rowan had been to Mongolia. The people there all commented on how tall he was. "So tell me something about this site. Something no one else knows."

"There is a pyramid inside." He pointed to the step pyramid at the center of the site. The *El Castillo*, or *the Castle*, as it was called was the most commanding of all the structures at the ancient site.

"Yes, I see the pyramid," Rowan said. "It's amazing."

"There is another one. Inside. *Dos pirámides*."

It took a second for Rowan to comprehend. "Two? Two pyramids. You're kidding me! Can I go in? Can I see it?"

Tuuk shook his head. "No. No one is allowed to enter. Too many people…" His hand moved like he was signing an autograph.

"Too many people were writing on the walls?" Rowan was stunned.

"*Si. Tuuk sera aquí.*"

"Oh, I got it. *Tuuk was here.*" Rowan did know a little Spanish.

"So, what do I have to do to get permission to film from the top of the pyramid?"

"*No esta permitido.*" Tuuk shook his head.

"Not even a famous television star?" Rowan looked at the camera.

Jean-René peeked out from behind the view finder. "I've already filed a request for a permit. We should know later this afternoon."

"Maybe famous." Tuuk grinned brightly.

"Maybe I'm famous?" Rowan shook his head. "Maybe I'll make you famous."

Tuuk stepped back, shaking his head. "Famous enough." He patted his own chest.

"I'll probably have to sign a hold harmless agreement, won't I?" Rowan said to the cameraman.

"I'm sure you'll have to sign a lot of things." Jean-René assured him.

THEIR TIME AT THE UNESCO WORLD HERITAGE SITE DID not go to waste. Tuuk gave them the full tour. Rowan and his crew spent their time making friends with other research teams. They shared notes and oriented themselves to the many buildings and carvings that could be found across the site.

They were about ready to leave to go find something for dinner in the little village just outside the site when Tuuk came and found the team, packing up their equipment. "Famous enough," he said, brightly. He handed Rowan an envelope. "*Mi amigo*, you are approved."

"Our permit?"

"*Si*," he said. "You can climb tomorrow morning."

"Can we stay here tonight? Can we camp?"

"*Si*." Tuuk pointed towards an area outside the walls of the site where campers and tents were assembled.

"This is great! Thank you, Tuuk! *Gracias*." He shook the man's hand vigorously and patted him on the shoulder. "*Gracias*! Now, can you tell us the best place to get some tacos?"

"*Si*." He nodded his head. "*Mi casa*. Come with me. My wife makes the best tacos in all Mexico."

"You're inviting us to dinner at your house?"

"*Si*." Tuuk grinned. He slugged Rowan in the arm playfully. "Famous enough, *mi amigo*."

Rowan grinned and threw an arm around his shoulder. "*Mi amigo*."

IT HAD BEEN A GOOD, ALBEIT SHORT NIGHT. ROWAN, JEAN-René, and Alejandro climbed to the top of the step-pyramid in the dark. Rowan wanted to be ready to film as soon as the sun broke over the jungle. Now, as the sky went from pale pink, to brilliant red, the glow of a golden orb split the world between night and day.

It was still a few days before the solstice. The crowds that were expected were limited to research teams from around the world. For now, only those who wanted to do their prep work ahead of the arrival of the public were permitted. If they wanted any vanity shots, they knew they better get them today. As the first rays of the morning sun cut across Rowan's features, Jean-René gave him the signal to go.

"The ancient site of Chichén Itzá on the Yucatán Peninsula was built between the 9th and 12th centuries on the outside of a ring made by a meteorite strike. The foundation was constructed, elevating the site several meters and you can see some examples of those piers that were excavated next to the Temple of the Rain God," Rowan narrated. His eyes turned toward the sun. It was so bright he had to squint to read the cue cards Alejandro held for him. "Considered to be one of the Seven Wonders of the World and a UNESCO World Heritage site, the name Chichén Itzá literally means, *at the mouth of the well of Itza* for the many sink holes in the area. I'm standing on top of the El Castillo, or the Castle, which is just one of many structures here at Chichén Itzá. But this ancient building has another name, the *Temple of Kukulkan*, the serpent god." Rowan was a master of the perfectly timed pause. He demonstrated it before he continued. "In just a few days, the Winter Solstice will herald the end of the Maya calendar, and thus, the end of the world. Some say the world will end in fire, some say in ice ... Not to quote Robert Frost, but I say it's just another day here in paradise. Join us for this special episode of *the Veritas Codex — The End of the World as We Know It.*"

"Cut!" Jean-René called. He clicked off the camera. "Nice job, Boss."

"Thanks." Rowan let out a heavy sigh of relief, wiping his brow with the back of his hand. This was the point where post-production would roll the opening credits. Normally the intro featured Lauren, and her journal filled with legends and truths. They might have to do something different for this episode since she wasn't with them. That was above even Rowan's pay grade to decide. He didn't have time to worry about that now. He'd made it up the step pyramid in the dark. With the sun now fully risen he could see how steep the climb down would be.

"Did anyone count the number of stairs on this thing?"

"Ninety-one," Alejandro said, tossing Rowan a bottle of

water. "I used to climb it when I was a kid. Back when they allowed anyone up here."

"I would have guessed more." Rowan put his hands on his hips, staring down the narrow steps. "Why do they have to be so steep?"

"Come on." Alejandro grinned. "I just got the call from Tuuk. The University Professor has arrived. He's waiting for you down there."

"Oh good," Rowan gasped. "I hope he knows CPR."

"I know CPR," Jean-René said. "Please don't make me do it on you. I'd prefer to save a hot blonde with big—"

"Pig." Alejandro cut him off.

"DR. ENRIQUE DELAFUENTES." THE MAN SMILED AS HE introduced himself.

"I'm Rowan Pierce," he said. Rowan then turned and introduced his small team.

The professor wasn't what Rowan had been expecting. He was a tall, lean man in his mid-forties. Beneath his hat, he had a thick head of hair that was dark. A bit of gray framed his square face at his temples. He wore a thin mustache but was otherwise clean shaven. He wore a lightweight white oxford cloth shirt, navy-blue pants, and a pair of red sneakers. "Nice to meet you. Welcome to Chichén Itzá." His English was excellent. "Welcome." He shook hands with each of them as they were introduced. "Is this your first time at Chichén Itzá?"

"For me, yes," Rowan said. "We were hoping you could tell us more about what archaeologists have discovered here." Jean-René had the cameras running. Thanks to Tuuk, Rowan already had a rather good idea what was going on at the site. This time he asked the questions for the cameras.

"Chichén Itzá is made up of several main buildings, and recently, we did some LIDAR scans on the El Castillo here."

"LIDAR?" Rowan shook his head. "Even we don't have LIDAR."

"No LIDAR?"

"I meant to grab a GPR, but in our haste to get here, I forgot to pack it. LIDAR is more than a little cable TV show can afford."

"That's too bad," the professor said. "We used LIDAR on an aircraft to scan the site and we found that inside of the El Castillo, there's another pyramid."

"Another one?" Rowan's brow lifted towards his hairline. Again, thanks to Tuuk, he already knew this. "Inside?"

"And that's only half of it," Enrique said. "There's a third pyramid inside the second one."

"A third one? Are you kidding me?"

"And all of that was built upon a complicated foundation to support the weight of structures because there is a cenote beneath the site."

A cenote was a natural reservoir formed when the limestone surface collapsed, exposing the water underneath. With no rivers running through the area, these deep caverns were a major source of water in the Yucatán. It was the lifeblood of the region, and such an important part of the Mayan civilization that precious objects such as jade, gold, copper and incense were often thrown into the cenotes as offerings. When times were especially hard, human sacrifices might also be cast into the seemingly bottomless pools. "The *well of Itza*." Rowan felt his cheeks dimple.

"Exactly. But the really interesting archaeology isn't happening here. It's happening in the jungle."

"More interesting than this?"

"I would like to take you to an area where we are actively working if you're up for a hike. There, I have something really special to show you."

Rowan turned to the camera. "It's just after sunrise, in Mexico. The temperature is somewhere between 90 and the surface of the sun. The humidity is about 140%. Sure, I'm up for a hike through the snake—and jaguar—infested jungle. Let's go."

Once the cameras were off, the professor put his hat back on. "I'm sorry for being late," he said. "There was a problem just north of here yesterday evening. The police had the roads closed."

"A problem?" Rowan queried. "What kind of problem?"

"I'm really not sure," he said. "I think someone must have died. They were very tight-lipped. It could have been a crash, but I didn't see them tow any cars away. I ended up sleeping in my car once I finally got to the site after midnight."

"Is it something we should be worried about?"

"I'm sure if it was, someone would have come and told us," he said. "Please, if you will follow me, I'll take you to a site of special wonder. It's just to the south. Not far from here."

"DID YOU KNOW, THE EL CASTILLO WAS ACTUALLY BUILT ON top of an older structure?" Enrique asked as they walked. Rowan was having a hard time keeping up with him and was breathless for his efforts. The professor wasn't even breaking a sweat.

"I had heard that," Rowan said. He'd already learned that the previous day.

"Yes, there was a much older civilization here before the Maya."

"Did their calendar run out too?"

The professor chortled at his joke. "More or less."

"So what do you make of all this...rigmarole?" Rowan asked.

"Really more of an annoyance," he mused with a dismissive wave of his hand. "It's usually more crowded here with tourists. We still have more company than we'd prefer. People want to learn and understand. We have so much yet to figure out."

"So tell me something about the Maya culture, something the average person might not know," Rowan said.

The professor stopped at the edge of the clearing. "There's a rumor... they were time travelers."

"Time travelers?" Rowan tried to keep a blank façade. They were into the unexplained, even the bizarre. But he hadn't expected to come here to learn about time travelers.

"Mexican archaeologist Alberto Ruiz discovered the tomb of King *K'inich Janaab'Pakal* or *Pacal the Great* inside the Temple of Inscriptions of Palenque in Chiapas. It's not far from here. At the entrance of the temple there were a total of 620 inscriptions. One of the most important aspects of the crypt was the cover stone. There, they found a Maya hieroglyph that has become known as *The Astronaut of Palenque*. Some believe this means they were modern astronauts that came from the future. Others jump to the conclusion that the Maya people were victims of a planetary ascension or abduction. Some say they acquired the knowledge of the advance architecture, astronomy, and numeric system from visitors from the stars. We have an astronaut here, too." He took out his cell phone and scrolled through the pictures, before turning it to Rowan. "See?"

Rowan took the phone and zoomed in on it, studying the square block, which really did look like an astronaut. It had a face in a round helmet with what looked like a breathing apparatus over the nose and mouth. It could have been a Yeti or a construction worker, but yeah, he could see why people might think it was an astronaut... or a time traveler.

He handed the phone back. "That's amazing," Rowan said.

"Just wait until you see what we found just off the *Old Chichén*." He smiled and motioned for the team to follow.

~

THEY FOLLOWED A NARROW PATH THROUGH THE JUNGLE, which turned into more rugged terrain. Nearly twenty minutes later, they came out to a clearing on a slight hill, where seven stones stood in a circle. To Rowan, it looked like the henges he had studied in Britain. In the center, stood a stone altar with a V-shaped notch in the middle of it. There was a series of stone channels that ran from the altar to each of the upright pillars.

"Wow!" Rowan studied one of the monoliths. It was covered in hieroglyphs. Each symbol was different. Some were faces, either in profile or front-facing. Others were nondescript shapes. Some were animals, but like none that he had ever seen. "Look at that," he said, breathlessly. "Looks like a 70's VW bus," Jean-René scoffed from behind the camera. "That one looks like an old Airstream camper."

A foot. A button... and yes, an Airstream camper. Rowan turned to Enrique. "So what do these mean?"

Enrique gazed towards the top of the monolith. "Reading Maya is like reading Korean. But there's no Rosetta stone to help us interpret the glyphs. We do know many, maybe even most of the symbols. The Mayan language isn't completely dead. Maya people still live here."

"We met some yesterday." Rowan used his phone to snap some pictures to send to Lauren. He knew she'd be interested in the henge.

"Ancient Mayan was usually written in blocks arranged in columns two blocks wide. Deciphering the writing is a long and laborious process."

"So you've deciphered some of these?" Rowan asked.

"This is the glyph for the word *b'alam*, or *the jaguar*." Dr. DeLaFuentes pointed at one of the markings. "That might mean this is an altar to honor the Jaguar King. The jaguar is representative of power, ferocity, and valor. He is the embodiment of aggressiveness. *Ek b'alam* is also called the Jaguar God, the god of the Underworld." He walked over to the tallest of the seven pillars. "This series of glyphs tell us about the Jaguar Queen. This has been the only one we found here that specifically relates to a woman. There is a jaguar goddess. She is related to childbirth, but this glyph is about an actual queen who lived during the height of the Maya empire. She was the bride of the Jaguar King. It says that she made the journey through the underworld and fell from the sky."

"Fell from the sky? Like an astronaut or like ... like a parachute?" Wonder filled Rowan's voice. The symbol in the center of the pillar did look a bit like a parachute.

"Well, this investigation may have just taken an interesting turn." Jean-René arched a brow. "Did anyone file a missing person's report lately?"

5

Lauren sat on the beach watching the last rays of the sun stretching over the ocean. It gave the sand a golden glow and made the waves sparkle as the water lapped at her toes. She missed Rowan, even though she got a lot of work done; for what little good it did. She could do research all day. Until Rowan returned with video in the can, and evidence to be analyzed she couldn't know what might be important. So she'd taken copious notes and logged the website sources. She documented everything so when she came back to it, she'd have the data.

It was going to be an awfully long few weeks with him gone. She had plenty to keep her busy. She had to update their website and record a podcast. She needed to work on an article for the Exploration Channel's magazine. It was due by Friday. She sat running through her mental list of other things she could do and what busy work she could find to occupy herself while he was gone. It wasn't going to be easy.

It was completely dark when she got back to the house. She'd stopped and picked up a pizza. She should have gotten a smaller one, she decided. Rowan usually ate most of it. She put a couple slices on a plate and poured herself a glass of iced tea. Carrying her meal into the living room, she turned on the television and sat back to eat. After flipping channels, she stopped on the local news. With all the interest in the upcoming winter solstice and the so-called Apocalypse, the national news stations had been carrying coverage on the upcoming event.

"In Crime Watch this evening, we're following reports of a violent attack against tourists in Mexico at the ancient site of Chichén Itzá. Just days before the winter solstice, a researcher was found dead on a rural road in the jungle near the ancient Maya site. While officials have not identified the victim, they did release a statement saying the victim had been shot in the head execution style. Mexican officials cite increasing violence in the area as local drug lords grow more powerful."

Lauren realized she was holding her breath when the phone beside her rang. She scrambled to grab it, nearly dropping it. "Lauren, what are you doing?" It was Bahati. Her voice sounded panicked.

"I'm watching the news," she said.

"Dammit," Bahati said away from the phone. "You saw it."

"Yeah, I saw it." Lauren snapped. "Was it our team?"

"I don't know," she said. "I tried calling on the sat-phone, but I didn't get an answer."

"Who else could it be?"

"A hundred other teams, Lauren," Bahati said curtly. "With all the hype over the upcoming solstice, scientists and television crews have to be flocking in from all over the world."

"Yes, but they said a researcher was killed."

"That doesn't mean it was one of our researchers," Bahati said. "Now turn off the television and go to bed. I'll let you know the minute I hear from them."

Lauren hung up the phone, flinging it into the corner of the sofa. She wrapped her arms around herself, as her brow drew tightly over her dark eyes, trying to figure out how worried to be, and what to do about it. She knew Bahati was probably right, but that glimmer of doubt was practically paralyzing. It was worse knowing she couldn't do a damned thing to help Rowan and his team. Not a damned thing.

She spent a second sleepless night fretting about what she couldn't do. She couldn't find a house, and she couldn't help Rowan. She hated not having control. She paced the floors, noticing the mirror in the bathroom had spatters of toothpaste above the sink. That's when the housekeeping began in earnest and she spent the entire night scrubbing the townhouse from top to bottom.

BAHATI WAS WAITING FOR HER WHEN LAUREN BLEW IN, looking even more disheveled than she had the day before. Her hair had been combed into a messy braid, with wisps escaping to frame her face. The dark circles under her eyes were more pronounced, and she looked like she was about to drop. The heaviness of her growing belly seemed to weigh her down; the worry curved in her shoulders.

"Seriously, woman." Bahati started to chide her, but Lauren held up a hand as she passed without saying a word. She dropped her purse in the corner and headed straight for the coffee service in the main conference room. She poured a large quantity of cream into a cup before topping it off with coffee. She took a few sips, to test the temperature, then promptly took a long drink, swallowing repeatedly as she tipped the cup back. She picked up the carafe and filled the cup again.

"I talked to Rowan this morning," she finally said. "They're fine. It wasn't them."

"See, I told you." Bahati crossed her arms.

"He called to ask me to help them with some research,"

she said. "There's a lot to do. I told him I'd call him back if I found anything."

"So tell me what we're working on. I'll help."

"Bring your laptop. I'll get my iPad. We can work in here today."

~

LAUREN TOLD HER EVERYTHING ABOUT THE JAGUAR QUEEN, and the glyph that looked like a parachute. She also told Bahati their theory about ancient Maya being time travelers.

"Missing persons' reports?" Bahati's nose twitched. "From how far back?"

"I don't know," she said. "When was the parachute invented?"

"Leonardo DaVinci's idea, right?"

"Seriously?" Lauren asked. "That would have been back in the 15th century."

Bahati went to the internet. "According to Wikipedia, that would have been 1485. But early parachutes may go back as far as 4,000 years."

"What?"

"The ancient Chinese noticed that air resistance would slow a person's fall from a height. There was a story I read about a Chinese emperor who ran away from his villainous father by climbing onto the top of a high building. When there was nowhere to go, he grabbed two bamboo hats and jumped off. He landed safely."

"Must have been two very large hats." Lauren snickered.

"More likely an exaggeration, if you ask me." Bahati agreed.

"No more so than ancient Maya being time travelers, though. Right?"

Bahati ran her hand over her cropped hair, as she let out a deep breath. "I think we've been doing this too long. I find it easier to believe in time travel than I do jumping off a building with a hat for a parachute."

"Physics and gravity are proven concepts," she said. "You have felt the effects of gravity before, ergo your brain recognizes it, and the concept is accepted. Time travel remains ... to date ... little more than science fiction."

"That makes sense," Bahati said.

"So. What about the modern parachute?" She pulled up her phone and held it out for Bahati to see. "Something like that?"

It was a picture of the hieroglyph Rowan had sent. Bahati studied the picture then turned back to her computer, scrolling down. Lauren zoomed in on the picture. As she studied it, something almost magical was triggered in her brain. She recognized the language within the picture. Each dot and swirl was one of two things. It was either a logogram that expressed meaning, or a syllabogram denoting sound values. She focused on the parachute, zooming back out. The words came to her in the same fashion the Cherokee language had found her in Washington State. It said *Sky god*. *Was that what the Maya meant?* She noticed the glyph beneath it on the right side of a double column and realized the two were connected. *Sky god woman*. She shook her head as Bahati pointed at her computer screen.

"Okay, so it looks like the more modern parachute came into being in the late 1700s, and continued to be improved upon through World War I. This one in the glyph," Bahati said. "It kind of looks like the traditional jellyfish-style chute."

Lauren shook off the odd sensation that had washed over her. "So anything after the late 1700s? Well, that ought to narrow things down a bit." Her sarcasm wasn't lost on her coworker. "Planes didn't come around until the more modern era, so if someone jumped out of an airplane ..."

"Or if a plane went down," Bahati said.

"Plane crashes," they said in unison. Lauren returned her

attention to her iPad. Each took their own approach to searches on the internet.

"How close to Chichén Itzá do you think we need to look?"

"I don't know." Lauren chewed on her lip. "Why?"

"There was a passenger plane that went down in 2006 about 125 miles north of there," Bahati said. "Twelve Americans, four Canadians and a crew of three. It took off from Playa Del Carmen. No survivors."

"But everyone was accounted for?"

"Yes," Bahati shook her head, moving on. "Never mind."

"WELL AT LEAST IT MADE THE DAY GO FAST," BAHATI SAID AS they headed toward the elevator.

"And we still have something to work on tomorrow." Lauren stretched her back. "I don't feel like we accomplished anything."

"Well, maybe tomorrow then," Bahati said. "Try to get some sleep tonight, okay?"

"I'll try," Lauren said.

6

The awakening of the ancient Mayan language and the mystery of possible time travelers had Lauren in a tizzy. She wanted very badly to spend the entire evening studying the Maya glyphs. She knew it was a rabbit trail. Like looking for a house. It would keep her up all night — again. Instead, Lauren decided a long walk on the beach would tire her out. It did, but it didn't help her sleep. She had calf cramps and her back ached. So, at midnight, she got up and made a cup of tea, and took it to the bathtub for a long soak.

Despite her best efforts, she spent another night searching the web and studying glyphs. With only a few hours of restless sleep, she was back at the office before sunrise. She even stopped and picked up breakfast for them on her way in. She had her work spread out over the conference table when Bahati came in. She had her laptop, iPad and a plate filled with food in front of her. She was wolfing down a bagel slathered with cream cheese.

"Still no sleep?" Bahati knew her too well.

"No, but lots of work," Lauren said, her mouth full.

"You're going to be sorry when that baby gets here," Bahati said. "You'll never get any sleep then."

"I'll cross that bridge when I get there."

"Uh huh," she said. "Are we working in here today again?"

Lauren nodded.

"Let me go get my laptop. I'll be right there."

Lauren was deeply engrossed in what she was doing. So much so that she never heard the head of the Network knock at the door. "Excuse me?"

She nearly came out of her skin. Lauren let out a yelp so resounding that he jumped too. "I'm sorry, Jacob." She clutched her hand to her chest, panting.

He seemed to recover quickly. "I stopped in to see how you were doing."

He wasn't much older than Rowan, but his hair was full white, and his eyes were as blue as ice. He cut a striking figure. He stood out in Southern California, but he was handsome, she had to admit.

"I'm doing fine," she said. "Rowan called this morning and asked me to do some research for him."

"I take it the team is doing well?"

"Aside from a little car trouble and missing their rendezvous with the professor in Mexico City, they're doing great." She intentionally didn't mention the news story.

"That's good," he said. "After our difficulties last season, I must say I'm impressed at how well this season is going."

Lauren sat back in her chair. She forced her expression to remain passive, even though she blamed Jacob for sending Rowan off without her. He knew they didn't want to work, and he'd come up with a project he knew they couldn't refuse. "Impressed, or surprised?" She hadn't meant to say it out loud. He pulled out a chair and sat down across from her, snickering. At least it amused him.

"A little of both, I'm sure." He chortled. "I was hoping I could have this conversation with you and Rowan both, but … oh well." Suddenly he was serious. Here it came. The tight budget speech. "I've been approached by one of our sister channels about doing a new show."

"A new show?" That wasn't at all what she was expecting. "Which channel?" She didn't want anything to do with the Science Channel at the moment.

"It'd be on Escape," he said. That was the network's travel channel. "It wouldn't be much different than the program you do now, except it would have more of a travel theme."

Lauren's brow narrowed. "That's what we do now. How would this new show be any different?"

"Lauren, did you know, 41% of Americans let their paid vacation days go to waste?" Jacob asked. "I should point out, that you and Rowan are among that statistic."

Lauren considered him for a moment. She wanted to shove it down his throat that they were trying to take a vacation now, but he'd insisted on this whole crazy Maya-thing. She bit her tongue, but did say, "We travel for a living. Why would we need to take a vacation?"

"Granted, you and Rowan are different," he said. "In more ways than one." He snickered. Lauren didn't even crack a smile. "Look, the US Travel Association believes that the average American doesn't travel because they don't see the value in it. They don't feel like they need adventure, or they don't feel like they can afford to be away from the office. A healthy work-life balance is critical. Not only to give workers a chance to enjoy their lives outside of the office, but also to recharge. It makes you more productive when you get back to work. We want this new show to inspire a new spirit of discovery. We want them to see what's out there to explore. To show that families of all shapes and sizes can travel together. We think you and Rowan would be perfect to show the world how easy travel can be."

Lauren's brow lifted. "Have you taken an airplane lately? Between over-booked flights, packed airports, long lines, and TSA check points? It's a freaking nightmare."

"But it can be simple," he said. "You have over 100,000 frequent flyer miles. I know. I checked. Rowan just racked his up to 150,000 miles. It's time to put those miles to good use."

Lauren pursed her lips and shook her head. Her hand went absent-mindedly to her stomach. "I'm not saying we're not interested, but... we have a baby on the way. We're looking to buy a house and put down some roots. You were the one who encouraged that, by the way. We want to take our maternity and paternity leaves soon. I think travel is probably the last thing on either of our minds."

He nodded and sat back. "I completely understand," he said. "Production wouldn't begin until next year. Making your growing family part of the experience would make it more authentic to the American public. Could you please think about it? Discuss it with Rowan and let me know if you have any reservations or concerns we can address."

"Like I said, I'm not saying no," Lauren said. "How long before we have to make a decision?"

"I wouldn't make the Network wait too long," he said.

"Thanks," Lauren said.

He stood. "Holler if you need anything while Rowan's away." He patted her shoulder. "If I can help, let me know."

"I will." Lauren stood. "Thank you."

Bahati snuck in from the other door as soon as he was gone. "What was that all about?"

"I'm not sure," Lauren said, sinking back into her chair. Her head suddenly ached, almost as bad as her back. She pushed her aches and pains, and any other concerns, to the back of her mind.

"Surely they don't want you to travel more," Bahati said.

"Surely not," Lauren said, completely disconnected. "Come on, let's get back to work."

∾

"Would you like another bagel with your cream cheese?" Lauren glanced up at Bahati, then looked at her empty plate. Half the cream-cheese had oozed off her bagel when she smooshed it together to make a sandwich.

"Sure." She pushed her plate over to Bahati, who glanced in the bagel box, and smiled, picking out the onion bagel, putting it on her plate.

"So what did Rowan say about the news story we saw yesterday?" Bahati asked.

"He said they didn't know anything about it, but that's what made the professor miss their rendezvous. He finally made it and he's the one that told them about the parachute woman."

"Have you had any luck?"

Lauren debated how much to tell her. "I don't know." Lauren decided to keep her whirring thoughts and mystic abilities to herself. She tapped on her iPad and brought up a story she'd found. "The only one that really stands out is a corporate jet that crashed into the jungle and was found later to be carrying large quantities of cocaine."

"Drug-running is pretty common in Mexico," Bahati said. "So I hear."

"True," Lauren said. "Is it time for lunch yet?"

"How many bagels have you had this morning? And you're worried about lunch?"

"Oh yeah, right." Lauren shook her head. "I need more coffee."

"Lauren." Bahati nudged her. "Lauren?"

Lauren glanced up from her iPad. "Huh?"

"Are you going to work late?" Bahati asked.

"No. Why?"

"It's after five," she said. "I'm going home."

"I think I found something," Lauren said.

Bahati stopped and took a step back. "Oh?" She crossed her arms and leaned her hip on the conference table. "Like what?"

"There was an American socialite traveling with her father in Mexico City when she was kidnapped and held for ransom in 2002," she said. "Her father, against the advice of the FBI, State Department and American Embassy, paid the ransom. Over $5 million."

"And?"

"And she was never returned," Lauren said.

"What makes you think that has anything to do with Rowan's parachute woman?"

"The men who collected the ransom were supposed to return her that afternoon, but they were captured when their plane crashed while landing at the airport in Progresso. She wasn't on the plane."

"So?" Bahati queried. "They told the police she escaped by jumping out of the plane with their last parachute."

"Well now." Bahati tilted her head a bit. "That does sound interesting. And the money?"

"Never recovered. The bills were marked … they've never turned up." Lauren reached for her phone. "I have to call Rowan."

7

The team spent all day documenting the circle of stones. They took measurements and examined the jungle around the mound where the monoliths stood. Rowan was hot, tired, and hungry. All that was forgotten when Lauren began rattling off information she and Bahati had found. She spoke so fast; he hardly understood a word of it.

"Lauren, wait." He finally got a word in edgewise. "Slow down and start over. I caught something about a kidnapping and an airplane."

He sat down on one of the stone blocks scattered at the edge of the site to catch his breath. She related the story with the calm measure he was accustomed to hearing in his wife's voice. "Are you kidding me?" That was the best thing he could think of to say.

"No. We verified the story from multiple sources," she said, as if she had to justify her research to him. "Her name was Stephanie Wentworth. She was sixteen when she disappeared."

"Wentworth?" Rowan's voice muffled. "Her father was William Wentworth? *The* William Wentworth?"

"Wentworth Petroleum's Founder and CEO until his death, a year ago... suicide."

"Wait, what?"

"He climbed to the top ledge of one of his offshore oil rigs — and jumped," Lauren said.

"Why?" Rowan asked. "Any suicide note?"

"Yes," she said. "He published a blog post about how he never recovered from the grief of losing his daughter. He was never the same. Shortly after Stephanie disappeared, his wife left him. He began abusing alcohol and taking pain killers. He spent months in rehab. Somehow, he was able to keep it from his board of directors... and the media. When oil prices plunged in '08, his company lost billions. He nearly lost everything. He started selling off assets to keep the company afloat. He sold his mansion in the Hollywood hills. He sold his Mercedes and his collection of muscle cars. He cancelled his membership at the country club. He canceled his subscription to Forbes Magazine. Then, he moved to Oklahoma City and bought a modest home and an old pick-up truck. He'd started his career in Tulsa, so he went back to the basics with his business. They were able to re-organize and recover from the recession. It's now in the top ten of the Fortune 500 companies in America. He was worth nearly $500 billion when he died."

"Who inherited his money?" Rowan asked the question sarcastically.

"He left most of it to the University of Oklahoma, for their petroleum engineering and football program. Even the marching band got a new building on campus and several customized tour buses and an equipment tractor trailer. All thanks to his generous endowment."

"Wow," Rowan swallowed hard. "So, now the hard part..."

"Which is?"

"Figuring out if the Wentworth girl has anything to do

with the Jaguar Queen of Chichén Itzá." Rowan swatted a mosquito. "Can you send some equipment for me?" He glanced up at the sky as the sun went behind a cloud. The air was damp. It made the jungle smells even more overt.

"What do you need?"

"Ground penetrating radar and some metal detectors," Rowan asked. "Dr. DeLaFuentes doesn't have access to a GPR, and I meant to pack them and the metal detectors, but in my haste... well, I forgot them."

"Not like your bag wasn't already full."

"Exactly."

"I'll have Bahati take care of that first thing in the morning," Lauren said.

"We've got hotel reservations at a nearby resort," Rowan said. "I'm ready to get a shower and a plate full of tacos. Then, I'm going to sleep in a real bed with air conditioning. I'll send the shipping info via email once we get settled tonight."

"I wish it was my bed." Lauren sighed.

"Me too," Rowan said.

"I wish I had tacos."

"I'd share mine with you if you were here."

"I know. I'll call if we find anything."

"I'll do the same," Rowan said. "Get some rest. You sound tired."

"You too."

8

It took four days for the crate with the equipment to reach them at the resort. They were working out of Rowan's room, using it for *basecamp*. It wasn't the luxury vacation one might think. The hotel had seen better days. They'd gotten the last few rooms left in the whole region. All the other hotels and resorts were filled with other research groups, and pilgrims who came to witness the end of the world.

To make matters worse, it had been raining for three days straight. Working in the rain was a challenge. Normally the Veritas team would work rain or shine, but the limestone gravel roads had turned to a hazardous quagmire. Enrique had to tow them out of the mud more than once. They finally gave up and returned to the resort. What had been intended to be a brief respite, had turned into a refuge. Here, they worked on their research, and performed maintenance checks and calibration on their equipment. Five guys crowded into a room meant for two.

"This symbol is the sign for water. In the jungle, the only reliable source of water is the cenote," Enrique said. Even the professor had taken shelter with the team. "There are dozens of them scattered around the jungle. They are giant caves, created in the limestone, carved by rainwater. These pools were sacred to the Maya."

"Water usually is," Jean-René said with a lift of his shoulder.

"When there are no rivers or lakes, they become especially so." Enrique nodded. "Do you scuba dive, Mr. Pierce?"

Rowan grinned. "Yes, I do. I love scuba diving."

"When the rain lets up, I will take you to one of the cenotes I found a few months ago a couple hours south of here. It's a long journey, but I think you will like it and it's worth the trouble."

"So what do we do until the rain stops?" Jean-René glanced out to the pool. Raindrops bounced several inches into the air with the force of their descent. It was raining so hard you couldn't see the tennis courts across the parking lot.

"The bar is open," Rowan licked his lip. "I've been in Mexico almost a week and haven't had a margarita yet."

"Is it even supper time yet?"

"It's five o'clock somewhere." Enrique grinned.

Rowan stood collecting his laptop and his papers. "Let's go have a drink then!"

OVER A LONG EVENING OF DRINKS AND TACOS, ENRIQUE gave Rowan and Jean-René a lesson in reading the Maya hieroglyphs.

"So this symbol is *u chan*. It means *his captive or his ward*." Enrique pointed to one of the stone carvings on his laptop. "But this symbol is *u bak*. It means *his captive or his bone*."

Rowan shook his head. He was overwhelmed and amazed at the multiple meanings of the blocks. "No wonder it's been so hard to translate these glyphs." He drained his fifth margarita.

"Barkeep, another round!" Jean-René called.

"Sorry, is last call thirty minutes ago." The Guatemalan bartender shook his head. "*No mas margarita* for you, *amigo*."

"Aw man! What time is it?"

"Three o'clock in the morning." Enrique glanced at his watch. "Rowan, Jean-René, we need to get some sleep. Maybe the rain will stop tomorrow, and we can go to the cenote."

"Here's to the cenote." Jean-René raised his sixth glass and tipped it back, nearly falling off the stool.

Enrique caught him and set him upright. The doctor reached for his wallet and pulled out a stack of bills, tossing them on the bar. "*Gracias Marti.*" He waved to the bartender who came and collected their empty glasses. "We'll see you tomorrow night."

"I will cut up more limes for you *gringos*." He guffawed. He'd been enjoying the Americans and their crazy stories.

"*Buenos noches.*" Rowan leaned on Jean-René. The cameraman was in no shape to stand on his own either. Enrique ended up holding them both up, getting them to their rooms, grinning the whole way.

LAUREN WAS AWARE THAT SHE WAS AWAKE, BUT SHE HAD NO understanding of why. The room was dark, except for the dim glow of the television. She rolled over and was immediately aware of what had woken her. A sharp stabbing pain pierced her back. At the same moment, the muscles in her stomach seized. Her belly went hard beneath her hand. She sat up gasping for air, but the pain sent her flat on her back. She was unable to move. Her hands wrapped in the sheets, holding on for dear life. The muscles finally relaxed. But the pain in her back didn't abate.

"Truth Seeker." She heard Tsul'Kalu as if he were sitting in the room with her. "You are in trouble."

"I'm okay." She tried to convince herself. She panted. "I'm okay. Just... Braxton-Hicks... I'm... sure."

"You need help." The voice came to her again. "You are not well."

"No." She gasped. "I'm okay. It's just a cramp."

"Call your friend." He calmly instructed. She didn't argue with the hallucination. She found her phone, but hesitated. It was two in the morning. "Call her."

She obeyed. "Bahati," she said, as clearly as possible.

"Lauren? Are you okay?"

"No. I don't think so." She panted, rolling flat on her back. "Something's wrong."

"Do you need me to call an ambulance?"

"Just... come get me," she said. "Take me to the ER?"

"I'll be there in five minutes," she said. "Is your front door locked?"

"Yes." Lauren groaned, panic washing through her. She wasn't sure she could get to the door in this condition, not by herself.

"Do you still keep a key in the ceramic frog in the flower bed?"

"Yes." Relief washed through her. "It's under the yellow rose bush."

"Okay," she said. "Hang tight. I'm on my way."

"Just hurry."

"MAY I HELP YOU?" THE NURSE DIDN'T EVEN LOOK UP FROM the computers as Bahati brought her into the ER. Bahati had the presence of mind to call and let them know they were on their way. Something was definitely wrong. Lauren had broken out in a cold sweat, and her hair clung to her brow.

"This is Lauren Pierce," Bahati said, curtly. "I called a few minutes ago."

"I feel like I've been run through with a claymore..." Lauren gasped. "My back is killing me ... my stomach just went hard like a rock."

"How far along are you?"

"Not far enough." She shook her head. "Thirty weeks."

"Did your water break?"

"No," Lauren said.

The nurse lay a clip board on the counter and barked instructions for her to fill the forms out and have her ID and insurance card ready. Bahati started to protest, but Lauren snatched the clipboard off the counter and gave the woman a shaded expression of irritation. She sniffed and made her way over to the bank of chairs nearby, sinking into one.

Lauren was relieved when a nurse brought a wheelchair and they moved her to it carefully. "Mrs. Pierce?"

"It's *Doctor* Pierce, actually." Lauren corrected her.

"You might be having Braxton-Hicks contractions, but we'll make sure you're not in labor."

Where are you taking her?" Bahati asked.

"We'll take her up to labor and delivery," the nurse said.

"OKAY, MRS. PIERCE." THE RESIDENT CAME IN, LOOKING over her chart.

"*Doctor* Pierce," she corrected him. "But ... call me Lauren."

"Okay, Lauren. We're going to hook you up to some monitors and check your baby and make sure it's okay. Do you know what you're having?"

"No." She was much more comfortable flat on her back, but the stabbing pain still made her feel like she was being ripped apart.

"Oh, you like surprises?"

"My husband wants to know, but... there's just not enough

mystery left in the world." Lauren winced as they went to work on her.

"Temp is 103.4," the nurse said.

"Have you been feeling okay lately?"

"Eh." Lauren managed weakly. "I came home from work early yesterday ... I was just really tired, but I haven't been sleeping much lately."

"Why not?"

"Couldn't sleep," she panted. "My husband's working ... in Mexico, and I don't sleep... well when he's .. gone."

"Well you're running a fever," he said.

"Is my baby okay?" she asked as Bahati came in.

"Let's find out." He peeled up her t-shirt. Taking the Doppler from the nurse he squeezed some gel onto her stomach before running the probe over her belly. A comforting whooshing rhythm came into focus, and Lauren recognized the baby's heartbeat, strong and steady. "That's a good sign."

"Is that the heartbeat?" Bahati asked.

Lauren smiled. "Yes." She sighed, cringing as her stomach went hard again, the muscles squeezing so tight, it took her breath away.

"Holy cow!" Bahati's face contorted. "That is a contraction, isn't it?"

"Sure looks like it," the resident said. "Let's get her hooked up to the uterine monitor. Let's go ahead and start an IV and get some fluids going, and some antibiotics." He continued his exam. "I want a full work up, and we'll start her on some Terbutaline to slow the contractions."

"Yes, Doctor." The nurse charted the orders at the computer terminal in the corner.

"Lauren, we're going to admit you until we can find out what's going on and make sure we can get these contractions under control, okay?" Lauren acknowledged him with a wordless tilt of her head. Bahati caught her hand, holding onto it tightly. Lauren's face was a study in focus as she held it in a permanent wince. "Where does your back hurt?"

She pointed to the right side of her back. He ran his hand along the spot, feeling for any injury. "Make sure we get a urinalysis," he said to the nurse. "I'm thinking UTI. Lauren, do you drink a lot of water?"

"Usually," she said between her teeth. "Haven't lately."

"Yeah." He nodded. "Could be kidney then." He patted her on the shoulder. "Hang tight and we'll find out what's going on and get you feeling better."

A FEW HOURS LATER, THE MEDICINE AND THE FLUIDS HAD kicked in. She was able to roll onto her side, at long last, comfortable. Bahati paced back and forth. "Should I call Rowan?" Bahati broke the silence.

"No," Lauren snapped, a bit too quickly. "Let's not worry him needlessly." She yawned. "I'm feeling better. He doesn't need to know yet."

The resident came back in. "Lauren, we got your test results back," he said. "There was blood in your urine, and your white blood count was elevated. That says kidney stone."

"A kidney stone?" Lauren wrinkled her brow.

"It's actually quite common. It's worse when you get dehydrated," he said. "I bet you drink a lot of coffee, tea, or soda, don't you?"

"Guilty as charged," Lauren admitted.

"I thought so. It also explains your contractions. Dehydration can do that too. So, from here on out, it's one cup a day, and at least 64 ounces of water," he said, leaning on the rail. "Any more contractions?"

"No," Lauren said. "Not for a while."

"That's good," he said. "I'm going to keep you on a twenty-three-hour observation, just to make sure you get plenty of fluids and antibiotics. We want to make sure the contractions are under control. I've called your OB. He said he will stop by this morning when he does rounds. So just get comfortable and try and get some rest."

"Thanks." Lauren yawned, ready for a nap.

"Do you need anything?" Bahati asked when they were alone.

"I need you to not call Rowan," she said curtly. "I don't need him worrying about me."

"I understand." Bahati smoothed her boss' hair back. "Get some rest and I'll be back in a little bit."

"Promise me." Lauren caught her wrist. "Say it."

"I promise," Bahati said. She even crossed her heart with her finger when Lauren glowered at her dubiously.

Lauren nodded and closed her eyes and surrendered to her exhaustion.

BAHATI SAT DOWN IN THE LOBBY AND DIALED THE NUMBER ON her phone. "Thanks for sending the GPR, Bahati," Rowan said without preamble.

"Rowan, Lauren's in the hospital."

There was a long pause before he said anything. "What happened?"

"She told me not to call you. But I figured I'd rather get fired by her than fired by you."

"No one's getting fired, Bahati."

"I know, but I can handle *her* being mad at me. If anything happened to her and I didn't tell you, I'm not sure I could handle *you* being mad."

"No, you did the right thing," he said. She could tell it was everything he could do to keep his composure. "What's going on? Do I need to come home? I can catch the first flight out."

"No," Bahati said, explaining everything to him. "You

don't need to come home. They're just going to keep her long enough to make sure her fever goes down. They also need to get her hydrated and make sure her contractions have stopped."

"Contractions?"

"Yeah, but the doctor thinks she's dehydrated more than anything. He told us that could cause contractions, as well as the kidney stones."

"Wow, this just keeps getting better. Kidney stones?"

"Come on, Rowan. I need you to focus. The point is, she's okay now. I don't need you coming home. If you come home, she'll know I called you and she'll kill me. She made me promise."

"So make a promise to me… if anything changes?"

"I'll call you first, and the airline second," Bahati said flatly.

"You're a good friend," Rowan said. "To me and to Lauren."

"I love you both," Bahati said. "I promise to make sure she takes care of herself."

"I appreciate that," he said. "I'll call you this evening. We're about to go diving in an ancient cenote in the middle of the Yucatán."

"Was that part of the plan?"

"Enrique wanted me to see something in this cavern."

"Lauren's going to be pissed," she scoffed. "You know how she feels about caves."

"Which why it's better that I go without her," he said. "And that she doesn't know. I'll make a deal with you. I will formally disavow any knowledge of this conversation if Lauren calls me, if you don't tell her I went diving in a cenote," Rowan said.

"Deal." Bahati agreed.

9

"Rowan? What are you doing here?" Lauren was startled by his appearance.

"If you think I wouldn't come home when I heard you were sick, you're crazy."

"Dammit Bahati," she muttered under her breath. "I didn't want her to call you and I didn't want you to come home just because I'm sick. I'm not even that sick," she moaned.

"You're sick enough that you've been hallucinating," he said, sitting on the edge of her bed.

"I have?"

He nodded. "Is the baby okay?"

"Yes," she said, putting her hand over his, moving it to where a foot pressed against her abdomen. "The baby's fine."

He looked at her cautiously, seeing the trouble in her eyes. "What's wrong?"

"I'm a horrible mother..." Tears flooded from her eyes. "The baby's not even here and I can't do anything right."

"What do you mean? You're not doing anything wrong."

"I let myself get sick." She sobbed.

Rowan shook his head. "You didn't do this on purpose,"

he said. "You can't blame yourself. You're going to be a fantastic mother."

"It's just... I never had a good relationship with my own mother" she sniffed. "She didn't need another kid. My father left because of me. I was an *oops*. She never meant to get pregnant with me. If it hadn't been for my extended family, I might have died."

She had told him before about how her aunts and older brothers had practically raised her. She had always fought with her mom, and the two hadn't spoken in years. Even at their wedding, Lauren and Diana had been distant. It was impressive the woman had even come.

Growing up, her brothers took her hunting with them, and taught her how to survive on her own, from the time she was little. The only brother she ever had issues with was Michael. They had a competitive and contentious relationship. He was always trying to one up her in everything. "You're not *your mother*, Lauren."

She reached for a tissue to dry her eyes. "I know, but what if?"

Rowan's hands spread over her growing belly and he leaned over and kissed her stomach. He rested his head on its swell, listening with an ear pressed to her bare skin. "I know many things in this world, and the one thing I know to be true, is that this child will be well-loved and well-cared for. We don't have to be perfect parents; we just have to love our child with all our hearts."

Her hand went to his hair. She loved running her fingers through it. The dim light played in the short cinnamon-gold locks. "If I love our baby half as much as I love you, that will be true," Lauren said, sighing.

"I love you." He lifted his head and rose, leaning down and kissing her.

"I love you too," she responded.

"Well, I love you, too." Bahati sat on the edge of her bed, with her hand on Lauren's hip. "Welcome back."

Lauren startled. She looked around; confusion written on her brow. "What?"

"You've been pretty out of it," Bahati said. "How do you feel?"

"I'm angry." She snapped at Bahati. "You called Rowan." She shifted in the bed, drawing up the covers.

Bahati's brow rose, but she held her ground. "Of course I did," she said. "He'd kill me if I let anything happen to you."

"Well he didn't need to come all the way home just for me," she said, looking over Bahati's shoulder toward the door. "Where did he go?"

"What are you talking about?" Bahati asked. "Rowan's still in Mexico. They went diving in a cenote." She clamped her hand over her mouth.

"He went diving in a cenote!" Lauren started to sit up, but Bahati restrained her with a gentle hand. "What the hell is he doing diving in a cenote?

"What makes you think he was here?" Bahati retorted.

"I saw him. He was just... here" Lauren rolled over onto her back, pushing back her damp hair. "I swear. I was just talking to him. Don't change the subject on me."

Bahati's hand went to her forehead. "You're still burning up."

"Why did Rowan go into a cenote? He knows how I feel about that." She pouted, pushing Bahati's hand away.

"Look, he's an accomplished diver. He wouldn't take any chances. Not now, with a baby on the way. I'm sure they took every safety precaution known to man."

"Oh." Lauren reached for the cup of water on the bedside table. She took a drink then shook her head. "I swear, it was like he was here. I could feel his hand on me... he kissed me."

Bahati smiled at her. "Well, if I was going to hallucinate, that wouldn't be a bad thing to envision."

"Ew! Get your own husband!"

∼

IT WAS LATE AFTERNOON BEFORE HER OB CAME IN TO SEE HER. "Full moon," he said, as if it were an apology. "How are you feeling?"

"Better," she said. "My back isn't hurting as bad as it was."

"Well, all your tests point to a kidney stone," he said, confirming what the resident had told her earlier. He went over to the uterine monitor and studied the read out. "No more contractions since early this morning?"

"No," she said as the nurse took her blood pressure and then her temperature.

"Fever's down to 102," the nurse said.

"Let's do another round of antibiotics," he said. "Lauren, I'm going to keep you one more night and see if we can't get that fever under control and to keep you on IV fluids. Dehydration can be to blame for the kidney stone, but also for the contractions. The stone may have passed, but it might have just shifted. We can keep you comfortable, but I want you to lay off sodas, coffee, and tea as well from here on out." Lauren nodded, but wasn't happy about it. "I'm also putting you on bed rest until further notice."

"Bed rest?"

"No physical activity, no sexual intercourse, and no more than twenty minutes out of bed a day. You can shower and make simple meals for yourself. You need to take it easy to make sure these contractions don't start back up. I don't need to tell you; 30 weeks is too early to deliver. Anything we can do to keep that baby in there for at least six more weeks, has to be done."

"Can I do research with my iPad?"

"Yes," he said. "But that's about it. Rowan will have to do the housework, the shopping, whatever else needs to be done."

"He's still in Mexico." Lauren pursed her lips, mentally going through her list of things she would need to have done for her, wondering how she would be able to do it.

"Is there someone that can help you until he gets home?"

"I'm sure I can get help," Lauren said, meaning Bahati. She was confident she could count on her best friend.

"That's good," he said. "I just need to do a quick exam to make sure you're not dilating."

BAHATI CAME BACK IN AFTER THE DOCTOR LEFT. "SO WHEN can you go home?"

"Not yet," Lauren said. "Maybe tomorrow ... if my fever goes down."

"Bummer," Bahati said.

"It gets better." Lauren sighed. "I'm on full bed rest for the next six weeks, at least."

"What does that mean?"

"No cooking, no cleaning, no shopping."

"No working?"

"I can do research from bed," she said.

"I'll take care of anything you can't do. You know that, right? At least until Rowan gets home."

Lauren smiled, taking her hand. "Thank you."

"I'm going into the office in the morning. I sent a request to the NTSB for a copy of the incident report on the socialite's plane that crashed. A courier is supposed to deliver it."

"Why the NTSB?"

"Because the FBI wouldn't release the foreign criminal files, even with a formal Open Records request."

"I wonder why?"

"They did tell me that two of the three kidnappers are currently up for parole," she said. "I've found a couple of old news articles where they were eligible before, but their parole was denied."

"I wonder why?"

"No telling," Bahati said.

"What happened to the third kidnapper? Why isn't he up for parole?"

"He escaped in 2009 and was never seen nor heard from again," Bahati said, pausing as she glanced out the window. "You know, this is probably a big waste of time. We don't have any reason to believe that she has anything to do with that pillar at Chichén Itzá."

"Just a glyph we can't explain and a myth about time travelers." Lauren conceded. "If nothing else, it makes for a good story."

"Now I know you're feverish," Bahati said. "You've never been happy with a *good story*."

"You're probably right." She yawned.

"TRUTH SEEKER?" THE VOICE CAME TO HER IN THE NIGHT. She was wide awake. The ceiling tiles above her were swirling in patterns, like Rorschach's blots. "Why do you not sleep?"

"I'm not sure," Lauren said. "My mind is restless."

"Among all the things you need, little one, sleep is the most important," he said.

"How is it you always come to me when I am troubled?" Lauren asked.

"You call to me," he said. "It is part of the ancient gift. It is the bond we share."

"What do you know of the ancient people known as the Maya?" Lauren said.

"They lived in the time of the All-Father when the gods walked among us. They shared their knowledge with the People," he said. "Show me the writings you saw on the pillar, Truth Seeker." The blots on the ceiling morphed in to assorted glyphs, but the only one that came clear to her was the one with the supposed parachute. "Ah, that is the Jaguar Queen. She was sent from the heavens to the Maya. She had the powers of foresight and prophesy."

"Was she a goddess? Or was she ... like me?"

"Like you. But she did not have the same gifts bestowed upon her," he said. "Her titles were given to her by the people of the region. She was cunning, and wise, and grew into a great leader. You have powers she could never understand."

"Like what?"

"Like your ability to summon me and to speak the Ancient All-Language," he said. "You summoned the Protector when you needed him. You have the ability to see beyond the dark and into the world of the gods. You who seek the truth, have seen it, and have made wise use of it; the gods smile upon you and show you favor."

"But how can I help Rowan?" she asked. "I can't even get out of bed."

"You must rest now," he said. "Your power grows stronger even as your stomach swells. It is in slumber that the visions will come to tell you what you must know."

The perfume of herbs filled the air around her, and it reminded her of the medicine woman who had tended them in the cavern beneath Mt. Saint Helen so long ago. Chamomile, willow bark, tansy... the heady fragrance was like an anesthetic. She breathed deeply. Her eyelids grew heavy. Sleep came with a feeling of peace and well-being.

10

"Wow!" Rowan glanced down into a crater that opened up in the middle of the jungle. "How far down is that?" Sunlight pierced the canopy and the whole cavern glowed.

"It's about six meters," Enrique estimated as he stopped and peeled off his backpack.

"How do we get down there?" Jean-René asked.

"Getting down is easy." Enrique bemused, gazing down into the cenote. His eyes lifted to Jean-René's. "Getting back up, not so much."

Rowan inspected the ancient tree trunk and the cantilevered jib. There was a rusted pulley and ropes made of natural fibers. They were dried, and the fibers turned to dust as the crew started rigging the ropes, preparing the equipment to be lowered. "I suspect getting back up has something to do with this. What is this? A jib crane?"

"Exactly." Enrique beamed. "The fun part is jumping in." He turned and waved a hand towards the crew he'd brought with them. "These guys get to hoist us back up."

"Is this thing safe?" Rowan inspected the jib dubiously.

"Please!" Enrique scoffed with a titter of a chuckle in the

back of his throat. "Would I joke about your safety? I have been down here a dozen times. It has never failed me."

Rowan wasn't sure he appreciated the professor laughing about something so serious. "If safety is a joke, then death is the punchline," he muttered.

"Of course it is safe," Enrique assured him with a hearty slap on the back. "Trust me. The modern Maya are just as good at engineering as their ancient ancestors. I promise you, it's safe."

"How ancient is this though?" The old rope ran through his fingers and fibers sloughed off into dust. Rowan stepped back and stood with his brows lifted and his hands on his hips. He glanced down in the hole, then back at the jib. "We could just send the ROV."

"Chicken." Jean-René cackled at him from behind the camera.

Rowan flashed a bright smile. "In the famous words of my wife..." He held up his middle finger at Jean-René and the camera. With a chuckle of resignation, he started peeling out of his backpack. "Let's do this."

"I'm not jumping with the underwater camera," Jean-René shook his head.

Rowan's head shot up as he turned and locked eyes with his Chief of Photography. "Who's chicken now?"

"You can hoist it down," Alejandro suggested.

"I'll stay up here and run the ROV," Jean-René volunteered, staying well back from the edge of the crater. "We can film video with it. Looks like the water is really clear."

"Alejandro? You want to come down with us?"

"No, I think I'll stay up here with the hoist team," he said. "You're a pretty big boy. I'm not sure these guys can hoist you up. Besides, if that pulley snaps, you're going to want me top side."

Rowan glanced at the four guys Enrique had brought along. Not a one of them was much taller than Tuuk, and

Rowan probably outweighed all of them. Alejandro, on the other hand, at least had a chance, especially with Jean-René to help.

"Okay," Rowan said. "Looks like it's you and me, Dr. Rick."

Enrique chuckled. "That's funny." The professor grinned. "I like that one."

"Suit up, let's go," Rowan said, looking directly at the camera, a look of annoyance on his face.

ONCE THEY WERE IN THEIR DIVE SUITS, ROWAN STOOD AT THE cavern's edge. He steeled his courage. "Six meters, huh?" He took a deep breath.

"More or less," Enrique said, with a wave of his hand. "After you."

"Uh, yeah." Rowan shook his head. He glanced at Jean-René and the camera. "What the hell, right? Here goes nothing."

Rowan took a running start and leapt out into the air. He seemed to hover at the apex of his jump for a split second before he fell straight down. He had the good sense to straighten his body like a pencil, rather than going for a cannonball. He cut through the water with almost no splash. He went deep but popped right back up, with an enthusiastic cheer. "Whew!"

"I told you that was the fun part!" Enrique called down as Rowan swam to the side of the pool.

"You didn't tell me it would be so cold!" Rowan called back. His voice echoed.

Enrique took a running leap himself. "Banzai!" He jumped and landed a few feet from Rowan, splashing him.

It took some time to get the equipment down to them, including their diving gear and the cameras. Rowan was shivering by the time they were all set to go. Enrique led him down into the dark depths. The water was as clear as glass. The effect was disconcerting. After a while, Rowan wasn't sure which way was up and which way was down. If it weren't for the bubbles, he could see how someone might get lost.

"How deep is the water?" His voice sounded hollow through the intercom built into his dive mask.

"About 38 meters," Enrique answered.

"That's what?"

"About 125 feet." The professor knew exactly what Rowan was asking about. "Americans and your lack of metric comprehension."

"Sorry," Rowan said. "They stopped teaching it when I was in third grade."

"There are a series of tunnels at 30 meters. They've started collapsing, so it's not safe to explore," Enrique said. "But I think you'll be interested to see something over here." Rowan followed him down all the way to the bottom. There on a stone shelf, they found an altar, much like the one at the circle of standing stones. A pile of human skulls lay on one side of it. Skeletal remains lay scattered on the other side. Below, was a second shelf littered with more bones.

"The Maya believed the humans were made from corn and the blood of the gods. In order to appease them, blood had to be shed. Human sacrifice was a common practice. You know this," Enrique said. "However, this site when it was in use, it wasn't under water. These altars were on dry, hallowed ground."

Rowan rolled to glance up so he could see how far up the water went, and was amazed to think about how much rain it had taken to fill this reservoir. "Where'd all the water go?"

"About the time of the height of the Maya civilization, it was believed there was a terrible drought," he said. "There is still much debate about if that was what caused the Maya to abandon the region and go north from Chichén Itzá to invade into the Aztec regions. It's possible that wars were fought for water."

"And there were wars, right?"

"Exactly," Enrique said. "The Maya would sacrifice their captives. The higher the rank, the more likely the gods were to be pleased with the sacrifice."

"So they'd bring their captives down here and behead them, and leave the bodies for the gods," it was less of a question, and more of a statement. "Gross and very disturbing," Rowan retorted.

"That's why I thought you'd like this place," the professor said. "There's one more thing I want you to see."

The cavern was massive. They crossed over to a pillar of stone off to one side. It looked like it might have been a large stalagmite at one point, but a huge chunk had sheared off and lay at the bottom of the cavern. Rowan fell in behind his dive partner as they worked their way up through the cenote. Rowan checked his dive computer on his wrist, then his oxygen gage. They were reaching the end of their dive time and would need to start their final assent soon.

As they came around the fallen pillar, it became apparent what Enrique had brought him here to see. It was a massive stone carving that was set in the side of the cenote wall. The sun beaming on it gave it an ethereal glow but didn't illuminate the entire circular carving. "Oh my gosh! That's amazing!"

"This is a recounting of the history of the reign of the Jaguar Queen," he said. "See the glyph here at the middle, that's the same as the glyph on the pillar at Chichén Itzá."

"The parachute." Rowan moved in to study it closer.

"Yes," Enrique said. "This tells of her fall from a burning disc in the heavens, and of her many powers. They called her a fire goddess when she came to live among the holy people of the Temple. Her arrival emboldened the Jaguar King, and he took it as an omen ... a sign of the gods' blessing. So he attacked a neighboring city, and here it says the streets flowed with the blood of their enemies. His victory brought him much power, and he claimed his seat upon the throne. He also had a right to any prize he desired, so he took her to wife, to be his queen. His prosperity lasted for decades."

"That is amazing." Rowan couldn't believe what he was seeing.

"Jean-René to Rowan." The radio squelched in his earpiece.

"Go for Rowan," he answered.

"Your air should be getting low. Are you on your way up?"

"Yeah," Rowan nodded, signaling Enrique to head up. Rowan turned the camera back on the carving. He made sure he got a good shot of each symbol, before falling in behind the professor and heading back to the surface.

IT WAS NEAR DAWN WHEN THEY RETURNED TO THEIR ROOMS in Mérida. After a few hours of sleep, Rowan and Enrique celebrated their successful dive with another night at the bar, this time with Mexican beer. The following morning, Rowan was sitting in the lobby with his sunglasses on. His head was throbbing when the rest of the team came back from the hotel restaurant where they'd had breakfast.

"Damn, Rowan," Jean-René said. He could laugh. He'd gone to bed early. "You look like death warmed over."

Rowan glared at him through the shaded lenses. His head hurt too badly to even bother with flipping him off. But a profanity-laced swear seemed appropriate for the moment.

"Cranky much?" Alejandro sneered. He'd come down for a couple of beers, but he hadn't stayed long.

"Just remind me never to take part in *pesos cervasas* night ever again," he groaned.

"What's on the schedule today?" Dr. Rick asked. He looked far too chipper for Rowan's taste.

"Ground penetrating radar and metal detectors," Jean-René said. Rowan could feel himself turn green; his stomach churning. He looked for a flowerpot or trashcan to puke in.

"Excellent," Enrique said. He caught Rowan by the arm and hoisted him to his feet. "How are you today, my friend?"

Rowan raised a finger to him, his eyes spinning in his head. "You... are not *my friend.*" He fought to keep his stomach contents down. "Not my friend."

"*Tecate* is not your friend, mi amigo." Enrique observed. "Neither is *Corona*, nor *Dos Equis.*"

"I am going to throw up in your shoe." Rowan promised. "Maybe not right now, but sometime today. I will. I will puke in your shoe. I swear it."

"Now, now, now," Enrique feigned indignation. "That is no way to talk to your best friend."

"You are *not* my friend."

"Give me the keys," Alejandro said. "I'll drive today."

Rowan fumbled in his pocket. He handed over the keys. He was in no shape to drive, and he knew it. "Don't hit any potholes."

"Don't puke in my shoe." Alejandro retorted.

IT DIDN'T TAKE LONG FOR ROWAN TO LIVE UP TO HIS PROMISE. Alejandro's shoes were safe, but Enrique was glad he'd left a second pair of boots in Rowan's Jeep. By the time the ground penetrating radar was assembled and ready to run, Rowan had gotten the worst of it out of his system and was ready, more, or less, to go to work.

"What is today?" he asked, as he calibrated the computer on the GPR.

"December 20th," Jean-René said. "Tomorrow is the end of the world."

"Did you notice how the sun in the cenote hit the disc yesterday?" Dr. Rick asked. Rowan nodded. "Tomorrow, the sun will be perfectly aligned with that carving. That is no accident. The Maya were amazing astronomers. They knew exactly what they were doing."

"So where are we going to scan today?" Jean-René asked.

"I want to go back up to the standing stones. I'm just not sure this thing will fit down the narrow path," Rowan said. The GPR was a series of tubes and wires that made a large grid. It took two men to carry it and when it was in use, it had to be carried flat, making it roughly 4' wide and 6' long. It weighed every bit of 50 pounds.

"I think it will work," Alejandro said. "The path was wide enough to walk two abreast most of the way ... just a few narrow spots. We can tilt it to get through."

"Then let's go," Rowan said.

Of course, he let Jean-René and Alejandro do all the work. He was sucking down water like there wasn't going to be any more, and he was still nauseated most of the day. By the time they were set up at the circle of stones, the clouds had returned, and a light mist fell.

"Did anyone see the forecast for the day?"

"Partly cloudy with a chance of Apocalypse." Enrique snorted. He was in rare form and quite pleased with himself.

OVER DINNER, THE TEAM SAT DOWN AND DISCUSSED THEIR plans for the end of the world. "So tonight is the last night of the Maya calendar." Rowan wasn't telling them anything they didn't already know. "I think we need to stay and do an overnight investigation."

"Where do you want to focus?" Alejandro asked.

"I'd like to start at El Castillo," Rowan said. "I think the Observatory is also worth dedicating some time."

"That might be the place to be at sunrise," Enrique suggested.

"I'd also like to go back up to the standing circle of stones and do some isolated EVP sessions," Rowan said. "I get the chills every time I enter that circle, and I think there might be something there."

"We've got approximately two square miles to investigate," Jean-René said. "We could check out some of the other ruins we haven't had a chance to visit yet."

"Okay," Rowan said. "It's about five p.m. now. We have a couple hours of daylight left so we need to get our equipment checked, and maybe catch a quick nap. Then we need to be ready to get cameras rolling no later than say 9:00. Let's hope the weather holds up, or we could be soaked by morning."

"I packed the rain gear," Jean-René said. "It's in the Jeep if we need it."

LAUREN'S FEVER RAGED THROUGH ANOTHER NIGHT AND INTO the day. The doctors ordered more tests, and changed the antibiotics, pushed fluids, and continued to monitor her baby, which seemed to suffer no ill-effects from its mother's fever. Contractions were effectively controlled, and she floated in and out of delirium as the fury burned. Bahati kept a constant vigil, mopping her brow and coaxing her to sip water from a straw in the fleeting moments she was lucid.

Lauren was aware of her plight but also aware of her presence in the world of shadows. She could feel the heat of the bonfire on her face and stood watching the ritual taking place before her. The priests chanted ancient words that were strangely familiar to her. The fever seemed to be making it harder to understand. The knowledge of the ancient All-language seemed dulled. Still, she knew what was happening.

Lauren dreamt of Tsul'Kalu. The old shaman sat before the fire. He had his eyes closed. The wrinkles around his eyes drew heavily downward as the flickering flames illuminated his face. Lauren sat beside him, cross-legged and bowed respectfully. She waited until he spoke. "There was a woman who slipped through the threads of time-and-being long ago. She was lost to memory. She became known to an ancient race. They recognized her crown of stars and placed her on their throne and named her their queen. There were many years of prosperity under her reign, but then the white-eyes came to steal her away. War came to the lands of these people. Prosperity came with war because it meant blood. Blood to be spilled for the Gods. And when the enemy was vanquished, the woman was exalted, and her name was carved into stone so that she might be remembered forever." Lauren could see the images of the story play out in the fire. A woman, with red hair and dark eyes sat on a carved throne. It was painted with vibrant colors, embellished with glyphs. The stone carvings declared her the Bride of the Jaguar King, Goddess of Fire, Jaguar Queen, and the Sky God Woman. Tsul'Kalu continued his story. "But then there was a season of no rain, and rot set into the crops. These people were hungry. The gods demanded more blood. With no enemies to give, they began to sacrifice the least of their ranks. Slaves, peasants, even warriors gave their lives to appease the gods, but to no avail. There were many who fled north, only to die at the hands of the warring Aztec tribes as their enemies moved south to bring more war, and more bloodshed."

Then, Lauren could hear the shouts and cries of these people as she found herself on the edge of the darkness. The drummers pounded out a deep cadence she could feel as a heaviness in her core. Her heart raged with equal forte. The tempo raced at a fevered pace.

A bare-chested Aztec warrior was brought to stand before the altar. He had been painted with bright colors to signify his worth to the gods. His hands were tied behind his back. He was a captive. "This warrior defeated a hundred men in the battle for Tikal," the acolyte announced. He projected his voice strong and loud. "When he was taken, he wounded five men in his struggle. He claims to be the son of the Snake King. He is brought hence. We give to the gods what belongs to the gods."

The priest stepped forward. The drums went silent. The crowd of onlookers settled. Even the jungle seemed to pause and grow deathly quiet. "Man is made from corn and blood, given to us by the gods. As the gods have given life to us, we must give life to the gods." His voice thundered over the waiting crowd. "This warrior has proven himself worthy. He has taken the lives of our warriors, which tells us he is strong. He has fought many battles, which tells us he is brave. He is the son of a king, which tells us he is noble. He is an enemy of high value and worth, to his own people... and to ours. May the gods welcome this gift that we may see our crops grow tall, and our children taller."

The priest raised an obsidian blade over his head as the warrior was brought to the altar. He didn't go willingly. He remained stone-faced and didn't cry out, or struggle against the ropes as he was laid over the stone table which forced his head back, and his chest up, bowing his body as his hands and feet were lashed to the four stone pegs at each corner of the alter. "Though you have warred in this life, may you find peace in the Great Beyond. Speak well of your enemies. We honor your life in your death." The blade came down and blood flowed into the stone channels, pooling around the base of the seven stones. Lauren could taste the tang of iron on her tongue.

She flinched when the priest dug open the man's chest and reached in for his heart, cutting it from his body. He held it up in front of the dying man's bulging eyes. The warrior gasped, convulsed. His life escaped his body. The sacrifice was finished.

The priest took the throbbing heart over to the raging bonfire in the middle of the circle of stones. He held it up for all to see. The blood ran down his bare arms, down his armpit, and along his side. "O hear me gods of the stars, from whom our lifeblood flows!" He called out. He walked the circle around the fire, presenting the heart to both the crowds and the gods. "Accept this, our gift, and be merciful to our people!" He tossed the quivering heart into the fire, and it ignited. Smoke rose from the flames as it came to lay among the glistening coals. Lauren could hear the flesh sizzling. The awful aroma filled her nose. Her stomach threatened to revolt.

She found herself standing before the fire, watching in awe. She turned and realized no one else could see her. On the rise above the circle, over-looking the scene, sat Tsul'Kalu; his eyes closed. His hands rested on his knees. "What is this?" Lauren asked.

"This is the truth of what you seek," he answered. "But it is only part of the story."

Lauren walked over to the woman by the throne. Two warriors had removed her from her place of honor and held her by the wrists. She made no effort to struggle. Lauren studied her. She, like everyone else, was oblivious to Lauren's presence. "Who is this?" Lauren inspected her more closely. Her green eyes were illuminated by the fire's glow. In the flickering light, threads of copper shown in her hair that was twisted into a haphazard knot. It was pinned back with what looked like a sharpened bone, decorated with feathers. "She doesn't look Maya."

"She's not," Tsul'Kalu said. "She is the Fire Goddess. The Jaguar Queen. Sky God Woman."

"She looks... *Anglo*. Is she?" Lauren stopped suddenly, remembering the story about the missing woman. "Why are they holding her? They don't intend to..." Lauren paused, realizing she might be next to face the priest's blade.

"You must ask her," Tsul'Kalu said.

Lauren turned back to look at her, studying the woman's terrified eyes. "But..."

"Call to her." Tsul'Kalu's voice came in a whisper from behind her. "Call to her, Truth Seeker." His voice was a breath, an echo in time. "Speak her name."

Lauren swallowed hard. She took a deep breath. "Stephanie? Stephanie Wentworth?" The woman's eyes turned to Lauren, seeing her for the first time. Suddenly the fire popped, and sparks erupted into the sky. The drums began beating feverishly, and the world spun around her.

"Who are you? Where did you come from?" The woman stared at her. A stunned expression overtook her face. Her eyes were wide with fear. The men yanked on her, moving her to the altar.

"I'm like you," Lauren said, though she wasn't sure where the words came from. She wasn't even speaking English. Still, there was comprehension between them. "They will kill you if they see you," the Jaguar Queen said, looking at the two men holding her. Clearly, she was just as puzzled as Lauren as to why no one else could see this... phantom.

One of the guards turned to the other and shook his head. "She is crazy. She speaks to ghosts."

"The gods will welcome her all the same," the other one answered. "They will rain down fire on our enemies, and water for our crops."

The Jaguar Queen looked back at Lauren, with fear and desperation in her eyes. "They are going to burn my heart. You must leave. Go back where you came from before your heart is consumed by the flames as well."

"Call her to you, Truth Seeker." Tsul'Kalu's voice resonated in her head.

"You must come with me," Lauren said. "I can save you."

"No one can save me now." The Queen looked sad yet stoic at the same time. She looked over at her King, who gazed into the fire, refusing to meet her eye. He had made the decision to sacrifice his bride. Though she seemed to understand, the feeling of betrayal was evident.

Lauren placed a trembling hand on the woman's shoulder. "I hear your words, but you must do as I say, *the Protector* waits for you on the other side. Go to him. He will see you safe. Find me in the Other World and we will help you."

Lauren moved suddenly, using all her strength to slam her fist into one of the guards' stomach. He buckled as the pain of it resonated down her arm. Lauren turned to the perplexed guard on the other side, bringing up her knee into his groin, elbowing him in the nose as he buckled.

The Fire Goddess stood transfixed, as everyone turned to look at her and the drums stopped. The fire seem to throb even without their beating. Lauren realized this was her one shot at saving the Jaguar Queen.

"Rowan!" Lauren shouted, hoping beyond hope that he could hear her through time and space, then looked back at the woman. "Run! Go to him!"

ROWAN STOOD ALONE IN THE CIRCLE OF STANDING STONES, gazing up at the clear night sky. Stars blanketed the velvet above him, and he could feel the power of the henge and its magic coursing around him. The moonlit hair on his arms stood as a sudden chill washed through him. His face went hot. Sweat beaded on his brow. He could almost feel the fire that would have burned in front of the altar. He glanced down at his electromagnetic meter, watching the needle sway wildly from one end of the spectrum to the other.

"Rowan!" He glanced up, thinking he'd heard his name in the wind. There was no one around.

"Hello?" He called out, listening for a response. He heard nothing more than the constant dirge of the jungle at night. There was a chorus of bugs and birds, singing their night-songs to the wind. He paused a moment longer. Hearing nothing, he paced slowly through the circle, studying the altar, and then the standing stones.

In the distance, the beating of drums began to echo in his chest. When he became aware of the feeling as a sound, he stood and turned around, trying to figure out where it was coming from, but then, they just stopped.

He turned, straining his eyes to see across the jungle in the dark. The main plaza of Chichén Itzá was nearly a mile and a half away. Surely someone's radio wasn't playing that loudly this time of night. Were they? A bright red glow across from the altar warmed his shoulders. It illuminated the stone in front of him. A scream erupted from the void around him and he turned abruptly to see what it was. A dark form blocked the red glow. It came crashing towards him and tumbled out onto the ground in front of him, rolling, like a bowling ball. There was no time to react. It took him down like a lone five-pin.

11

Rowan realized he was lying twisted with his throbbing head against the standing stone. There was a weight on top of him. "Base camp to Rowan," the radio lying on the ground just out of reach squawked as he came to his senses. The pounding in his head was horribly persistent.

His hand reached out in the darkness for the radio, but came to rest on something soft, warm... human.

"Base camp to Rowan! What's going on up there? Was that you screaming?"

He managed to sit up and roll the body off of him. He lay the person aside, finding his flashlight. "Rowan? Come in Rowan?" The desperate call went unanswered as he sat on his knees, inspecting the form. He fought to remain upright against the spinning world around him.

She was unconscious. There was no evidence of physical injury from his cursory inspection... no blood anyway. She was tall but well-formed; more robustly made than his wife. She was dressed in what appeared to be a historically accurate representation of an ancient Maya woman's outfit. The cloth band around her breasts was red, and the skirt around her hips was a slightly darker color, though it was hard to tell for sure what color it was in the dark. Crimson, or possibly a muted black. She had metal cuffs around her wrists, and a beaded thong tied around one bicep. She had a gold hoop in one ear, and her hair was tied back and adorned with feathers and shells. A half-disk of what appeared to be gold, or possibly brass, was tied at her neck with a leather cord. She had been painted in bright colors all over her exposed body.

"Rowan!" This time the voice wasn't from the radio, it came from the path below. "Rowan! Are you hurt?"

He still didn't answer. He was breathless and confused. The woman stirred, wincing as she rolled her head. Rowan's neck and shoulders were already starting to grow stiff from the impact, but he was more concerned for her. He took her hand as she groaned. He looked around to see where she had come from. He was quite sure he'd hit his head when she crashed into him. *Had he been hallucinating? Had she really come from a burning orb of fire in the jungle, or did he have a concussion?*

"Rowan," Jean-René was at his elbow. Dr. Rick and the team arrived just behind him. Alejandro had the camera running. "Are you okay?"

"Who is that?" Alejandro asked. Jean-René took Rowan's arm. He lifted his friend to his feet, but Rowan's knees buckled. He sank back to the ground, as the world tilted, and consciousness escaped him.

ROWAN WAS LYING FLAT ON HIS BACK ON A STRETCHER under the lights that had been set up for the scientific teams that had come to Chichén Itzá to see the end of the world. He could hear voices around him, long before he could get his eyes open. When he did, he realized the whole team was standing around, looking down at him.

"Welcome back, Sleeping Beauty." Jean-René squatted down beside the stretcher. "We thought you were dead."

"I almost wish I was." Rowan winced. Every muscle in his neck and back were screaming. "What the hell happened?"

"Where'd you find the girl?" Enrique appeared over him.

"She found me." He grunted, rolling his eyes. "Came running at me out of nowhere."

"Who is she?"

"Looks like one of the historical reenactors," Enrique said. "But the group I met earlier... they don't recognize her. She's not with them."

Rowan rolled over onto his side, wincing as he pushed himself up with his elbow. He was stiff and unable to turn his head. "Where is she?"

She wasn't far. Paramedics were loading her into the back of an ambulance. Rowan managed to get up, with a hand from Jean-René. He staggered over to the ambulance. "Where are you taking her?" He asked, noting they had her in restraints. An IV had been started and Rowan suspected they'd given her something to keep her calm. As a former paramedic, he knew the protocols if she'd been combative when she came to. Alejandro came over and asked the same question in Spanish.

"They are taking her to the hospital in Mérida," he said to Rowan. "He says if you want to see her, you can go there."

"Shouldn't they be taking Rowan to the hospital too? He's been unconscious for like twenty minutes. Look at him, he can't turn his head. He's got a goose-egg on his scalp the size of a softball." Jean-René protested.

"I'm fine," Rowan said, at the same moment the paramedic said something seemingly to the same effect in Spanish. He turned away as the door closed, and the ambulance pulled away. Rowan nearly fell over as he stumbled to a large flat rock and sat down on it.

"Rowan, you're not fine," Alejandro said. He and Jean-René were each at his side as Enrique came to look him over. "You're as white as a sheet." Rowan pushed him away.

"That was the craziest thing I ever saw." Rowan sat with his head in his hands, shaking. "I don't know what happened."

"Tell me what you *think* happened," Jean-René said, his hand on his friend's back.

"I had the weirdest feeling, like I wasn't alone. I set up the digital recorder to try to do an EVP session," he said. "Then the EMF detector started going crazy. I thought maybe I'd walked over some sort of ley line or hot spot. Then I heard ..." he hesitated. His voice was unsteady as he closed his eyes, trying to collect himself.

"What did you hear?" Jean-René asked.

"I heard... Lauren," he said. "She called my name." He glanced up at Jean-René. "Then I heard the drums, and I turned around. It was like a ball of fire, right in front of me. A shadow came flying out of it. It hit me with so much force... and then I was on the ground, with her on top of me."

"Lauren?"

"No, that woman..." he said. "She came out of the fire... and the drums stopped."

"Are you sure she didn't just shine a flashlight in your face and try to tackle you?" Enrique asked, also at his knee.

Rowan shook his head. "I could smell something burning."

"You smelled the fire?"

"It was like... it smelled like..." he struggled to find the words, hanging his head. "You know how it smells when you go to a barbecue? Like wood and smoke... and…"

"And flesh?" Jean-René said the words he could not.

ROWAN AND HIS TEAM WERE AMONG THE THOUSANDS THAT gathered to observe the phenomenon as the sun rose on the eastern horizon. The glow of it cast a shadow on the stairs of the temple, creating the illusion of a snake descending on the stair-stepped sides of the El Castillo. "For this reason, this structure was also known as the Temple of Kukulkan, the feathered serpent," he said, looking into the camera. "Kukulkan was just one of the 250-some gods worshipped by the ancient Maya, and as the sun rises on the day that was supposed to be the end of the world, I can't help but hear the words of the song by REM... it's the end of the world as we know it, and I feel fine. How about you, Jean-René?"

"I feel like a margarita." He chuckled.

"That sounds good." Rowan gave him a thumbs up as the red light on the camera went off. "Let's get out of here."

IT WAS LATE AFTERNOON BEFORE THEY GOT PAST THE congested roads and back to the resort. Because it was still early, they had the bar to themselves. A margarita wasn't nearly enough to soothe the tight muscles in Rowan's neck and back. A second margarita in the hot tub finally provided minimal relief.

"I'll go to the hospital tomorrow and see if I can talk to the woman," Enrique said, setting a third margarita on the concrete deck next to Rowan's half empty glass. He climbed in and sat beside Rowan.

"I want to go with you," Rowan said, unable to turn his head, he had to look at Enrique sideways. "Maybe they'll give me some muscle relaxers."

"If I had some, I'd give them to you," he said. "Tequila is the best I have to offer."

"And I'll take it." Rowan reached for his half-empty glass and drained it. He then reached for the glass Enrique had brought him and drained it too.

"I know this señorita in Mérida who gives the most amazing massage," Enrique said, sitting back and closing his eyes. "So freaking hot..."

"I'm a married man," Rowan said. "I've been away from my wife too long. Please don't do that to me."

Enrique grinned, wickedly. "Sorry dude," he said.

"So I take it you're not married or otherwise attached?" Rowan asked. In the few days they'd known each other, they'd talked of little else but work.

"No." Enrique shook his head. "I haven't found a woman who will wander the jungle with me. Most girls aren't into books, or jungles or underground archaeological dig-sites."

"Not true. They are out there," Rowan said. "If Lauren could be here, she would."

"When is the baby due?"

"Not until February," Rowan said.

"Is this your first?"

"Yes." Rowan's expression grew wistful. "We were at a meeting trying to get a permit to film an episode at the Arab Split near the Sea of Azov. That's in Crimea... well technically, Ukraine. Anyway, Lauren suggested we set up for us to film at a nearby dig sight at sunrise. I had no idea the whole thing was a set up." Rowan closed his eyes. Just thinking about Lauren and that joyous moment made his muscles ease. "Jean-René had the cameras rolling when the team invited me to come help them dig out an artifact. They handed me a brush and a pallet knife. I set to work while they moved on to other objects they'd identified. After a moment, I freed the object buried in the sand and brushed it off as I picked it up. It was a pregnancy test... a positive pregnancy test."

Enrique nearly snorted in his drink. "That's how you found out?"

Rowan nodded. "It took me a moment to figure out what was going on, but when I looked at Lauren, I knew. I lost it. Right there on camera, I started bawling like a big baby. I've never been so happy. I crawled out of the excavation and hugged her so hard I thought I might break her."

"Boy or girl?"

"We won't know until it gets here," he said. "She didn't want to find out."

"Old fashioned woman, huh?"

Rowan's face lit up brightly at the thought of her. "You'd have to know my wife."

"Bring her next time you come back," he said. "The stones will still be here."

"She's going to be pissed when she learns we went diving in a cenote," Rowan said.

"Maybe it's for the best she didn't come along then," Enrique said.

They sat in amiable silence for a while. "I heard Alejandro say something about flights back to the States. Will you be leaving soon?"

"Yeah," Rowan said. "The world didn't end and there are bills to pay. What about you? Are you expected back at the University?"

"My role as a research professor gives me a lot of flexibility," he said. "I'll probably be back to my office by Tuesday or Wednesday."

"So what else are you working on?"

"I'm preparing a few papers for peer review. Thinking of writing a book."

"A book huh?" Rowan tried to stretch out his sore neck. "I've been thinking about writing a book too."

"Do it, my friend. There will come a time, when it becomes more painful not to write. That is when you will become a writer."

"I write all the time, but mostly articles and scripts. Maybe someday, I'll have time for a book." Rowan drained the margarita. "We'll start analyzing our evidence from last night and reviewing all the research when we get back. I want to make sure I have your number before we leave. If I find anything interesting, I'll call you."

"I would welcome that, my friend. And I will send you a copy of my book, when I get it published, of course."

"Autographed, right?" Rowan quipped.

"Of course," Enrique said.

"I need sleep." Rowan moved slowly, struggling to get out of the hot tub. His stiff muscles were no help. "Good night."

"Of course." Enrique nodded. "*Buenas Noches.*"

~

Enrique found Rowan outside the ER, where he'd left him. "Feeling any better?"

"Not really," he groaned. "Still waiting for the meds to kick in." He picked up the pill bottle and rattled it, showing Enrique the label, before tucking it in the breast-pocket of his jacket.

"Well, we better tend to business. In thirty minutes, you will be flat on your back," Enrique caught him under his armpit and helped him stand. He was in worse shape than he had been the night before. "She's in room 201."

Rowan was impressed with how modern the hospital was. He wasn't sure what he'd been expecting, but he was surprised at how nice it was. The doctor that had tended to him in the ER spoke English better than most people and had determined he had a concussion and a severe case of whiplash. It wasn't serious, but it would take a few days on muscle relaxers before he'd be himself. Hopefully, he would be home soon. A few nights in his own bed, with Lauren tucked safely against him would do him good. That was the balm he needed right now. Unfortunately, there was still work to do. He needed to learn the identity of the woman who had t-boned him into a rock.

As he entered the room, with Enrique behind him, Rowan hesitated. She was laying with the head of the bed slightly elevated. Someone had taken care to clean her up and she wore a white hospital gown. Her red hair lay limp on her shoulder, and her eyes were closed. Rowan tapped on the door frame, and she startled, lifting her head off the pillow. He was immediately struck by how green her eyes were—like jade.

"I'm sorry to bother you," Rowan said, but she looked at him blankly.

Enrique stepped through the doorway and introduced himself to her, speaking what sounded like Spanish. Her whole countenance changed. He continued speaking, clearly introducing his non-Spanish-speaking friend. Rowan presumed he was explaining how they'd come to find her.

"Are you Stephanie Wentworth?" Rowan finally asked when Enrique finished his prolonged introduction.

She turned and looked at him sharply.

It took a moment before she spoke. Rowan didn't recognize the language. "Is she speaking… Maya?" Enrique had given him a primer in the language, but he couldn't be sure. It sounded like Maya.

"Yes," Enrique grinned. "You were paying attention."

"What'd she say?"

"She says she was lost in the jungle, for a long time. She thanks you for finding her and she's sorry for your aching back and head." Enrique smiled. He said something to her in her own language and she looked at him warily. He glanced back at Rowan. "My Maya may be rusty, I'm not sure I said that right."

"What'd you ask her?"

"I asked her if she was the daughter of an oil man, and was she kidnapped," Enrique said.

The woman said something back to him, speaking in a frantic long string of glottal syllables chained together. She looked agitated by the question, and her eyes were as wide as they could be.

"Are you Stephanie Wentworth?" Rowan repeated.

"*Má in woojel.*" She looked straight at him.

Rowan looked to Enrique. "No," Enrique said. "She isn't."

"What's her name?"

"*Áantení,*" she answered.

"She's not the woman you're looking for," Enrique said, turning to Rowan. Rowan looked at her, seeing something in her eyes he couldn't explain. "She's not the oil baron's daughter, Rowan."

Rowan felt defeated. He'd wanted to believe the story so badly. He nodded and smiled, politely. "I'm sorry we bothered you." He'd felt like they were on the verge of an amazing discovery, but the reality of the moment was too much to bear. Enrique made their farewells behind him, as he turned and walked out.

1 2

"How's that? Better?" Bahati helped Lauren get settled into her own bed. Her fever had broken two days before, and they'd finally discharged her from the hospital.

"Yes, thank you."

"What sounds good for dinner?"

"After a week of hospital food? I could..." she started.

"Most of which you didn't eat, by the way." Bahati cut her off, sitting down beside her.

"Fair enough," Lauren conceded. "I could really go for a pizza."

Bahati hadn't been expecting that and said as much. "Really?"

"Really." She stretched out and ran a hand over her belly. "Baby wants pizza. The menu for Isa Bella's is on the fridge."

"The usual?"

"Please?"

"Okay," Bahati said.

Lauren adjusted the pillows so she could sit up in bed. She reached for the remote but laid it back down. She wasn't in any mood to watch television. The past couple of days had been trying, to say the least. She'd spent a couple of days in and out of fevered dreams, some of which hovered just outside of her ability to recollect. Others were as vivid as the painting on the wall over her dresser. What she could remember made her all the more fretful about what she couldn't. Tsul'Kalu usually made her feel better when he came to her, but something about his recent visits had her feeling unsettled.

Bahati returned with a bottle of water. "Looks like your fridge is a bit empty. The cupboards are bare too."

"I haven't had time to go to the store lately," Lauren admitted. "With Rowan gone, it was just easier to go pick up a meal."

"Well if you'll make me a list, I'll run to the store before the pizza gets here."

"Sure," Lauren reached for the notebook by the table. She and Rowan were both writers—it was part of their jobs—so there was always a pad of paper or a journal nearby. This one was full of notes for the show they'd done on Atlantis. "Just give me a minute."

She jotted down some things that would be easier for her to manage on her own. Not knowing how much longer it would be until Rowan came home, she figured she'd better get used to being self-sufficient while doing as little as possible. She gave the list to Bahati. "That ought to hold me," she said.

Bahati inspected the list. "Doesn't seem like much," she said.

"It'll do."

"If you say so. I'll be back in a bit. Got your phone handy?"

"Right here." Lauren held it up.

Poor Bahati. Lauren knew she had been by her bedside through the worst of her illness while she was in and out of delirium. She knew she could count on her co-worker. She curled up around her pillow, wishing it were Rowan. She needed him home, so she didn't have to burden her friends.

She sighed, picking up the remote. She flipped through the channels.

Six weeks of this? Could she do it? Lauren wasn't sure.

～

THE MUSCLE RELAXERS KICKED IN WITH A VENGEANCE. Rowan was knocked out cold. Jean-René sat beside him on the airplane and prayed to God the thing didn't crash. There wouldn't be any way he could get over Rowan's limp form if he had to evacuate in a hurry. He'd never imagined himself going out of the world that way. It wasn't beyond the realm of possibility with as much traveling as they did. Alejandro had won the draw for the window seat, leaving Jean-René stuck between the two of them. He barely had enough room to set his iPad up on the tray table. With his earbuds stuck in his ears, he began replaying the video they'd collected, watching for anything they hadn't noticed before.

Rowan, with his chair leaning back as far as it would possibly go, snored so loud Jean-René could hear it through his so-called noise-cancelling headphones. It made Jean-René's task more difficult. He finally gave up. They'd be in Houston before long, and he'd have a chance to get up and stretch his legs... assuming they could wake Rowan and get him up and moving.

"So..." Alejandro nudged him. Jean-René lifted the headphones from his ear. "Who do you think the girl was? If she wasn't Stephanie Wentworth?"

Jean-René made a purely French noise in the back of his throat. "No telling. Dr. Rick said he'd keep in touch with her and see if he couldn't help her."

"Have you gotten to Rowan's body cam footage yet?"

"No," he said. "I've still got a hundred hours of my own footage to review."

"I'll be anxious to see what you find," Alejandro said.

"Me too."

~

Once she had her fill of pizza, Lauren got up long enough for a warm shower before she put on her pajamas. She found Bahati camped out on the sofa, watching television. "What are you doing here? I thought you were going home."

"I decided I'd just crash here tonight," Bahati said. "If you don't mind of course. It's storming and I really don't want to get out on the roads at a time like this."

Lauren glanced out the window, realizing the wind had picked up and the rain was coming down in sheets. It reminded her of growing up in Oklahoma where weather like this was more common. A rumble of thunder punctuated Bahati's story, and Lauren nodded. "I wouldn't want you out in that," she said. "The sofa makes out into a bed, if you want me to show you how."

"No," Bahati said, inspecting the sofa. "This is fine."

"Well the blankets are in the trunk over in the corner. There's a pillow in there too."

"Thank you," Bahati said. "Did the shower help?"

"Yeah," Lauren said, yawning. "See you in the morning."

"Good night." Bahati got up to fetch the blankets and a pillow.

Lauren paused to open the blinds in her room so she could watch the storm. She wasn't sure she'd sleep any time soon. The lightning over the harbor was more interesting than anything on television this time of night. She lay down and made herself comfortable. A crackling bolt of lightning raced across the sky, illuminating the room, followed by a crash of thunder.

She fell asleep much quicker than she expected, and she had been thinking of Rowan, when she nodded off. At some point in the night, she rolled over and found him lying beside her. She curled up into the crook of his arm, resting her head on his shoulder, running a hand down his chest. She sighed, breathing deeply, smelling the faint hint of his cologne beneath the musky smell of unwashed male. He pulled her in and kissed her head, before they drifted back to sleep in each other's arms.

13

The sun was up when Lauren woke. She thought it odd the blankets on Rowan's side of the bed had been tossed back, as if he'd just left it. Lauren rolled over and blinked back the strange dreams. She closed her eyes, knowing there was nowhere she needed to be. Even if she wanted to go somewhere, she couldn't. She began to drift back to sleep. The dreamy moment of bliss lasted only a moment when she realized she could smell bacon. That was odd. Bahati didn't like bacon. She never made it. Why would she? Lauren threw back the covers, and rolled over slowly, making her way to her feet, pulling on her bathrobe, and stepping into her slippers.

She shuffled into the living room and froze as Rowan came around the corner, holding a plate of golden, steaming pancakes, slathered with butter, and drizzled with syrup. A side of crispy bacon confirmed her senses. Lauren let out a yelp and stumbled backwards, catching herself on the door frame. "Rowan! You're home?"

He looked pained as he sat the plate down and reached for her, drawing her into his arms. "I got in a couple of hours ago," he said, holding her, realizing she was shivering. "You curled up next to me and slept on my shoulder. Don't you remember?"

"I thought I'd called you into my dreams," Lauren sniffed. "I'm so glad you're home." She leaned back and kissed him fiercely. He winced but made no noise. He didn't try to pull away. "You're hurt?" She backed away, holding him at arm's length so she could inspect him. His neck was still stiff, and he had a wicked bruise on his forehead, right at the edge of his hairline. His left eye was black and blue. "What happened?"

"I took a tumble during one of the night investigations. Nothing serious," he said. "But you're supposed to be in bed. I was just bringing you breakfast."

"And it smells wonderful." She conceded and returned to bed. He brought the plate and handed it to her. "I'll go make you a cup of coffee."

"I can't have it," she said. "Just some juice or better yet, water."

"No coffee?" Rowan stopped mid-turn. She realized he had to turn his whole body to look back at her. "Really?"

"Doctor said no caffeine. No tea, no coffee, no sodas."

Rowan gazed at her, stone-faced. "That's probably better for you and the baby anyway," he said, headed back to the kitchen.

He returned with a glass of orange juice and had a plate for himself. He climbed into bed beside her and sat cross-legged as they ate in companionable silence. It was good to be home. Nothing could make him go off and leave her again. He'd given the crew the rest of the week off. They'd pick back up analyzing the data the following Monday. They were due some downtime. And after the curious turn of events with the mystery woman on the night of the solstice, he needed the rest too. Hopefully in a few days, his back would be better. He had enough muscle relaxers, he hoped, to make that happen.

"There's more, if you're still hungry," Rowan said.

"No, thank you." She handed him her empty plate.

He finished his. "So, Netflix and binge today?"

"Not like I'm going anywhere." Lauren glanced out the window. She scooted down under the blankets, pulling the comforter up over her shoulders. He took their plates away and returned, climbing into bed beside her. He took another muscle relaxer and settled where she could curl up next to him. "How are you feeling? Better?"

"Tons." Lauren sighed. "I guess Bahati told you how sick I was."

"She did," he said. "More than once, I wanted to come home... investigation be damned."

"I'm glad you didn't." She yawned. "You couldn't have done anything. Now, tell me about what you found?"

Rowan proceeded to tell her about their adventures. "The coolest part was this cenote we dove in," he said, telling her all about the skeletons and the altar. He was prepared for the scolding he knew would follow. She hated caves and diving in them was even worse. Because she was afraid, she worried for him, and hated him taking unnecessary risks. Much to his surprise, though, she didn't say anything, so he continued. He didn't leave out the part about the carving at the bottom of the cenote, or the ancient Maya glyphs that the sun had illuminated. He talked all about their margarita nights and some of the unique things they found, but he trailed off when he realized she'd nodded off, as he lay flat on his back. He'd been daydreaming as he talked, realizing he was drowsy too.

ROWAN WAS SNORING VIGOROUSLY WHEN SHE WOKE UP. SHE got up and went to the kitchen to get something to drink, finding his backpack on the kitchen table. They usually brought one another little trinkets when they traveled separately. She grinned, wondering what he'd brought her. She unzipped the bag and recoiled at the smell before rummaging through the pack, pulling out a sweaty t-shirt, damp socks... and a pair of swampy boxer shorts. She had to wonder how long they'd been in there. Still, she couldn't just leave them to mildew. She pinched her nose carrying them to the laundry, tossing them in and set the washer to run.

She shook her head as she washed her hands and then went back to her search. She found his favorite camera and his digital voice recorder. She studied them both, realizing the battery on the voice recorder was completely drained. She took it over to the charging station at his desk and plugged it in. She then went to his camera and scrolled through the digital images. He was a good photographer. After years working with Jean-René, he'd better be. He was a good writer too. Combined, he'd used his talents to host a blog for the Exploration Channel.

It reminded Lauren about needing to talk to him about the travel show the Network bosses were interested in. She was bound and determined to talk them out of it. The last thing she wanted to do was travel with a newborn. Traveling was difficult enough without diapers, baby wipes and breastfeeding. She cringed thinking about all the times she'd been trapped in a plane with a baby. The changing pressure in the cabin usually sent them wailing as their little ears popped. She'd been seated next to an exhausted mother on one flight. The poor woman ended up changing a particularly stinky diaper right there in the aisle. The smell was so bad the flight attendant passed out free bottles of booze. It kept the rest of the passengers from revolting.

Lauren had ended up with the baby on her shoulder long enough for the woman to go dispose of the diaper and wash her hands. When she returned, Lauren had calmed the child and it had fallen asleep in her arms with her hair wrapped in its chubby little fist. They spent the rest of the flight that way, and the child's mother managed a brief nap before they got into LAX.

A week later, a bouquet of flowers arrived at her office with a *thank you* note from the mother. The woman recognized Lauren from her TV show. She hadn't done it for the thanks. She'd done it because she secretly loved babies. It'd been a long time since she'd gotten to hold one. She never expected to have one of her own someday. She'd resigned herself early in her career to being married to her job. Rowan had changed all that. Having a baby of her own hadn't even been on her radar.

A foot caught her in the ribs, reminding her of the little one she would hold soon. She returned to her rummaging. At the bottom of his backpack, she found a tiny parcel wrapped in layers of paper packing material. Inside, was a terracotta ceramic tile, a Maya glyph, intended to be used as a coaster. She inspected it with a bemused huff of amusement. "Cute," she chortled.

Rowan found her standing there. "Aren't you supposed to be in bed?" He came up behind her, snaking his arms around her middle, resting his head on her shoulder, sighing. "Oh, I see you found your present."

"*Ek Balam*, the jaguar god," she said. "I love it."

Rowan's head cocked sideways. "How did you know it was the jaguar?"

She gave a half-hearted lift of her shoulder. "I don't know, but that's what it says." She ran her thumb along the pattern. "Literally, this means, *he who kills with one blow.*" She pointed out each of the syllables and markings spelled out in the square.

"Since when did you learn to read ancient Maya?"

She lifted her shoulder again. "I don't know. I've been doing a lot of reading and research while you were gone. I feel like I've been reading in my sleep."

"I thought you dreamt only of me while I was gone." He kissed her cheek.

"I did dream of you," she said. "You came to see me in

the hospital. Bahati said you were diving in a cenote, but you were here. You kissed me, just like that."

"I guess my secret is out. You weren't supposed to know about the cenote."

"Uh huh." She chortled. "Just promise me you didn't take any unnecessary risks."

"Would I do that?" Rowan gasped, a titter of nervous laughter escaped his throat.

"Yes, and we both know it." She wormed her way out of his grasp. She finally made it to the kitchen, which had been her original plan.

"There's one other present for you." He stepped around her, pulling the backpack across the table. He rummaged through pockets, trying to find it. It took him a moment, but he finally produced a small plastic zip-top bag with a form in it. He handed her the bag. She looked at the paper through the plastic, puzzled, then flipped the bag over. Inside, a silver cartouche with Maya hieroglyphs caught the light of the sun coming through the sliding glass doors nearby. A wide smile spread across her face.

"It's your name in Maya," Rowan said and took the packet back. He opened it.

"It's beautiful," she said. "Thank you." She didn't have the heart to tell him it wasn't her name. It was just a series of symbols equating to little more than gibberish.

He leaned in and kissed her, pressing her stomach to his. "I'm glad you like it."

"I'm going to make a salad. Do you want some?"

"No," he said, taking the head of romaine from her hand. "You're going to go lay down. I'm going to make us salads."

"With some grilled chicken?"

"I'll even make my homemade creamy garlic dressing."

"Yes, please."

"You want everything on it?"

"Of course," Lauren said. "Bahati went to the store for me yesterday. Should be plenty of fixings."

He reached in the refrigerator for a bottle of mineral water. "Your favorite." He held it up. She snagged it from him and returned to her bed, straightening up the blankets before climbing back in.

SHE SAT PICKING LINT OFF THE DUVET COVER, GLANCING OUT the window. The ocean was a deeper blue than the sky. The sliding door leading out to the patio was open, letting in the warm breeze. The air smelled of salt and the sea. She sighed as she sank back into her bed. She still found it hard to believe it could be so warm this late in the year. In Oklahoma, it was usually cold in December. It rarely snowed on the plains, though at least once in her life she could remember a white Christmas.

Sand was as close as you could get to snow in Southern California, and she couldn't even get close to the sand. Last year, they made sandcastles instead of snowmen. This Christmas would be different. Lauren knitted her brow, thinking about Christmas for the first time in days. She picked up her phone and opened the calendar. Christmas Eve was tomorrow. She hadn't done any Christmas shopping, and her annual care packages of homemade cookies and peanut butter fudge would be missing from everyone's stocking. She was fairly sure the crew would understand.

AFTER LUNCH, ROWAN LEFT LAUREN TO DO THE ONLY THING she could do, lie in bed, and surf the web. Meanwhile, he tidied up the house. He put the laundry into the dryer before he returned with his laptop, and camera. He stretched out beside her and set to work. He linked the camera to his laptop so he could download the video that'd been shot the last day in Mexico.

"Did you get anything good?" Lauren asked, snuggling up next to him when he sat back to watch the footage. She took one of the earbuds from his ear and stuck it in her own.

"Yeah," he said. "I think we did. Jean-René and Alejandro interviewed some of the local Maya that had come to Chichén Itzá in the hopes of welcoming their ancestors. We got underwater video from the cenote. There are literally hundreds of hours of video that needs to be reviewed."

"Plenty for me to do," Lauren said. "What else?"

"Well, there's video from my body cam we need to look at. I didn't get a chance to tell you about what happened."

Lauren listened to him tell the story. She was transfixed by his account. By the time he was finished, his hands were shaking. A mist of sweat had broken on his brow despite the cool air coming through the screen door. The skies had gone dark, despite the hour. A flash of lightning made him jump and a rumble of thunder echoed over the bay, leaving him even more shaken. She caught his hand. "Rowan, that's unbelievable," Lauren said. "But then again... I've seen stranger."

Rowan shook his head, looking at her warily. "I know, right?"

"And you're sure it wasn't Stephanie Wentworth? Did you talk to her?"

"I've got audio of our interviews with this woman. She was a reenactor."

"I want to hear the audio," Lauren said.

Rowan got up and closed the sliding door. "I'll go get my recorder."

"It's on the charger," she said.

Rowan went to the other room then returned. "Huh. The battery's at like 10%." He shook his head, plugging it into his computer, uploading the audio, draining the battery at the same time.

"It was dead when I found it." She noted.

"I just need this last conversation..." he said as he waited.

Lauren took the headphones and put them on. Once he had it ready, Rowan hit the play button. He sat watching her reaction as she listened to the conversation from the woman's hospital room. She locked eyes with him as she sat up, holding her hands to the headphones. "Could you replay it and turn it up?"

"Sure." Rowan did as she asked.

"Sounds like it was in your shirt pocket," she said.

"It was." She knew him too well.

She listened again as he replayed it. Her face remaining stern, puzzled. "Who's your translator?"

"That was Dr. Enrique DeLaFuentes," Rowan said. "From the University. He was immensely helpful."

Lauren looked at Rowan like he was insane. "He lied to you."

"What?"

"She didn't say what he said she did. You asked her if she was Stephanie Wentworth," Lauren said. "He asked her to shake her head *no* and not speak in English. He said they couldn't talk with you there and he needed you to go away."

"What?" Rowan's brow drew down making a deep wrinkle over his nose. "Why would he do that? He was nothing but helpful the entire time." Rowan sat, perplexed. He ran it all through his mind before he looked at Lauren sharply. "Wait, how do you know what he said? Last I remember your Spanish was limited to ordering from the *Casa Del Taco*."

"It's not Spanish," she said. "He spoke to her in Maya. His words were a local modern dialect, different from what she speaks. I can tell it's not Spanish."

"Since when do you speak Maya?" He stood, pacing the room, pausing to glare at her.

"I told you, I've been studying..." she swallowed hard. "You know I have a penchant for languages."

"Like how you picked up Cherokee while you were missing in the Pacific Northwest? Yeah, I'm still baffled at how you do that."

"I wish I could tell you it was a gift from the ancient gods, but that would just be crazy, right?"

"Yeah, right," he said scornfully. He still didn't know everything Lauren had learned from Tsul'Kalu, her imaginary shaman. She'd convinced him she'd been hallucinating about him after she was kidnapped and nearly had her arm ripped off.

She couldn't tell him it was a Bigfoot who was her spirit guide. He wouldn't understand. He didn't know she still spoke to him. He certainly didn't know she could summon him when she needed him. Or could she? Had it just been the fevered dreams of a sick pregnant woman? Maybe she *was* losing it.

"Why would Dr. Rick lie to me?"

"Dr. Rick?"

"Yeah, that was our nickname for him," Rowan said, sitting down with his back to her, his hand on his knee and his thumb against his chin. Lauren rested her hand in the middle of his back, and he seemed to soften. "I thought we were friends."

"Is there a way to contact him?"

"He gave me a phone number." Rowan glanced at his watch. He took his cell phone out of the pocket of his cargo pants. Lauren could hear the ringing as Rowan waited for an answer that never came. "Dammit," Rowan snapped when the call didn't even go to voicemail.

"You said he was with the University?"

"Yeah," Rowan said. Lauren took his laptop and searched the web.

"Which one?" Lauren asked.

"The one in Mexico City," Rowan said curtly.

"There are like five or six different universities," she turned the computer towards him.

"I think it's in my dossier." Rowan shook his head. "Let me see if it's in my backpack."

He came back a minute later and had a file. "*Universidad Nacional de México*," he pointed to it, showing Lauren. "That's the one."

"Okay," she said, going to the link. After a few minutes, she found his name on the faculty list, and a phone number.

Rowan took the number she jotted down on a pad she kept by the bed. He punched the numbers into the phone. "I don't speak... *hola?*" He was interrupted mid-sentence.

Lauren reached for the phone and he surrendered it. "*Buenos Días. Mi nombre es la Dra. Lauren Pierce. Soy una investigación que intenta llegar al Dr. DeLaFuentes. ¿Podrías conectarme con él?*"

"Oh, you speak Spanish now." It wasn't a question. "Great, suddenly my wife speaks Spanish." He turned to the window, watching it rain, listening to the faint, muffled response over the phone, not understanding a word of it.

"*Lamento mucho oír eso. Mis condolencias a la familia. ¿Puedo preguntar, cuándo murió?*" Rowan turned, his brow arched, and he wasn't sure, but he thought he caught part of that. He had to wait while she listened intently on the phone. Nodding, then shaking her head. "*Gracias. Aprecio tu tiempo. Tenga un buen día.*"

"What?"

Lauren looked grim when she hung up. "Dr. Enrique DeLaFuentes was murdered on the road to Chichén Itzá the day he was supposed to meet with your team. His car ran off the road north of the site. His body was found a few yards away, with a single gunshot wound to the head. He was sixty-nine years old. He left behind a wife of forty-two years, five children and six grandchildren."

Rowan's whole countenance sunk. His knees failed. He sat more quickly than he had intended, nearly missing the edge of the bed. "What the hell?"

Lauren scooted over, leaning against him. She rested her head on his shoulder and took a deep breath. "Whoever that was you were working with... I'm going to assume, was not Dr. DeLaFuentes."

Rowan shook his head, still in disbelief. "Then who was he?"

"Yet another mystery we have to solve," she said.

"Well, no one's better at not solving mysteries than we are, huh?"

"Are we still using that tagline?" Lauren shook her head, kissing his cheek.

14

Rowan called the team together ahead of schedule. They met in the conference room with their laptops, iPads, video cameras and other equipment. Bahati was barking orders. She provided instruction on what Rowan was looking for. She covered everything they needed to find to advance the investigation. Normally, this was Lauren's job. As her second, Bahati stepped in, effortlessly. This team had been on dozens of investigations together. Everyone knew what to do.

Rowan waited for her to finish her instructions and for the team to get their coffee, grab a donut and get settled in before he stood and filled everyone in on the latest turn in their mystery.

"The world didn't end on December 21st, but for the real Dr. Enrique DeLaFuentes, it was over before the day even began. What I want for Christmas is to find out who that jerk was that pretended to be our friend." Rowan's anger was evident by the poison in his tone. "I want to know who he is. I want to know where he is. I want to know why he did what he did. If he had anything to do with the real Dr. DeLaFuentes' death, I want him brought to justice. I want no stone left unturned." Rowan took a deep breath. "Now, let's put in a good solid four hours going through the video and audio recordings. I need a clear photo of Slick Rick. Then we'll quit early and pick up after the holidays."

The team jumped into action. Everyone did exactly what they were supposed to. When they went home, they were no closer to answering the many questions they'd come in with, but at least the ball was rolling.

LAUREN WAS NAPPING WHEN ROWAN CAME IN. IT GAVE HIM THE opportunity he needed to wrap her Christmas presents. There was no tree to put them under. The potted palm plant on the balcony had been decorated with red ribbons and miniature twinkling lights. Rowan brought it in and set it in the corner of the living room. He wrapped the few presents in colorful paper. There was something for the baby too. He couldn't help himself. He put them under the palm, smiling as he imagined the look on Lauren's face when she opened them.

"Rowan?" She called from the bedroom. He stashed the wrapping paper in the closet and went to check on her.

"I didn't wake you, did I?" Rowan asked, coming in and setting down on the edge of the bed.

"No." She yawned, stretching. "I've been awake for a while."

"That's odd." He tilted his head. "I was just in here about fifteen minutes ago and you were snoring."

"I don't snore." She feigned being affronted. "Maybe you snore, but I don't."

His eyes went wide in an expression of mock indignation. "Oh, I snore?" He chuckled.

"Yeah you do." She insisted. "It's okay. I don't mind."

"Uh huh." He shook his head. She ran her hand up his arm to his cheek and drew him in for a kiss. "So what's the rest of your Christmas Eve look like?"

"It's Christmas Eve?"

"Yeah," he said. "I thought I might go get us something to cook for dinner. Then we could watch Christmas movies and drink hot chocolate with marshmallows. I could even bake cookies for Santa."

"Since when do you bake cookies?" She scoffed.

"Honey, I've got skills you haven't even seen." He puffed out his chest.

"Okay …" Lauren grinned, dragging out the word. "I'd like to see you bake cookies. Let's do it?"

"Deal," he said. "Have you been out of bed today?"

"No," she said, adding a salute. "In accordance with orders."

"Well then, why don't you go take a warm bath, and I'll put clean sheets on the bed. I'll make you a sandwich for lunch. Then I'll go get everything for dinner, cocoa and baking cookies."

"Sounds like a good plan. Clean sheets would be wonderful."

ROWAN WAS MUCH HAPPIER BEING DOMESTICATED THAN SHE was. Lauren was already like a tiger in a cage. A week spent in bed was torture for a woman who lived for two years in a tent in Yellowstone without seeing another soul more than once or twice a month.

Rowan not only changed the bedding, but he put the linens in the wash, ran the vacuum cleaner and brought her a fresh towel from the linen closet. He put it on the bench by the tub, while she soaked in the warm foamy waters.

By the time she got out and dressed in a pair of pink shorts and lilac t-shirt, he'd dusted and tidied up the bedroom and had the bed turned down for her.

Once she got settled, he came in with a bed-tray. On the

plate was a sandwich, tortilla chips, green grapes, and a cup of tapioca pudding.

"Think that will hold you until I get back?"

"Yes, thank you." She popped a grape in her mouth.

"Anything else you need from the store? Anything sound good?"

"I could go for more of those grapes... any fruit, really, sounds good," she said. "And meat. Any kind of meat.

That made him smile. "I have my phone if you think of anything else," he said, leaning in to kiss her forehead.

"TRUTHSEEKER," TSUL'KALU WAS STANDING AT THE FOOT OF her bed when she looked up. She froze, watching Rowan's shadow move as the door closed behind him. She turned to the shaman in disbelief.

"What are you doing here?" She asked, lowering her voice as if anyone might hear her.

"You summoned me." He folded into a lotus position.

Lauren sat back against her pillow crossing her arms, biting her thumbnail. "How'd I do that?"

"I am here when you need counsel."

"What I need is... I need to get out of this house," she said, heaving a sigh.

"As you wish." He stood.

The next thing Lauren knew, they were standing at the top of the El Castillo, looking out over the jungle. The sun shone down on her. She could feel the humidity in the surrounding air. Lauren looked down, realizing she was still in her pajamas. "What the hell?"

"This is what you wished to see," Tsul'Kalu said. "You wish to speak to the Jaguar King. Come, I will show you to the portal."

"Portal?" Tsul'Kalu took her hand and she took a step

towards the stairs. The next thing she knew, they were entering a clearing in the jungle where a circle of engraved stones stood. There were seven of them. They were magnificent. The largest stood higher than seven feet tall, and at least three or four feet wide. It was white quartz. Maybe granite.

She felt her breath escape her body. Her head wanted to swim, but Tsul'Kalu had his hand on her arm. He steadied her. "You... you called this a portal?" She asked.

"Yes." He led her into its center. "This is a sacred place where the veil of time is thin. There is little to separate this world from space and time."

The perfume of the jungle filled her nostrils. It was a combination of humid moss and ancient magic. She walked over to the largest of the seven pillars. Putting her hands on the ancient stones, she studied the glyphs. The carvings had once been deep. The stone had been weathered away, leaving only a trace of the markings.

It no longer surprised Lauren that she could read the glyphs. It told a story of the ancient king who took to wife, a goddess who fell from the sky. She gave him sons and brought much prosperity to the land. For a time they were happy and there was peace in the realm. But there came a year with no rain. Warring nations came to their lands. One year turned into five. These People grew hungry. Crops withered on the stalk.

There was talk of men with hair like corn-silk. Their eyes were like sapphires and emeralds, much like the Jaguar's bride. Clearly, the gods were displeased. It was their wrath that made the crops wither. The angry gods drove the game from their lands. There was only one thing to placate the divine beings and restore order. That was blood.

Lauren could see the story unfolding even as the world around her went dark. The only light came from the fire in the center of the circle. The King took his throne and watched as the blood of their enemies flowed. War had been waged against neighboring tribes and the light-eyed men to appease the gods. Time seemed to blur the details as months passed, and more battles were fought. More captives were brought to the altar and their hearts removed while they still beat. The smell of roasting flesh and wood smoke mixed with the perfume of the jungle, created a nauseating miasma. It made the bile rise in Lauren's throat.

A priest at the King's elbow began whispering. Lauren listened to the voice over the crescendo of the drums. Over the screams of the tortured captives. His voice echoed in the air. Blood pooled at their feet. Lauren caught every word, but the rising smoke made her dizzy. The circle began to spin around her. "Give back to the gods what they have given to you." The words echoed in her mind. "Man is made from corn and blood... *is made from corn and blood...* given to us by the gods... *a gift for us from the gods...* as the gods have given life to us... *life to us...* we must give life to the gods... give her your queen... the gods demand blood... give her your queen..."

The world spun in Lauren's head. A piercing scream threatened to split the lobes of her brain. She covered her ears and crouched. She couldn't block the dirge from her mind. She could feel her grasp on time and place slipping away, and the world fell away. The blackness came for her. Then, there was nothing.

15

Rowan arrived home later than he'd expected. Traffic had been snarled. The grocery store was packed. He was soaking wet as the skies outside continued their onslaught, drenching him on the brief dash from the car to the door. *By God! Their next home would have an attached garage.*

He was surprised to find the condo dark. Lauren must have gone to sleep. He envied her ability to sleep anywhere. It didn't matter if it was in a plane or the back of a truck. The minute she lay down she was usually out like a light. He smiled to himself as he unpacked his grocery bags. He put everything away, except for what he needed to make dinner. He paused to put on some Christmas music, setting his phone on the counter top as he set to work mixing dough for his favorite homemade calzone. It wasn't traditional Christmas food, but he and Lauren weren't traditional people. They were anything but.

It would take about an hour for the dough to rise. He found a bottle of beer in the back of the fridge and cracked the lid open. He grabbed his phone. Taking it to the sofa, he flipped on the light and reached for the remote as he sat down.

He had at least a dozen emails and messages from fans, studio execs, partners, and extended members of the team, wishing him and Lauren Merry Christmas. He smiled and sent back a dozen reciprocal wishes. There was a text from his parents in Denver, asking him about the baby. They were excited to become grandparents. They promised to come out for a visit after the baby arrived. He couldn't decide if he should be pleased or offended. They'd never come to visit him. They hadn't even come to his military retirement ceremony. But now, suddenly it was convenient to come all the way out to California to see their first grandchild? He could see where he ranked.

His mother was especially amusing. Every text from her started with, "Hello, son. It's your mother." Like he didn't have her set in his contacts. "It's been a long time, and your father and I miss you." Every single time. If they missed him so much, why didn't they just call? His father was getting hard of hearing and Mom—she just didn't like talking on the cell phone. Every text ended with "Love you, Mom and the Colonel. PS: Your father says hello too." Every. Single. Time.

Rowan drained his beer and decided not to take it personally. He'd been a decent son, though he always felt like he could have done better—like he should do better. His father had retired as a Colonel from the Air Force after 30-some years in the military. Mom had been the perfect officer's wife. She hosted the weekly Bunco night for the other officer's wives, as well as the garden club and the book club too. When Rowan and his sister were older, their mother had gone to work at the public library in Denver. She worked for twenty-some years before she finally retired to spend more time with her husband. Still, they'd been too busy to come out and visit.

Rowan, unlike his father, had gotten out of the military much sooner, thanks to an unfortunate series of events. He had been more than ready to take an early retirement. Many of his friends continued to go back into the fray, only to end up with a more serious case of PTSD. Rowan knew when to let it go, and move on with his life, regardless of whether his father understood.

Whatever. Rowan got up, casting aside bad memories. He tossed the empty beer bottle into the recycling bin. He decided he better check on Lauren.

He could only see shadows of the room, the daylight growing dimmer as the hours had passed. He flipped on the light on their dresser. The room was empty. "Lauren?" He switched on the overhead light. It chased the shadows away. Still, there were no signs of his wife. "Lauren?" He checked the bathroom. She wasn't there. She wasn't on the balcony. In their cramped townhouse, there wasn't anywhere else for her to be. Panic coursed through him. He found his phone and tried to call her, but it went straight to voice mail. He called again, tracing the sound of the ring tone back to the bed. Her phone was beneath her pillow. *Dammit*! She was nowhere to be found. She'd left without her phone—or her purse. It was still hanging on the hook on the back of their bedroom door.

Calm down, think, man! Rowan ran a trembling hand over his head. Panic threatened to overtake him. Where would she go? She was supposed to be on bed rest. She wasn't supposed to go anywhere! He looked down at his phone. He dialed Bahati.

"Hey Rowan, Merry Christmas," she answered brightly.

"Hey," he managed. "Have you talked to Lauren today?"

"I called her this morning. I haven't talked to her since. Why?"

"I went to the store and when I came back… she was…" His voice failed him. He took a deep breath to keep the room from spinning. "She isn't here." he managed.

"She's not supposed to leave her bed, much less the house …" Bahati's tone changed. "Did you call her cell phone?"

"Yeah," he said. His heart thudded in his throat. "It was under the pillows. Her purse is still here too."

Bahati was silent for a moment. "I'm coming right over."

"Have you noticed anything... different about her lately?" Rowan sat down, no longer able to keep his feet.

"Pregnancy changes a woman," Bahati said.

"It's not just that." He shook his head. "Never mind, maybe I'm just seeing shadows that aren't there."

"I'll be there in ten minutes," Bahati said. "Just hang on. I'm coming."

ROWAN WAS AGITATED BY THE TIME BAHATI WALKED IN. HIS face and eyes were red. He paced feverishly back and forth behind the couch when she walked in. After losing her in Washington State, he was having flashbacks and all those same feelings of fear and dread had overtaken him.

Bahati pulled him into her arms. He held onto her tightly. He tried not to sob into her damp hair, but it was no use. Bahati led him over to the sofa and made him sit down. He took the tissue she handed him. "How long were you gone to the store?"

"An hour and a half, maybe more. I don't remember." He sniffed. Bahati handed him a tissue. "I came in and put everything up and started dinner. I sat down to have a beer. When I got up to check on her, she just wasn't there." He was panting. "I thought she was asleep."

"How was she before you left?"

"She was fine," he said. "She had a bath. I put clean sheets on the bed. I fed her lunch."

"You said something about her being different. What did you mean by that?"

"I can't put my finger on it. The other day when I got home from Mexico, she picked up this Maya glyph and read it." He picked up the coaster off the coffee table. "Do you know what this says?"

Bahati inspected it. "No," she said.

"It's the Maya symbol for Jaguar," he said. "Lauren knew exactly what it said."

"We have spent a lot of time studying the glyphs," Bahati nodded.

"That's what she said. And then when we called to talk to Professor DeLaFuentes in Mexico. She carried on a complete conversation with the operator in Spanish. Did you know she spoke Spanish?"

"No," Bahati said.

"That's because she doesn't... didn't. Yet suddenly, there she is talking like a local, right down to how she rolled her r's."

"Lauren? Rolling her r's? Now that really is weird." Bahati backed away. She shoved her hands in the pockets of her jeans.

Rowan looked at her sharply. "Really? That's what surprises you about all that?"

"There are a lot of things about Lauren that amaze me. The least of which is how she rolls her r's. I've said it before. She's always been a bit of a mystery to me. She continues to surprise me."

"I don't like surprises. I don't like not knowing where my wife is." Rowan crossed his arms. He was frustrated. *Why did she always do this?* "I didn't like it any in Washington and I certainly don't like it now."

"We should call the police," Bahati suggested.

"She has to be missing for twenty-four hours before they'll take a missing person's report," Rowan said.

"I don't think that's true, but where would she go?" Bahati asked. "Maybe we can figure out where to look for her."

"I don't know," Rowan grabbed a handful of his hair and tugged at it. He was frustrated and helpless to do anything about it. Bahati reached up and caught his hand, pulling him into her.

"It's going to be okay, Rowan."

"You don't know that." His voice cracked.

"Let's start calling the team. We could see if anyone's talked to her or seen her today. Maybe she's at the library, or the Asian market. We can check there."

There was a pounding knock on the door. Where Bahati seemed to melt with relief, Rowan lept to his feet. He was at the door before Bahati could even turn. He took a step back when he realized there were two police officers, holding on to his soaking wet wife. She was shivering but didn't look up at him. Someone had thrown a blanket over her shoulders. Her hair hung in dripping cords around her face. She trembled violently.

"Lauren!" Bahati rush towards her, catching her arm and pulling her into the townhouse. The police officers stepped in behind her. "We've been worried sick." She made eye contact with the officers. Rowan seemed too stunned to move.

Lauren pulled away and stood, frozen. Her eyes never moved from the spot on the floor where she stared. Finally, Rowan reached out for her. He pulled her into him. She didn't shy away from him. She didn't melt into him as she usually would. He kissed her head before he looked to the police officers for answers. "Where did you find her?"

"She was in the San Diego Zoo after closing time. That's where the security patrol found her," one of the officers responded. "She was just standing there, staring at the animals."

"We couldn't get her to answer. We were about to call the paramedics to come take her to the hospital for a psychological evaluation. Then, she just looked at me and said I'm looking for Rowan Pierce," the police officer explained. "Are you Rowan Pierce? How do you know her?"

"I am Rowan Pierce. That's my wife Lauren."

"Does your wife usually go out for a walk in the middle of a rainstorm?"

"Nothing my wife does is usual," Rowan said. "Lauren is... different. This pregnancy has been hard on her."

Rowan rubbed her arm. He felt the subtle movement of her body as she rested her head on his chest. His shirt was immediately soaked. He didn't mind. He kissed her wet head again. He could feel her arm snaking around his waist. "Mrs. Pierce?" The first officer raised his voice.

Lauren turned and looked at him. "It's okay. I'm home."

It took several minutes of additional questioning before Bahati got fed up and came over, taking Lauren by the shoulder. "Come on," she said. "Let's go get you into something a bit... drier."

Lauren moved obediently, and Rowan was left to answer questions.

LAUREN WAS SOAKED TO THE SKIN. A PUDDLE COLLECTED ON the tiles around her as Bahati peeled her out of her damp clothes. Even her under garments were drenched. Lauren didn't protest. She didn't exactly participate either. Bahati turned on the shower, setting it to warm before wrapping Lauren in a dry towel to get her to stop shivering.

Bahati helped her with a quick shower. By the time she had her hair washed, the shivering ceased. When she got her out, Bahati helped her dry off and paused to find Lauren's bath robe, getting her limp arms into it. Then, she herded her towards the bed. Lauren veered off to the living room, where Rowan was being questioned.

"Are you all right, ma'am?" One of the officers eyed her warily.

She nodded. "I am home now."

"Come on, Lauren. You're tired," he said. "She needs sleep."

"Of course." The cops glanced at one another. "We'll

follow up if we have more questions, but... it can wait. The Zoo doesn't intend to press charges, so I suspect this will be the last of it, unless they change their minds."

"Press charges?" Rowan's brow tightened.

"For trespassing," the second officer said.

"Oh," Rowan said. "Well I'm sorry about that. She hasn't been herself lately. We'll talk to her doctor, so we make sure nothing like this happens again."

"Thanks, Mr. Pierce."

LAUREN CURLED UP AND CLOSED HER EYES. ROWAN AND Bahati stood over the bed. Both of them were puzzled. There were no words between them.

Bahati finally broke the silence. "I'll call and check on you both in the morning," she said. "Get some rest."

"No promises." Rowan pursed his lips.

Bahati managed little more than a worried smile. "I'll let myself out."

Rowan slipped out of his wet clothes. He put his pajama pants and t-shirt on then climbed into bed beside her. She made no protests when he pulled her into his arms, and let his body warm her. His hand came to rest on the swell of her abdomen. He could feel her relax into sleep. The child within her kicked against his hand.

It was a comfort, but it wasn't enough to help settle his racing heart. Lauren had never been one to sleepwalk. Not in all the years he'd known her could he recall her ever having an issue. Just when he thought he knew all her secrets; he'd learned something new. He knew exactly how Bahati felt.

When he woke up, the bed beside him was empty. Rowan bolted, breathless and terrified. He realized Lauren was standing on the balcony, watching the waves, kissed by the first rays of the morning sun. The rain had let up and the skies were as clear as they could be. The ocean hummed in a rhythm as it lapped against the shore in the distance.

Rowan smiled as the cool ocean breeze met him when he stepped outside and put a hand around her waist. "Sleep okay?"

She nodded, sighing. "I miss the beach," she said. "Remember our honeymoon?"

"How could I forget?" He smiled, inhaling the perfume of her hair. She'd already had a shower and had dressed in a pair of shorts and a t-shirt. "No clothes for a week," he grinned. Just the thought of her dark brown skin made him smile. SPF 50 had been his best friend. That and the shade from the cabana had saved him from becoming a lobster.

"I miss the piña coladas, and laying in the sand... the warm sand..."

"So put on your bikini and we'll go lay on the beach all day," he said, as she leaned against him.

"But..." She started to protest.

"I know you're supposed to be on bed rest, but what's the difference between laying in the sand and laying on the mattress?"

"May I have a *bahn mi*?"

"So, do you think the Vietnamese restaurant is open on Christmas?"

"I still can't believe it is already Christmas?"

"How could you forget Christmas?" He gasped. "Come on, I've got presents for you."

"For me?" Lauren caught his hand and let him lead her into the house.

"Make yourself comfortable," he said, pointing to the sofa. He was willing to break the rules for a short period, but she needed to comply with doctors' orders as much as possible. She didn't argue. He handed her one of the packages from under the palm tree, holding the other one as he sat down in the chair beside her.

"You didn't have to get me anything," Lauren said, blushing. "But... I didn't get you anything."

"I have everything I need," he said, meaning it.

"What is this?" She got the wrapping paper off of it and was amazed at the red velvet box.

"Open it," he said, lifting his chin.

She hesitated, eyeing him warily, then lifted the lid. There, on a bed of red velvet was a silver charm with a heart-shaped diamond at the top of a disk. "Another necklace?"

"The cartouche was actually a gift from our guide at Chichén Itzá. He gave it to me to give to you. I found this one at a shop in Mérida. I couldn't resist." She looked at him blankly, clearly trying to guard her emotions. It was a compass, and the diamond looked like a North Star above the circle. There was a lot of symbolism behind the North Star, and she recognized that fact immediately. "It's to remind you that you are my True North. Wherever you are, that is my home." He took the box out of her trembling hand. He took out the silver chain, reaching over her to clasp it behind her neck. The charm hung just below the hollow of her throat, and it was cool against her skin, but promptly warmed as her hand went to it. The cartouche that wasn't her name hung in the hollow between her breasts. They were both silver.

"Rowan, it's... it's beautiful." She trembled. "Thank you." She threw her arms around him, kissing his cheek. She hugged him fiercely. When he let go of her, she glanced at the second box. "What's that?"

He handed it to her. "Open it," he said, smiling when she did. There was a similar pendant. This one was a bit bigger. The diamond was in the middle. It hung from a black leather thong, with a silver clasp. "That's the matching one for me, so you know, and to remind me, should I ever forget... that you are my heart."

Lauren managed a faltering smile. She pursed her lips to keep the tears from rolling down her cheeks. Nothing could stop the flood. He let her help him put it on, and she climbed up into his lap, putting her arms around his neck, resting her head on his chest, toying with the charm as she inspected it. "You are the sappiest son of a bitch I ever met." Her lip trembled. She lifted her face to his. "And God, I love you."

He leaned in and kissed her, drinking deeply of her. "I love you too." He sat back, and settled in with her in his arms, his hand running over her stomach. "This other gift is for the baby." Rowan took up the small, flat box. Lauren reached to open it and brightened when she saw the outfit looked exactly like one of Rowan's favorite hiking outfits. There was a pair of olive drab shorts, a plaid shirt, and a matching vest, with a hat just like the one he wore. There was also a white undershirt printed with *The Veritas Codex* across *the front*.

"Thank you," she said. "It's perfect."

"Now. Are you going to tell me how you ended up at the San Diego zoo, in a storm... after hours... when the gates were locked?"

"Huh?" Lauren lifted her head off his chest. She looked at him as if he'd lost his ever-loving mind.

"Do you not remember anything from last night?"

"No, but... I did have the weirdest dreams."

"Tsul'Kalu again?" The undertone of frustration was evident in his voice.

"Yeah," Lauren said. "How did you know?"

"Lucky guess." He offered. "Tell me about it."

"Well, he told me he was taking me to talk to the Jaguar King," she said. "And it was like I was walking... through a portal. It was one of those places where the boundaries between time and space are thin."

Sure. Very dreamy, Rowan thought. "Did you see the King?"

"Yes," she said. "But I saw him once before."

"When?"

"The night of the solstice... I thought it was just the fever, but... it was so real, seemed so real. I can't explain it."

"Tell me what you saw," Rowan said.

"I saw a circle of stones... and an altar," Lauren said. "I could hear the drums beating deep in the jungle. It was so dark, except for this great bonfire in front of the altar." She told him what Tsul'Kalu had told her, about the wars and the famines, along with the drought. He told her how the gods demanded blood. He'd heard the same stories from Enrique, or whoever the hell that had been. "The King knew the gods would only hear his prayers if he gave what was most precious to him. Since his sons had already died of war or disease, he gave the only thing he had left, his Queen. But... the fire never got a taste of her flesh because she was stolen away. Some say it was the gods, who had given her to the King in the first place, who had taken her back. They spared her heart from the flames, but..."

"How much of the footage from our expedition did you watch yesterday?" Rowan queried.

"None," she said. "Why?"

"I've heard that story before," he said. "Or a version of it."

"From whom?"

"The impostor." He crabbed.

"It wasn't the gods who stole her back, though," Lauren sighed, holding her charm in her hand, learning the feel of it by touch.

"Oh? And who was it?" He asked, puzzling over their whole conversation.

"You did," she said.

"I did?" Rowan lifted his brow. "How did I do that?"

"You were there on the solstice," she said, leaning her head back against him, her hand back on his chest.

Rowan sat up, lifting her effortlessly so he could look at her. "Are you telling me, the woman I found in the standing circles on the solstice was the Jaguar Queen? Do you realize how crazy that sounds?"

"I'm not crazy, Rowan." Lauren looked mortally wounded by his accusation. "I know what I saw."

"Seriously," he said, finding it hard to believe she'd seen what he'd seen, and knew things… things he'd only heard in tales of lore. He had chalked his perception of the events up to the concussion from hitting his head on the stone. Now he wondered how they could both share in the delusion. "I've known you to come up with some pretty crazy stuff, especially since the whole Bigfoot fiasco. But all this is hard, even for me, to swallow."

Lauren stared at him blankly. Her expression was one of utter disbelief. She turned away and stood. She walked out on him without another word, slamming the bedroom door behind her. He heard it click and realized she'd locked it.

"Lauren?" Rowan immediately realized his error and followed her. He jiggled the handle and put his shoulder into it with a thud. "Honey. I'm sorry. Please just... let's talk about this?" He could hear her crying. "Lauren?"

There was no answer.

～

ROWAN DECIDED IT WAS BETTER LEFT ALONE, AT LEAST FOR the moment. Clearly, he'd hurt her feelings. Fortunately she wasn't one to hold onto things like that for long. She was tired, and uncomfortable. The whole situation had them both out of sorts. He left her to rest.

Making a pot of coffee, he sat down at the kitchen table with his laptop and went to work. He watched the video from the first days of their expedition. Hesitating, he went looking for the video from the night of the solstice. He had to thumb through the hundreds of files until he found the one from his body cam.

They'd recently converted to a new type of camera system. The new ones were similar to the ones police officers wore, except the studio had gone all out to get multifunctional cameras. The new ones could film not only night vision, but infrared, as well as regular day-time film. That night, Rowan had set his up for night vision. The screen glowed green against his skin as he watched the film for the first time. His jaw dropped as the scene unfolded. He paused the film, rewinding it. Holding the headphones to his ears, he listened again. There it was! He could hear the throb of the drums in the distance. He could hear his name being called. The cameras captured a strange glow coming from behind him. When he turned, it was so bright it washed out everything on the night vision camera. A dark form erupted from the light, and the camera jostled as he was sent tumbling headfirst into the stone. Then, the camera went dead.

"Holy Mother of God..."

"Now do you believe me?" Lauren stood in the open

doorway but turned and returned to bed. Her eyes were still red.

"I'm sorry I ever doubted you," he said, standing. He followed her into the bedroom and pulled her into his arms. He buried his face in her hair and breathed in. "I don't know how you did it, but I knew I heard you call my name."

"I'm not sure I can explain it either. I just need you to trust... whatever this is, this gift, this magic I have... I never asked for it, never wanted it. I can't control it. But it's a part of me now. I have to use it."

Rowan held her and felt his own heart racing. "You're right. I trust you."

1 7

Rowan arrived at the office early Monday morning after the holiday. He set to work, re-arranging the conference room. Jean-René arrived just in time to help him move the conference table to one end, and a sofa from the executive office to the other. Jean-René was puzzled by the boss' strange behavior but said nothing. When Bahati arrived with Lauren in tow, the purpose became evident. If he couldn't keep her in bed at home, he'd at least put her on the sofa at the office. At least here, he could keep an eye on her.

The coffee table served as their conference table as everyone gathered around with their laptops and other equipment. Lauren had the printer going within minutes of getting her iPad up and running. Bahati served as gopher, bringing her everything she printed.

"Okay." Rowan called the team to order. "I'm quite sure Lauren's doctor isn't going to like this. It's a compromise that was necessary to keep her resting and get her help to figure out what the hell happened in Mexico."

"I'm going to be bossy, needy and whiny, so get used to it," Lauren said. "I've only got a few more weeks of this before *Rowan Jr.* gets here, so let's get to work."

"*Rowan Jr.?*" Rowan's brow arched as he looked at her, puzzled.

"Or *Lauren Jr.*," she said, realizing they hadn't even talked about names, at least not seriously. His suggestion had been to name their child Indiana Jones Pierce, regardless of whether it was a boy or a girl. She'd already put the kibosh on that. "Whatever."

"Let's just get to work," Rowan said. "Jean-René, you coordinated with the University. How did you get the name of this Professor DeLaFuentes?"

"I talked to the Dean of the Archaeology Department, Dr. Pedro Alvarado," Jean-René said. "I found him from a series of blog posts he'd published on the Maya Apocalypse. I'd hoped he would come and meet our team. He said he was just too busy. He had his own research teams to lead. I thought he was going to brush me off all together, but then he said he'd have one of his professors meet us. He said DeLaFuentes was the best man for the job."

"I did a background check on Dr. DeLaFuentes and confirmed what I had learned when I called the University the other day," Lauren said. "Enrique DeLaFuentes was a graduate of the University of Bogotá in Colombia. He got his masters at Stanford, and his PhD from the University of Cairo."

"My dream college." Rowan sighed wistfully. Lauren had applied for their PhD program long ago. She hadn't gotten in. She'd ended up getting her PhD in California.

"Rub it in, Mister." She continued. "The Professor was supposed to retire at the end of the semester in May." Lauren handed Rowan a printout of a picture. "This is the real Dr. DeLaFuentes."

It was a much older gentleman than the one Rowan and the team had met. This man was rotund, with a head full of hair that was clearly dyed pitch black. It stood out on his round head like a chia pet. He had a bushy black mustache and wore a pinstripe suit that must have been twenty years old. He looked more like a drug lord than an archaeologist.

"Yeah, that's not Dr. Rick." Jean-René studied the picture over Rowan's shoulder.

Lauren continued. "Stephanie Wentworth was sixteen when she came with her father on a business trip to Mexico. They stopped to meet with a petroleum geologist at the University of Mexico. William was interested in the oil reserves off the coast of Venezuela. His company was working on a deal to start drilling. It was supposed to be a working vacation for the father and his daughter. They had planned to go to Playa Del Carmen and catch the ferry to Cozumel upon conclusion of his business at the University. Stephanie, however, met some college kids at a party. They offered to take her sight-seeing the following day while her father worked. When William returned from his meetings, Stephanie was gone. There was a ransom note on the bed in the hotel."

Lauren handed Bahati the picture of William Wentworth. He had been a robust man, tall and well-formed, even for a man in his early 50s. He had a mane of sandy blond hair and piercing green eyes. Laugh-lines cut through his tanned skin. His teeth were perfectly straight and bone white.

"Bet he was popular with the ladies," Alejandro said as the picture came to him.

"It's the dimples," Jean-René said. "Girls love the dimples."

Lauren glanced up at Rowan, who was grinning so hard his dimples were unmistakable. She blushed behind her bangs and returned her attention to her iPad. "He contacted the authorities. But against their advice, he paid the ransom."

"How was the drop made?" Rowan asked. He glanced up at Jean-René. He didn't know how much it had cost them to get him out of that jail cell in Mexico, but it was probably a lot less than the ransom William Wentworth had paid for his daughter.

"A backpack with unmarked bills was left in a trash dumpster, as directed. Police made an arrest, but it turned out to be a vagrant looking for food. While the police were otherwise occupied, the bag disappeared."

"Cops in Mexico." Rowan snickered nervously. His eyes darted at Jean-René. "They're so stupid."

"It's the oldest trick in the book." Alejandro pointed out. He couldn't even look at Rowan. He stifled a peal of laughter.

"Not too stupid." Lauren continued, oblivious to the joke. "They had the foresight to put a tracking beacon in the lining of the backpack," she said. "The kidnappers were already in the air by the time the authorities picked it up. The flight plan indicated the plane was going to Tulum. Authorities were waiting for it when it came into land, but the plane was in trouble long before it turned for approach. A fire started in one of the engines. The pilot declared a mayday over the jungle."

Lauren handed the picture to Rowan. "That's Stephanie Wentworth."

Rowan held the picture. His whole countenance changed as he gazed on a familiar face. "Oh, my God..." It wasn't the same photo Lauren had sent early in her investigation.

Jean-René snatched the photo out of his hand. He and Alejandro inspected it. "*Tabernaque*! That's her!" The teenager was bright-eyed, and beautiful. Her hair was auburn, and her eyes, green, like her father's.

"You're sure that's her?" Bahati asked. Lauren didn't need confirmation. She could tell by the look on Rowan's face. He'd seen her before. Lauren had too.

"She is older now, but yes. That's the same woman. I'm certain of it."

"So, what happened to the plane?" Alejandro asked.

"The pilot made an emergency landing, and he did a decent job, but then the landing gear failed, and the wing broke off. The remaining fuel ignited. The plane burst into flames. The pilot was killed. The kidnappers were able to escape the wreckage, only to be picked up by the authorities and arrested at the edge of the airfield."

Lauren had pictures of each of the kidnappers that she passed around. "Emilio Juarez, Javier Sanchez and Santiago Mateo. The authorities determined their motive was just what you'd expect. They saw a rich girl and knew they could get daddy's money."

"But what happened to Stephanie?" Alejandro asked.

"We don't know for sure. But I have a theory," Lauren said. "I just don't have an explanation." Rowan looked at her, puzzled. "Whether by choice or by force, Stephanie Wentworth was able to parachute out of that plane somewhere near Chichén Itzá. She might have had a rough landing in the canopy, knowing how thick the jungle is."

"Seems fair enough," Rowan said.

"Here's where it's going to get weird. I really need you guys to keep an open mind about this," Lauren said. She paused long enough for everyone to nod at her, indicating they were with her. "Somehow, she made it to the standing circle of stones, which some say is a portal. It's a place where the veil of time is thin."

"A portal?" Bahati asked.

"A tear in time and space," she said. "Stephanie Wentworth fell through that rip, and the Maya saw her as a fallen goddess. Sky God Woman." She held up the glyph she had translated.

"With hair like that, I see why they called her a fire goddess," Alejandro quipped.

Jean-René's face contorted with his skepticism. Of all the people to question her theory, she'd least expected it from him. "If I didn't know better, I'd think Lauren was the one who hit her head on the altar."

"Hear her out," Rowan spoke up for her. "Tell them the rest of the story, Lauren."

She took a deep breath and swallowed hard. "On the night of the solstice, while Rowan was doing his investigation, Stephanie Wentworth escaped the bonds of time and returned to the modern world."

"How did she do that?" Alejandro asked, almost demanded.

"She was summoned," Lauren said.

"By whom?"

"Rowan," she said. "Stolen from the Jaguar King. Just in time too. They were about to sacrifice her."

"And how do you know this, Lauren?" Bahati asked.

"I was there," she said.

Bahati shook her head vigorously. "You were raging with fever on the night of the solstice." She protested. "I sat with you at the hospital that whole night."

"I don't know how it all works, but, maybe in my fever, I was able to escape the bonds of time too," she said. "I remember being there with Stephanie as they prepared her for the altar. She was terrified. I called to Rowan, seeing him through the tear. Somehow I was able to help him summon her from her fate..."

Everyone sat staring at Lauren in disbelief, she was certain they must be wondering if the boss had utterly lost her mind. Rowan finally turned to the group. "Look, I know it seems bizarre, but... you've got to see the footage from my body cam." Rowan had his laptop hooked up to the big screen television on the wall. "Someone dim the lights, would you?"

Jean-René got up and switched the lights, sitting back down while Rowan pulled up the video. He hit play. He didn't say a word as the video clip played. It all happened pretty fast. It left the team sitting with their jaws agape. Rowan hit reboot, and played it again, turning up the audio. "Again." Bahati insisted, after the second viewing.

After the third run through, Rowan turned off the video

and they sat in the dim light looking at one another. Jean-René looked at Lauren, blankly.

"Holy crap, Prometheus! Look at you go!" Alejandro made an obscure reference to Greek mythology, holding up his hand up to Rowan for a high-five that went unanswered. He lowered his hand, dejectedly. No one got his joke about Prometheus stealing fire... or in this case, Rowan stealing the fire goddess.

"Boss, I'm sorry I doubted you," Jean-René said to Lauren.

Jean-René turned the lights back on, as the last set of pictures came around for everyone to inspect. Rowan shuffled through them. The debate about what might have happened to Stephanie Wentworth raged around him. He glanced up at Lauren and turned one of the pictures around, holding it against his chest. "This one," Rowan said. The room silenced.

"You think?" Jean-René snarked.

Lauren leaned forward and took the picture. "Santiago Mateo," she said. "He'd been an under-grad student at the University when he met Stephanie at the party. He tried to get a plea deal and turn states evidence against the other suspects, but the local authorities didn't offer any quarter. He got the same verdict and conviction as his cohorts. They were sentenced to life in prison for the kidnapping and murder of Stephanie Wentworth."

"Life? For kidnapping?"

"Murder." Rowan gulped. "But they never found a body, did they?"

Lauren shook her head.

"Someone with the resources William Wentworth had could have paid a lot of money to ensure they got locked up," Jean-René pointed out. "It doesn't take that much money to buy your freedom in Mexico, so getting someone sent away for life wouldn't have put a dent in the Wentworth fortune."

"You think Wentworth bribed the judges for a conviction?" Lauren queried.

"Maybe."

"Can we go to the jail and interview him?" Bahati asked.

"Not likely," Lauren said. "He escaped from jail in 2009 and hasn't been seen since."

"Until last week." Rowan took the picture back and held it up for everyone to see. "Picture him a little older and unshaven."

Jean-René looked at him dubiously as he took the picture. He studied it a moment. "Yeah. That's him.

"No way!" Alejandro snatched the picture away. His expression dropped as he looked at it. "Holy hell..." he realized he'd been mistaken. "That *is* him. That's Slick Rick."

"That's the impostor?" Bahati asked, taking the picture. She looked at it, then looked at Rowan. "If you've seen a fugitive from the law don't you need to report that to somebody?"

A foul word escaped Rowan's lips. "Yeah, we do. I better start with the Network execs. They'll need to get legal involved."

"Oh man! Not legal!" Jean-René groaned. A long chain of expletives in French followed. Lauren glared at him. Rowan did a double take when he saw her expression... and realized what it meant. The Network was not going to be happy. Not one bit.

"*Ce n'est pas un problème, mon ami*," Lauren said to Jean-René. It was little more than a platitude. She turned to Rowan. "Better call Jacob."

18

Lauren came out of the meeting with the legal department, looking pale. Rowan was just angry. Jean-René, Bahati and Alejandro stood when the bosses came out of Jacob's office. They waited for someone to say something... anything. Lauren just walked past them. She had exceeded her allotted time up and had explicit orders from the Chief Legal Counsel to go home and go to bed. She was not to come back to work until she had a medical release, or a twelve-week-old baby in her arms.

"So?" Jean-René asked.

"We're off the case. I have orders to contact the Mexican authorities and be prepared to return to Mexico City."

"You have to be kidding? Does Lauren know?" Jean-René's accent thickened.

"The last thing I want to do is go off and leave her again. But what choice do I have?"

"Surely there's another option," Bahati offered.

"Don't be so sure," Rowan twisted the tuft of hair beneath his lip between two fingers. "Going to Mexico isn't even the worst of it."

"Oh?" Alejandro asked.

"No, not at all. The worst of it is, the whole episode is on hold and we've been ordered to lock up all the video, all the photographs. We are required to turn over anything and everything that might be considered evidence to Legal."

Legal would take care of notifying the State Department and Federal authorities. "We have been ordered not to go anywhere, and not to discuss the case between ourselves or to anyone else until further notice."

"Oh boy," Alejandro rolled his eyes.

"Oh boy, indeed." Rowan added.

LAUREN SAT IN THE CAR WAITING FOR ROWAN. SHE LAY THE seat back, feeling like she'd just been run through the wringer. She knew he would have to pack up all the materials he had control of and explain orders to the team.

This was probably one of their most successful investigations, short of actually finding Bigfoot—which only Lauren knew about. Yet, it would be censored as another successful mission they'd never be allowed to talk about. She hated that more than anything.

She alone had made the decision to protect Tsul'Kalu and The People. She had never revealed what he'd taught her or the wonders he'd shown her. She made the team promise not to tell anyone about the cave full of diamonds located under Mt. Saint Helens. It was also the cavern The People called home.

Rowan knew some of it. He didn't believe half of it. She still hadn't told him everything she knew. It gnawed at her. But the safety of The People rested on her shoulders. It was a burden she willingly carried, even though it meant the truth she'd worked so hard to prove could never be known. That gnawed on her too.

. . .

"SO YOU SPEAK FRENCH NOW?" ROWAN ASKED AS HE GOT IN the car.

"The All-Language of the ancient gods." Her voice had that weary, but misty tone. It was like that after the incident in Washington. "No, I don't know how it works. Yes, it is weird. No, I didn't ask for this."

"Oh so you read minds now?" He groused, starting the car. He met her eye as he reached for his seat belt.

"You can snipe at me all you want, Rowan, but you're directing your frustration at the wrong person." She snapped back.

Rowan put the car back in park. He turned it off as his expression softened. "You're right. I'm sorry." He reached for her hand, half expecting her to pull away. She didn't. He drew her hand into his and pressed it to his lips, then to his chest. "I'm just..."

"Frustrated?" She suggested.

"You know, that's just not even a strong enough word." He shook his head and sat back.

"Well, the good news is, we're now free for New Years' Eve." She scoffed.

He turned the car back on. "Well we can't leave town, and we can't have champagne, and we can't celebrate any other way." Rowan rolled his eyes.

"Promise me our next house will have a bath-tub big enough that we can celebrate New Year's Eve with a champagne bubble bath. Together." Lauren closed her eyes and dreamed aloud.

Rowan glanced back at her. A curl formed in the corners of his cheeks and his dimples deepened. "It's a deal."

"Maybe we can find something to do this year." She suggested.

"When's your next doctor's appointment?" He asked. "Are you sure I can't convince you to find out if I'm having a son or a daughter?"

"Does it matter?"

"No, not really," he said. "But the suspense is killing me."

"My appointment is tomorrow, and you've only got a couple more weeks to wait, so chill." She sat her seat back up, settling in for the drive home. "We'll find out soon enough."

～

"ROWAN, YOU'RE BACK FROM MEXICO," THE DOCTOR SAID AS he came through the door. Rowan grasped his hand and gave it a hearty shake. "How was your trip?"

"Typical business trip," he said. "Same old, same old.

"I know how it is when you're working for *the man*," the doctor said in jest. Lauren wasn't sure how much he knew about what they did for a living. Like many Californians, Rowan listed his occupation as *entertainment*, or put down that he worked for a television production company. Lauren always listed her occupation as *biological anthropologist*, even though she didn't practice it as much as she would like.

Still, the doctor didn't seem to recognize them, nor did he ask many questions beyond the polite conversation they engaged in. "Lauren, how are you doing?"

"Much better," she said.

"Any more contractions?"

"Not a one," she said. He pulled out the table and had her lay back. He peeled up her gown and measured her abdomen with a tape measure.

"Kidney function?"

"Peeing like a racehorse." She rolled her eyes, as he donned his gloves. "Especially when I sneeze."

The doctor grinned and proceeded with his exam. "Stress incontinence is very common in late pregnancy," he said. "Have a good Christmas?"

"It was nice." She winced. "Rowan brought me presents from Mexico."

"What'd you get him?"

"I figured he could wait a couple more weeks for his present," she glanced at Rowan as he finished up.

"We just have to get you to thirty-six weeks, at least," he said, peeling off his gloves. He patted her leg and offered her a hand to help her sit up. She pulled down her gown and covered her legs with the paper drape. He pulled out a disc from one of the drawers, lining up one wheel with another. "You're measuring about thirty-two weeks, so the last week of bed rest has been good for you. The baby's growing quickly. Probably about five pounds or so by now."

"I'm restless though," Lauren said. "I don't have to keep doing that, do I? Bed rest?"

The doctor leaned back crossing his arms. He looked dubiously at her. He glanced at Rowan who just shook his head. "You know what," he said. "I'm willing to consider light duty, provisionally."

Lauren's brow lifted. She hadn't expected any concessions. "Four hours a day on bed rest. That is in addition to a good night's sleep. No heavy lifting. No exercise. No sexual intercourse."

"Well if she has to spend four hours a day in bed..." Rowan started to protest, in jest. The look on the doctor's face told him it was not the time for jokes. "Never mind." He withdrew his mock protest.

"You must continue to stay well-hydrated, and you have to take it easy," he said. "If you have even a single contraction, you're back on bed rest. And if you do have any contractions, you're to report to the hospital for monitoring immediately. I'm only allowing this because you haven't started dilating at all. I will see you every week from here on out."

"I can do that," Lauren said. "And just to clarify, is lying on the beach in the sunshine considered rest?"

He eyed her. "Is there a mattress on the beach?" He retorted. "Bed rest means just that. Resting in bed. But laying on the beach is considered an acceptable activity for your time out of bed," he said. "Not swimming. No Bay Watch slow-motion-running. No volleyball. No rollerblading."

"Sandcastle building?"

"As long as Rowan hauls the sand," he said, patting her arm. "Call me if you have any problems."

"Thank you," Lauren said.

Rowan followed the doctor out to the hallway, leaving Lauren to dress. "So be square with me, Doc. How sick was she?"

The doctor summoned him into his office so they could talk. "I'll be honest," he said. "She was very sick."

"She acts like it was nothing." Rowan took a seat across from him.

"She was pretty out if it." The doctor pulled up her chart. "She had a high fever and was in and out of delirium when I got the call. It took three days of antibiotics and IV fluids to stabilize her condition. We did an ultrasound to verify the kidney stone passed. She got lucky."

"People die from kidney stones?" Rowan asked, scratching his chin with his thumb.

"No, but they die from fever and infection," he said. "She wasn't in any imminent danger; I will give you that. If she'd been stubborn and stayed at home to suffer in silence, she could have been in much more dire straits. She's lucky she conceded and got her friend to bring her in when she did."

"You know her," Rowan started, but hesitated.

"I can tell something's bothering you," the doctor said. He swiveled in his chair. "Spit it out, son."

"She's been *sleepwalking*, at least once that I know of," he said. "Is that... normal?"

The doctor gazed over the top of his glasses. "Nothing about pregnancy is normal," he said. "Hormones can make women do all kinds of odd things."

"Should I be worried?"

"Hang a jingle bell on the door... and sleep lightly." He tried to reassure him.

"I haven't been sleeping at all." Rowan realized now why he was so tired.

"I wouldn't worry too much. She's a tough lady, and we're rounding the corner for the home stretch." He smiled, glancing up as Lauren came to stand in the doorway, tugging her black t-shirt over the swell of her stomach. "I'll see you next week?"

Rowan stood and met her at the door. She saluted him. "I'll make my appointment on the way out."

"Happy New Year." He chirped with a wave.

"SO WHAT DO YOU WANT TO DO BEFORE YOU HAVE TO GO BACK to bed?" Rowan asked as they got back in the car.

Lauren paused a moment. Rowan could see her gears turning. "I don't know," she said. "It's such a pretty day. Oh, I know..." she looked at him with a wicked grin.

"What?" He looked scared.

"I want to go to the zoo," she said.

"What?"

"Well, we can't do any work. Right? So we might as well go see what took me out of the house in the rain," she said. "You said I went to the zoo, right?"

"Right..." he drew the word out, hoping she'd explain.

"I didn't even get a caramel apple or cotton candy," she said. "That's no fun."

"Cotton candy?"

"I want to go see the big kitties," she moaned playfully. "Maybe have a word with the jaguars. Maybe they know why I was there."

Rowan's face went blank a moment before his brow lifted inquisitively. "Oh yeah?"

"Yeah," she said. "I have a lot of questions. If I can't go to Mexico, at least I can talk to the natives." Rowan looked skeptical, but he humored her... and took her to the zoo.

～

CARAMEL, MIXED WITH APPLE JUICE, RAN DOWN HER CHIN AS Lauren stood in front of the habitat. She watched for the illusive jaguar. Rowan elbowed her and pointed. Her gaze followed his finger to a branch where one of the great cats lay in the shade, napping on a limb. Lauren smiled. "*Hola, Señor Guapo*," she said to him.

"Do you speak Jaguar too?" Rowan asked. His tone this time was more playful than snide.

"No, but I can read," she said, pointing at the sign in front of the enclosure. "That's *Guapo*," she said. "The female is *Nindiri*, and their cubs are *Tikal* and *Maderas*."

Rowan studied the sign and realized she was correct. "Well, what does the Jaguar King say?"

"He says *m'row*." She mimicked the jaguar sound, and much to Rowan's surprise, the great cat lifted his head. He turned his green eyes towards her and replied with a similar sound. The female appeared from the bushes. She walked over to the pool of water and glanced up at Lauren. The spotted kits appeared from the brush, chasing their mother's tail, missing, and tumbling to the water's edge, jumping back from their mother's swatting paw. Lauren bowed to the king.

"Greetings your majesty." She gushed. The female barked at her, and she feigned. "My apologies, my Queen. Greetings to you too."

"Ask them if they know what happened to the Maya civilization," Rowan sneered.

Lauren made some very cat-like noises. The male jumped down from his spot in the tree and came over to the edge of the habitat, a ticking mewl came from his chest. The female barked at him. Lauren's brow lifted. "Interesting," she said.

"What did he say?"

"He says he doesn't know," Lauren turned to Rowan, taking a bite of her caramel apple. "He was too busy making sweet, sweet love to his queen, and chasing fish in the river."

Rowan's eyes narrowed, but when she busted out laughing, his façade cracked. His dimples appeared. He caught her hand, pulling her caramel apple to his mouth, taking a huge bite. The juices dripped down his beard and onto his shirt. "Come on," he said. "Your time is running out. I have to get you home before your carriage turns into a pumpkin."

"Kind of like my belly?" She patted her stomach.

"That's what happens when the king makes sweet, sweet love to his queen," he said. He darted in for a kiss, then hooked his arm in hers, turning back towards the entrance.

"I have to get my cotton candy before we go." She protested.

"We'll get it on our way to the car," he said. "I'm ready for some real food."

"Mmm. Me too." She fell in beside him. "Chinese sounds good."

"We'll get it to go," he grinned.

"I'll call Grand Palace on our way, so it's ready when we get there."

THAT NIGHT, THEY ATE CHINESE FOOD IN BED. ROWAN CUED up the latest superhero movie on Netflix. They fought over the last dumpling and Rowan ended up trading his second egg roll for it. That made Lauren happy.

After Rowan carried away the empty containers, they curled up to finish the rest of the movie. Lauren dozed off before it was over. She snuggled up against him in her sleep.

"Hey Tsul'Kalu," she muttered in her sleep.

Rowan sat up on one elbow studying her. "Hey," he nudged her. "Ask Tsul'Kalu to come back later. I'm trying to watch the movie."

"M'kay." She smiled in her sleep and rolled over.

And that was the end of it.

Rowan watched another movie after that. He got up just before midnight to polish off the last of the sweet and sour chicken and steamed rice. He was tired, but he was still miffed about the whole DeLaFuentes deal. He debated going for a run and decided a beer on the balcony would have to do.

19

Lauren was sitting on the balcony the following morning with a bottle of water in her hand. She gazed off across the ocean. "Penny for your thoughts." He startled her when he opened the door.

"You were up late," she said, inhaling the perfume of his coffee, yearning for one sweet *crème brûlée* kiss of it on her lips. Rowan provided, but it left her yearning for a sip.

"Restless," he said.

"I know the feeling." Lauren nodded.

"How long have you been up?"

"A while," she said. "I watched the sun rise as it came over the hills and hit the ocean. It was beautiful."

"Squandering your time out of bed?" He asked, taking the chair beside her.

"No. It was worth it," she said. "I've been doing a lot of thinking this morning."

"About what?"

"Time," she sighed. "How there's never enough of it to do all the things you want to do. Aristotle said, *what is eternal is circular and what is circular is eternal.*"

"Pretty deep thoughts for so early in the day." He took a long drink from his mug.

"And that got me thinking about Maya calendars... and time travel."

"And what did you come up with?"

"Time travel is paradoxical," she said. "The minute you step foot outside your own place in time, you alter history. It's like ripples on the surface of the water."

"Or the butterfly effect." Rowan added his thoughts.

"Exactly," Lauren said. "Like the Greeks, other ancient cultures including the Maya and Egyptians believed there was a cosmic, eternal time where their gods resided. The Greeks and the Maya both believed that time was cyclical, whereas Christianity and many modern religions hold with the belief that it is linear."

"Alpha and Omega... beginning and the end." Rowan said.

"Albert Einstein for example, believed that the past, present, and future all exist simultaneously. It was the basis for his theory of relativity."

"You know the whole story of *Urashima Taro*, right?"

Lauren glanced over at him. "No, I don't guess I do."

"It's an ancient story about a man who was said to visit the underwater palace of the Dragon God *Ryujin*. He stayed there for three days. When he returned to the surface, 300 years had passed."

"There's a similar story in the Quran." Lauren's face brightened. "It's about the cave of *Al-Kahf* and a group of young Christians who tried to escape persecution and retreated, under God's guidance, to a cave where God put them to sleep. They woke up 309 years later."

"That would be an interesting cave to explore," Rowan said, seeing her bristle. She hated caves, especially exceedingly small ones. But he also saw something else; some realization washed over her. It was so strong, she couldn't hide it.

"Lauren?" She came back to herself with Rowan's eyes peering into hers. "You okay?"

"Fine," she said.

"You were a million miles away," he said.

"I was thinking about the cave of diamonds in Washington State. I sensed an energy there. I was just wondering if the cave of Al-Kahf had the same type of energy."

She put a hand on his forearm as she shook off the thought. She tried to downplay the revelation she'd just reached. "I was just thinking." She swallowed hard. "I need to go back and read more about the Philadelphia Experiment."

Rowan looked puzzled. "Do I know that one?"

"How could you not? It is one of the best-known stories of accidental time travel. How true it is? Well... that's anyone's guess."

"What happened?"

"It was an experiment done by the US Government back in the 40's before or during WWII. I can never remember exactly when," she said, sitting back. "The experiment was centered on using a cloaking device to make a ship invisible to an enemy radar. Unfortunately, something went terribly wrong. The ship not only vanished from Philadelphia but reappeared in Norfolk... 10 seconds later. Some of the crew members were physically fused to the bulkhead of the ship. Others developed mental disorders. A couple disappeared completely. Some of them reported traveling into the future and back."

"No way! How have I never heard this one?" Rowan exclaimed.

"Well, there's still some debate over whether it really happened. The government disavows any knowledge."

"Of course they do," Rowan shook his head. "We need to put that one on our list of mysteries to explore."

"Well, since we can't work on the *Investigation That Must Not*

Be Named, we might as well work on something else," Lauren said.

"Since we're on the subject," Rowan said. "What do you know about the physics of time travel?"

"Some scientists think using faster-than-light-travel is feasible to journey back in time. If you think about it... if time slows as an object approaches the speed of light, then exceeding that speed causes time to flow backwards, right?"

"So now you're some kind of physicist? Who are you? Sheldon Cooper?"

Lauren rolled her eyes. "Then I guess I won't get into theories on warp speed technology and how accelerating an infinite mass any faster than light speed is impossible."

Rowan grimaced in disbelief. "Thank you, Mr. Spock."

"It's okay honey. It's just rocket science. Not everyone gets it."

She rose and went into the house. Unable to stand it any more, she walked straight into the kitchen, and took out her favorite coffee cup. She blessed the cup with the *crème brûlée* creamer before filling it with coffee. She stood at the counter, taking a few tentative sips before she tipped the cup back and drained it completely.

Rowan followed her into the house and stood back watching the scene. She put her cup in the sink and headed to the bedroom. Rowan refilled his cup and followed her, finding her struggling to tie her bikini behind her back. He took the strings, tying it for her. He paused to kiss her copper shoulder. "Are we going to the beach?"

"Yes, please."

Rowan grinned. "I haven't seen you in your bikini in a while." He ran his hand over the swell of her abdomen. "I like it like this."

"I feel fat." She grunted, sticking out her belly purposefully.

Lauren might have thought of herself as fat, but all Rowan saw was beauty. He said as much. "Besides... you've gained what? Less than ten pounds," he said. "At least five of that is baby."

"My belly button's going to pop like a turkey timer any day now." She rubbed cocoa butter over her skin that was stretched tight. She was carrying in front. Her hips were still narrow. Her bosom strained the ties of the bikini top.

"You know what sounds good?" He hugged her from behind as he took over the job of rubbing the cocoa butter in for her.

"What?" She smiled at his reflection in the mirror.

"A box of fried chicken and some biscuits," he said. "We could have a picnic on the beach."

"Mmm," Lauren said. "But isn't it a bit early for fried chicken?"

"It's almost eleven," he said. "By the time we get food and get settled on the beach, it'll be lunch time."

"You don't have to convince me," Lauren said. "Get your swim trunks on and let's go."

LAUREN TIED HER SARONG AROUND HER WAIST, THEN GATHERED up her beach bag, and slipped into her flip flops. Rowan came out in his baby blue swim trunks and a white t-shirt. He slid his feet into his sandals. "Ready?" She smiled, reaching for the door.

A man in a black suit stood in the arched entryway, reaching for the doorbell. He startled and quickly recovered. "Agent Miller?"

"Dr. Grayson?" He took off his sunglasses.

"It's Pierce now," she said. "Dr. Pierce."

"Congratulations." He offered, brightly.

Lauren stepped back. "Come in," she insisted, as Rowan

shook the FBI agent's hand. They hadn't seen Andrew Miller since the incident in Washington.

"Double congrats!" He grinned at her protruding tummy.

"Thank you," she said. "It's good to see you."

"I wish I could say this is a social call," he said. "But I'm afraid it's business."

"We were just going to go down to the beach, but..." Rowan said. "We can go later."

"Please, have a seat." Lauren motioned to a chair. She sat down on the sofa. Rowan sat beside her. "We've been expecting a visit from authorities, but... we weren't expecting it to be someone we knew."

"I understand you had a run in with a fugitive down in Mexico," Miller said, taking out his note pad, and a picture. "Is this him?"

Lauren and Rowan examined it. It was more current than the mug shot Lauren had found online. "Yeah," Rowan said. "He claimed to be an archaeology professor from the University of Mexico. I spent several days working with him at Chichén Itzá."

"Do you know who he is?"

"I do now," Rowan said. "Lauren was working at home and figured it all out."

Miller turned to Lauren. "Are you sure we can't convince you to come work for the FBI?"

A wry smile crossed her face. "I'm flattered. But I'm fixing to take a hiatus from the job I have."

"If you change your mind, let me know." He grinned.

"So why is the FBI working on this case?"

"About a year ago, I transferred to the FBI's International Violent Crimes Unit. My father used to be the Special-Agent-In-Charge, and I always wanted to follow in his footsteps."

"I don't guess I've ever heard of that division," Lauren said.

"We oversee criminal investigations of international

kidnappings and hostage-takings. Our main goal is the recovery of kidnapping victims. We pick up a lot of business in Mexico and South America, as you might imagine."

"Makes sense."

"Once we return the victim, our secondary goal is the prosecution of the bad guy. We never did recover the victim, even though we prosecuted the suspects. Since my father worked on this case back when Stephanie Wentworth was kidnapped, someone in authority decided I should follow up on my father's work. I'm happy to take the case. I want to see my dad's work completed."

"Your dad worked the Wentworth case?"

"Yeah." He nodded. "He retired from the FBI three years ago."

"We think Rowan saw Stephanie Wentworth," Lauren said, noting the look on Miller's face.

"She was presumed dead after... her body was never found."

"After she parachuted out of the plane over the Yucatán Peninsula?"

"Yeah. It's been twenty-some years since anyone has seen her."

"Been almost as long since anyone saw Santiago Mateo," Miller said.

"Since he escaped from a Mexican jail," Lauren added.

Miller's smile told her he was impressed with her knowledge of the case. "So you heard about that?"

"We've put in a FOIA request for the NTSB report on the plane crash," Lauren said. "We haven't had any luck."

"Well, if she's alive, my question is, where's she been all this time?" Miller said, thinking aloud. "You don't think he's still tryin' to find her?"

"Or the ransom," Lauren offered, not sure how much to tell him.

"If our suspicions are correct he found her," Rowan said, with a side-long glance at his wife.

"Can you help us with the FOIA?" Lauren asked.

"I'll see if I can't get it for you," Miller said. "I did get my father's files. There's evidence that suggests the plane changed altitude not far from Chichén Itzá. It slowed. We believe that was where the engine trouble began."

"If the engine was already on fire at that point, wouldn't it have been a perilous jump for someone with a parachute?" Rowan asked.

"Depends on which engine," Miller said.

"If someone was desperate to escape, they might be willing to take a chance," Lauren said, thinking aloud. "I keep running it through my head. What I would do if it were me… everything I've read about Stephanie tells me she was a pretty strong young woman. Stubborn to a fault. Independent… brave."

"Sound like anyone we know?" Rowan tilted his head towards his wife.

"That was my assessment too," Miller said.

Lauren glanced at Rowan, then turned to the agent. "So how can we help the FBI find Stephanie…Mateo?"

"I'd ask you to come with me to Mexico, but it doesn't look like you'd want to do any traveling right now." He glanced overtly at Lauren's stomach.

"No," Lauren said. "I'm on restrictions until the baby arrives in February."

"Think you'll make it that long?" Miller made a face.

Lauren couldn't decide for a moment if she should be offended or take it as a compliment. "That's the goal," she said.

"Then I have an alternative proposal," he said. "With approval from my superiors, I can designate you as a special government employee. I can authorize you to help me review records and files. If you're willing and able."

"Really? That's an actual thing?"

He nodded. "It is," he said. "It doesn't give you any authorization to act as a law enforcement officer. It doesn't come with any pay, but it does allow me to swear you in. It requires you to hold everything you find in the strictest of confidence. You report directly to me. You can't discuss your findings with anyone else."

Rowan stood, pacing behind the sofa. "Wow, I'm kind of jealous."

"Don't be," Miller said. "I've got a job for you too."

20

"You're going back to Mexico?" Jean-René asked. "What does Lauren think about that?"

"She's not happy about it. She knows she can't go. She also knows I don't have a choice."

"I can't believe the FBI is ordering you to leave the country." Bahati scowled.

"I'm just glad they're letting us work our own investigation," Rowan said. "Look, I need you guys to keep an eye on Lauren while I'm gone. I don't expect to be down there more than a week or two at the most. I fully intend to be back before she goes into labor. I will be here for my baby's birth."

"Of course. We'll make sure Lauren's okay," Bahati said. "If there's anything you need, all you have to do is ask."

Rowan nodded, as she went over to sit with Lauren on the patio at the restaurant overlooking the harbor. Jean-René caught his sleeve. "Something is bugging me, boss," he said.

Rowan looked at him dubiously. "What is it?"

"Ever since Mexico, I've had this nagging feeling in the pit of my stomach. I just can't shake it," he said. "The fake Dr. Rick was pretty insistent that we get that ground penetrating radar. I thought it was odd at the time that a big university like his didn't have access to one. Now that we know what a fraud he was, I have to wonder why it was so important."

Rowan had to think about that too. What major University didn't have a ground penetrating radar? He'd thought that at the time Slick Rick had asked if they had one or could get one. He'd made excuses that the other teams had already hoarded all the good equipment and the only one he had left was in pieces on a workbench in the engineering lab while they tried to figure out how to fix it. It also occurred now to Rowan that Enrique DeLaFuentes didn't introduce them to any of his fellow research teams. Now that he thought about it, Enrique seemed to intentionally avoid them. "You think maybe he was looking for something? Not like something archaeological?"

"Who knows?" Jean-René scoffed. "It may be nothing, but... it keeps bothering me. That makes me think it's important."

"I'll see if I can't get some answers for you on that," he said, patting Jean-René's upper arm. "Keep an eye on Lauren."

"I will," he said. "Come on, I'll buy you a margarita."

"First round of tacos is on me," Rowan retorted.

"So when do you leave, Rowan?" Bahati asked as the men joined them at the table.

"Tomorrow," he said.

"Man, they aren't wasting any time. Are they?"

"Time is one thing we don't have much of," he said. "We're losing evidence with every passing day."

"The sooner he gets down there and helps them figure all this out, the sooner he can get home," Lauren said, her hand went absentmindedly to her abdomen.

"What? Three more weeks?"

"That's minimum," Lauren said. "I'm not due until February."

"Well," Jean-René raised his glass. "Here's to mysteries to solve, and margaritas to drink."

"Slainté," Lauren said, raising her water glass.

"Slainté," Rowan rolled his eyes. *Now she knew Gaelic too?*

"*Taco Bueno*," Jean-René joked.

Rowan sat down his glass abruptly. "That bastard got us drunk..." he said out of nowhere.

"He got *you* drunk," Jean-René said.

"Why would he get you drunk? And more importantly... why is that important?" Bahati asked.

"Dammit," Rowan sat back in his chair. "He grilled me about everything from how the GPR worked, to..." his face went red. "I told him all about Stephanie. Dammit all to hell."

"Do you think he already knew about her? About what happened to her?"

"He might have had some theories. I found an old article that had speculated about where searchers had looked for her — or her body—and he asked a lot of questions about the investigation to find her, and how long they looked and where they searched..."

"Okay, here's a question," Jean-René said. "Do you think it's even remotely possible that she sabotaged the airplane in an attempt to escape?"

"I mean, anything is possible," Bahati said. "But would she have that kind of skill set?"

Lauren lifted a shoulder. "No telling."

"I'll see what I can find out when I get there," Rowan picked up his glass again. He looked around for the waiter. "So, what's a guy got to do to get some tacos around here?"

ROWAN WAS UP BEFORE DAWN. HE WAS QUIET IN HIS EFFORTS to shower, dress, and pack the last of his supplies and equipment. He always did his best to travel light. But going solo meant he had to carry everything he would need. Loading up extra equipment made it difficult.

When everything was packed, he sat his bags by the front door. He went back to the dresser and picked up his wallet and pocket change. He checked to make sure he had his ID and some cash. Then, he paused and put on the necklace with the compass on it, before putting on his wedding ring. He grabbed his sunglasses and passport, tucking them into his jacket pocket.

He hesitated a moment at the door. He came back to the bed where his wife slept, leaning down, he kissed her head. She smiled in her sleep. He watched her for a moment. A sense of melancholy washed over him. He hated having to leave her, but what choice did he have?

He rose, halted by a hand catching his shirt. She pulled him back down as she rolled onto her back. Lauren pressed her lips to his. He snaked his hand over her stomach. "I love you," he said, when her lips released his.

"Come home safely," she said. "The last thing we need is you locked up in some Mexican jail or lost in the jungle."

He grinned nervously. "I'll be working with the FBI. I'm sure I'll be fine."

"Got the sat phone?" She asked.

"It's in my pack," he said. "Call if you need anything."

"Hurry back."

Rowan kissed her again. "I will."

ROWAN SHOULDERED HIS PACK, GATHERED HIS THINGS, AND slipped out silently. The Uber driver was waiting for him when he stepped outside. Before the sun even rose, he was off to the airport. The refrains of John Denver's *Leaving on A Jet Plane* echoed in the back of his mind. *Oh babe, I hate to go.*

After getting through security, he stopped and got a muffin

and a cup of coffee. He found a comfortable spot and took out his iPad. He set to work on notes for the post-production script.

He could hear Marlon Perkins in his head when he was doing voice-overs for his episodes. He grew up watching *Mutual of Omaha's Wild Kingdom*. It was one of the reasons he loved doing a show like *The Veritas Codex*. While Marlon talked about lions and zebras, Rowan got to talk about Bigfoot and *Chupacabra*.

As a young man he'd join the military because he'd wanted adventure. He discovered that sort of adventure was a little more than he was able to handle. He liked being a medic. He liked helping people. But when he realized he was spending more time with a gun in his hand than his first aid kit, it started to weigh heavily on him. The more time he spent in combat, the more futile it all seemed. He began to question his career choices.

After he nearly got blown up by a roadside IED, he was ready for retirement—the sooner, the better. He got his honorable discharge. They even pinned a couple of medals on his chest. The best part of the deal was the one-way ticket home to Colorado. Life was peaceful. It was safe—and completely boring.

Meeting Lauren had been the best thing to ever happen to him. She'd introduced him to a world of exploration, excitement, travel—a new kind of adventure. He hadn't been shot at in a long time. While his skills as a medic were only of occasional use, his creative writing, and other gifts made him a valued member of the team.

He also fell in love with his co-host. While the relationship had been rocky at times, most of the turmoil stemmed from her desire to keep it under wraps for so long. Neither of them was a good enough actor to hide the attraction. Now that they were married—with a baby on the way—he didn't have to.

A baby was a dream come true for Rowan. He'd always

wanted to be a dad. While Lauren might have her doubts, Rowan was never surer of anything in his whole life. He would do whatever it took to be a great dad. He couldn't wait to show his son or daughter the world.

THE FLIGHT TO MEXICO CITY TOOK ABOUT THREE AND HALF hours. He was able to catch a nap once they got to cruising altitude. He'd been lucky that it wasn't a full flight. He was able to move to the exit row, where he had the row to himself. It gave him more shoulder room, as well as leg room.

As the flight attendants prepared for landing, he shook the cobwebs out of his head. He found his agenda in his carry-on. He took a moment to review it before they landed, so he knew where to go and how to get there.

The FBI had taken care of all his travel arrangements. A courier had delivered his credentials designating him as a special government employee. Agent Miller didn't think he'd need to show them anywhere but wanted to make sure he had them in case there was any trouble.

THE HOTEL WAS IMPRESSIVE, AND ROWAN COULDN'T REMEMBER the last time he'd stayed in a decent hotel; one that wasn't a total dive. Most of the time they were roughing it in the jungle, the woods, or the desert. He certainly wouldn't be sharing his bed tonight with rodents, snakes, frogs, or insects. The Bonvoy Mexico City was a modern hotel in the heart of downtown. The decor was sleek, though Spartan, yet totally comfortable. He stowed his gear, collected his camera, and headed out to see about finding some lunch. He was starving.

"Rowan!" He hesitated at the sound of his name echoing across the expansive lobby. Agent Miller walked towards him in a pair of khaki slacks and a white button-down shirt. He wore a Panama hat and looked perfectly at home with the locals.

"Hey." Rowan grinned. He was dressed more like Crocodile Dundee. Rowan, in his wrinkled shirt and cargo pants, had the appearance of a worn-out traveler.

"I'm glad to see you got in okay," Miller said. "I just met with the local authorities. They have given us the authority to follow up on the Wentworth case. I'll stay in contact with them if we find anything else. I came to see if you were here and if you'd had lunch."

"I am and I have not," Rowan said. "Know a good place for tacos?"

"I was just going to follow my nose and see what I could find." Miller tapped the tip of his nose and smiled.

"Sounds like a plan." Rowan fell in behind him.

OVER THE RAUCOUS BUSTLE OF THE STREET, THEY DISCUSSED their plans for the next few days. Miller wanted to get a look at the original records. "I figure we'll get a good night's sleep tonight and start fresh tomorrow," Miller said. "If we get a chance, there might still be some people who know Santiago Mateo we can interview. Maybe one of them knows what his motives were for the kidnapping, beyond money."

"Isn't money the most powerful motive there is?"

Miller chuckled. "True, but the more money they have, the more people focus on themselves. They become less sensitive to the welfare of others. People want money for many reasons... to pay off a debt, to escape their personal troubles, or to live a life they could only dream of. Mateo and his accomplices needed money for something. Knowing that reason might help us understand why kidnapping a girl like Stephanie was their path to fortune."

"There certainly are easier ways to make a few bucks." Rowan could think of a dozen or more.

"It's amazing what people will do to get rich."

"Everything except work hard for it." Rowan chortled.

"Man, you got that right." Miller shook his head.

WITH A STOMACH FULL OF TACOS, AND A COUPLE—OKAY, MORE than a couple—of *Dos Equis*, Rowan was ready for a late afternoon siesta when he got back to the hotel. A long day of travel had drained him to the point of exhaustion. He was also sweaty and hot and decided he needed a shower to wash away the travel funk before he took a nap.

It was fully dark in the room when he startled awake. He lay in the inky blackness, recovering and allowing himself to drift just beyond the realm of dreams. He lay sprawled out like a starfish across the king-size bed. It was luxuriously comfortable.

With a deep breath, he could feel himself slipping under when a cool hand caressed his cheek. A warm body pressed itself to his side. The familiar hand snaked down his chest and stomach, slipping beneath the sheets. A long, soft leg hooked over his. His whole body chilled.

He started to bolt, but the hand warmed to his flesh. His will was no longer his own. He tried to protest, but she spread herself on top of him. Her hair brushed against his skin. He completely melted, surrendering to the shadowed vision.

Lauren always wore her hair down when she wanted to seduce him. It worked every time. The long raven locks were as soft as a prayer. He inhaled the perfume of her body as he wrapped his fingers in her tresses. He pulled her lips to his. He drank of her sweetness. His free hand slid up her leg to her flank, finding her skin as smooth as cocoa butter. It all seemed so real. A fleeting thought that he was dreaming came and went just as fast.

He knew every inch of Lauren's body. She knew his. She used that knowledge against him, taking advantage of his fragile state. His body responded to hers as she nuzzled against his neck, nibbling his ear. Untangling his hand from her hair, he reached out in the darkness for her. He pulled her into his arms, hungry with longing. It was a need that had gone unspoken—unfulfilled—for far too long. As his hands explored her flesh, he decided he *was* dreaming, and he did not care.

But this was not his pregnant wife. This was her body when it was pristine, as it had been some months ago. Her breasts were taut. Her hips were full. His hands found the dimples at the base of her spine. Her stomach, flat.

"Lauren." He breathed her name through his teeth like a prayer. He pressed his lips to her skin. He needed to hear her voice to be sure it was really her.

"Have you missed me?" She purred in his ear, grinding her hips against his. It *was* her.

Emboldened by that knowledge, he flipped her over onto her back. He caught her hands and held them over her head as he inspected her in the dim light. "This is a dream," he said flatly, bowing over her. His lips took her's in a fever.

Her hips arched to meet his. A hungry groan escaped her throat as she took him. "Then..." she breathed, as he released her hands and pulled her body to the circle of his arms. "... it's a good dream..."

"A very good dream." He whispered in her ear.

They hadn't been intimate since before his last trip to Mexico and probably wouldn't be again for some time. His need exceeded his control. If this was a dream, he intended to make the most of it, as her body moved with his, and their lips battled for authority over the other. He took what he needed with fervor.

"Oh God!" he gasped, rolling her back on top of him, sinking into the bed. He let her take command, surrendering while he still had some control.

"I needed you too," she said between the rise and fall of her hips. "I need you... now."

Release came all too quickly, but it was so satisfying that his body was left trembling. Suddenly, he was cold. And she was gone.

Rowan sat up, startled, breathless and confused. His body still ached from her touch, but he was left with a troubling emptiness he'd never felt. He got up and turned on the light. His knees felt weak. Leaning heavily on the wall, it was everything he could do to regain his senses. He realized he'd just experienced something very real—very disconcerting. He went to the door and found it locked from the inside. He was on the 22nd floor and he knew Lauren hadn't rappelled from the roof and disappeared just as quickly as she had come.

A long shower wasn't enough to steady his racing heart or ease the feeling that he'd just cheated on his wife—with his wife—or her doppelgänger if that kind of thing were even possible. She'd said she had come to him in Mexico before. *Had she done that again? Christ, that woman was something!* As he toweled off, he forced himself to chalk it up to an amazing dream spawned by tacos, Mexican beer, and unbearable longing.

MILLER WAS WAITING FOR HIM WHEN HE ARRIVED IN THE LOBBY the next morning. Rowan hadn't gone back to sleep. He was hungry, grouchy and in need of a cup of coffee. He could use something for his aching head too.

A car waited outside for them. Rowan wasn't at all talkative as they made the 30-minute commute to the University. Miller carried on a one-sided dialogue the entire way. He went over the list of people they were scheduled to meet with. He covered what he hoped to accomplish with each interview. The longer he talked the more Miller sounded like the teacher on Charlie Brown. And the more Rowan's head hurt. He was still out of sorts from his encounter the night before and all he wanted to do was call Lauren. Even better he wanted to go home to her.

She had some kind of force over him that made him long for her even when he was just running to the grocery store. Being a thousand miles from her physically made his heart hurt. It was no wonder he was having such erotic dreams about her. It was the draw of her spirit on his. The compass necklaces had been purely symbolic. Neither of them needed such charms for their souls to find one another, even in the darkest night.

THE FIRST MEETING OF THE DAY WAS WITH THE DEAN OF THE Archaeology Department, Pedro Alvarado. The man was a stuffed shirt, typical bureaucrat. Clearly, he'd been coached by the University's legal team and skirted all their questions. He provided few answers.

"We sent Enrique because the rest of the team doesn't like him." He finally answered something straight. "He's old and crotchety. He thinks he knows everything there is to know about the Maya."

"We needed someone who knew everything about the Maya," Rowan said. "Old and crotchety... well, not so much."

"The man always smelled of moth balls and cat piss." the Dean added. "But... he didn't deserve to die; not like this."

Clearly, the man was moved. Whether or not anyone liked the Professor, they felt his loss. "What was the rest of your archaeology department doing that you couldn't have sent them to work with us?" Rowan asked. It was the only question he cared about.

"The goings-on at Chichén Itzá were just a minor annoyance, really. We sent a team, but we had other priorities. We made an exciting discovery near Tikal. A hidden pyramid was uncovered using LIDAR satellite mapping. It took us six days to hike into the jungle, just to reach the base of it, it was so overgrown. You wouldn't believe the size of it. It puts the El Castillo to shame." Rowan's brow lifted. He sat back in his chair. "Well, that probably was more important than the end of the world."

"We knew the world wasn't going to end. We're educated people, Mr. Pierce. Surely you didn't buy into the hype."

"I am very much relieved the world didn't come to an end. I didn't expect it to. But now I'm left with more questions than answers. Did you know Santiago Mateo when he went to school here?"

"The name doesn't ring any bells."

Miller pushed his picture across the desk. "It would have been 2002 or so."

"Well, I've only been here since 2005. I wouldn't have known him," he said before looking at the picture.

"But you watch the news?"

"I prefer to read." The scholar finally looked at the picture, and Rowan noted a glint of recognition in his eyes.

"What?" Rowan asked.

"That's DeLaFuentes's research assistant," he said, wrinkling his nose. "He quit when DeLaFuentes refused to take him along. We figured he ran off with one of the other professor's lab assistants. She hasn't been into work since about that time."

Rowan looked over at Miller. "Coincidence?" Miller asked.

"I don't believe in coincidences," Rowan said.

Miller turned back to the professor. "Has anyone talked to either of them? Since the night of the so-called apocalypse?"

Alvarado got up and went to his file cabinet, pulling out two files. He came back to the desk and opened the first one. "Matt Iago, that's the name he was using." He pushed the file over to Miller, while he opened the second one. "Ria Flores-Cortez," he said. "Dr. Soto's research assistant." He pushed that file over too, and sat back in his chair, rubbing his eyes. "We suspected someone was skimming antiquities from the warehouse and selling them on the black market. It now occurs to me that nothing's gone missing since those two ran off."

"You think they were selling antiquities?" Rowan's brow lifted.

"We have thousands of artifacts and there's only one piece DeLaFuentes has been working on for the past year, but he's signed out over 100 artifacts for examination. I can only assume that was Iago. But some of the missing artifacts were signed out by Soto, Haas or some of the other professor's or their assistants."

"What was the artifact DeLaFuentes was working on?"

"An ancient Maya Codex," he said. "It's called the Grolier Codex."

"You have the Grolier Codex here?" Rowan's brow shot up as he leaned in.

"You've heard of that?" Miller turned from the file.

"They found it in a bar," Rowan said. "I can't believe it's here."

"Would you like to see it?"

Rowan's jaw dropped. "Could I?"

Alvarado made a phone call. "If you'll excuse me, I have a meeting down the hall. It shouldn't take but a minute. By then, the archivist should have the document here for you to see."

"Of course," Rowan glanced at his watch.

"Missing artifacts, missing lab assistants, and a murdered professor," Miller thought out loud, pushing Iago's file over to Rowan. "Do you think DeLaFuentes caught them and they killed him to keep him from ratting on them?"

"I suppose it's possible," Rowan said. "But something doesn't add up."

"What do you mean?"

"Well, if they killed him and then ran off, doesn't that make them look guilty automatically?"

The professor came in, and Rowan recognized at once something was wrong. "What is it?" He asked.

"It's gone," Alvarado's voice cracked, and he paced behind his desk. "The codex... it's not in DeLaFuentes's office, and its not in the archive."

"Have you reported any of the missing artifacts to the police?" Miller asked.

"No," he said. "We didn't have enough evidence."

"I'm going to need a list of everything that's missing. Go ahead and call the police, it's their jurisdiction. I can coordinate with them."

Alvarado balled up his fist, his color rising. "Late bloomer, indeed!" His fist pounded the desk. "I knew that guy was too old to be a lab assistant!"

∼

THREE MORE INTERVIEWS FOLLOWED, AND BY THE TIME THEY sat down for a late lunch in the student commons, Rowan was more than a bit irritated. It showed. "What's eating you, friend?" Miller asked.

"I can't help but think we're wasting our time," he said. "Whether or not the missing artifacts are related to our investigation is still secondary to what happened to Stephanie Wentworth, though it does make me all the more determined to find Mateo."

"I couldn't agree with you more," he said. The two were silent for a few moments. "I'm with you, I don't think any of this is coincidence."

"I think we need to go to Mérida and talk to the people at the hospital there," Rowan said. "We need to find out what happened to Stephanie. We need to find her."

"Think she'll lead us to Mateo?"

"I think it's our best chance."

Miller considered this for a few minutes. "I'll check with the airline and see when the next flight to Mérida is."

"God, I wish we'd flown the last time I was here," Rowan said, tipping back his bottle of Coca-Cola, draining it.

"Why didn't you?"

"It surprises people how tight the budget is when you're working on cable. It was cheaper to drive."

"Well, don't expect anything fancy on the government's dime. We won't be flying first class."

"As long as the plane isn't a bucket of bolts, I can promise you it will be better than some of the planes I've had to fly in."

THE RANGE ROVER THEY RENTED AT THE AIRPORT IN Mérida was one of the nicer rentals Rowan had gotten lately. It had four-wheel drive which would be handy if the skies grew any darker. The air smelled damp. There was a chance of rain. Rowan could only hope it would stay south of them.

Their first stop was a check in with the local authorities. Miller and Rowan were introduced to a detective named Phillipe Gutiérrez. "How may I help the American Federales?" He asked, jovially, as they were seated in one of the interrogation rooms. Rowan inspected the surroundings and was immediately taken back to Peru. He'd been in a room like this before and was amazed at the similarities.

Miller pulled out the photos of Stephanie Wentworth he'd

printed up and pushed them across the table, giving the detective the whole history.

"It's my understanding you're working the murder of a scientist named Enrique DeLaFuentes?" Miller asked.

"Yes," he said. "But we haven't had any decent leads."

"What can you tell us about the murder of Dr. DeLaFuentes?" Rowan finally asked. He'd allowed Miller to brief the detective, but he was anxious for answers to his questions too. Unlike the University staff in Mexico City, this Detective was extremely helpful. He answered every question the US Federal Agent and his assistant had. He pulled files and shared the records freely. The detective admitted they had no suspects, and no motive. The real doctor still had his wallet in his hip pocket. "He had the equivalent of 300 US dollars in it, and nothing appeared to be missing from the vehicle." He admitted it was likely to be a senseless attack by the local drug cartel. Poor Dr. DeLaFuentes had been caught in the crosshairs.

"Well, there's another theory," Rowan retorted.

The detective glanced between the two men. "Is there one I haven't considered?"

"We discovered the professor's research assistant was suspected of skimming and fencing Mayan artifacts on the black market. He and another assistant have gone missing." Miller said.

"Except, I've seen him," Rowan said, stabbing the photograph between the eyes with his index finger. "My team was here when DeLaFuentes was murdered, and we worked with Dr. DeLaFuentes while we were here."

"Before he was killed?" The detective's face contorted into a puzzled expression.

"No, after ..." Rowan said.

The detective laughed. "You're joking, right?"

"No," Miller pushed the picture of Santiago Mateo across the desk. "This is the man who was working as his research assistant. He gave the name Matt Iago, but, you know him as Santiago Mateo."

The detective looked up with a stunned expression. Rowan could tell he recognized the name. "You worked with this man?"

"You know him?" Miller asked.

"He's on our bureau's Most Wanted list."

"Oh he's on my list too," Rowan said. "We want to help you find him."

"You think he killed the professor?"

"Yes, and if he still has any of the antiquities he's stolen, we want to return them to the university too." Rowan added. Murder was one thing but scalping historical artifacts on the black market was just as bad in his book.

"Do you think he had something to do with the professor's murder?" the detective asked.

"Technically, we're not here to investigate this murder. Our primary objective is to locate the girl ... and if possible bring a fugitive of the law to justice, with aid, I hope. Perhaps we can help you solve your murder investigation and tick a name off your Most Wanted list."

The detective had listened patiently. When Miller finished he sat back and sniffed. "You're in my jurisdiction," he said, without preamble.

"Which is why we came to see you," Miller said. "I've already met with Mexican Officials in Mexico City," he said. "Your government has agreed to cooperate. I have all the authority I need, but, as a courtesy, I prefer to make this a joint effort."

"So, how can I help," he asked, picking up Stephanie's picture again, then Mateo's.

"This woman was last seen in the company of a fugitive from the law just a few weeks ago," he pushed Mateo's picture back at him. "I need a BOLO on Mateo...and Stephanie Wentworth."

"This I can do," he said. "I'll have every officer on patrol looking for them." He turned and glanced at Rowan then back to Miller. "What else?"

"Can you recommend a good hotel?" Miller gave him a crooked Texas smile.

Gutiérrez smirked and nodded. "I know the best place, but … it's New Year's Eve," he said. "There is a fiesta, and the rooms may be booked. Let me make a call and see if I can pull a few strings."

"Thanks," Rowan said. "Gracias."

"De nada."

THE TWO AMERICANS WERE STILL IN THE PARKING LOT WHEN Detective Gutiérrez picked up the phone and dialed a now familiar number. He lowered his tone before he said anything, making sure everyone else in the bustling detective's room was too busy to overhear. "That problem you thought might come back to haunt you? It's back."

"So soon?" The voice on the other end said.

"And this time, he's brought back up," Phillipe said.

"What kind of back up?"

"Federales," the detective said. "The kind who can easily get extradition if it came to that."

"Let's make sure it doesn't," he said, drawing the words out.

"And you should know … they know about the antiquities … and DeLaFuentes."

There was a long hesitation before an answer came. "Remember that favor I said I might need?"

"Yeah?"

"I'm going to need it. Walking papers and a plane ticket to San Diego."

"I'll have the courier bring it over as soon as I get it," he said, glancing at the photo his recent visitors had left behind. "I even have a photo for the passport."

"Excellent."

"Just make sure my compensation is sent back." The detective turned his back as he spoke gazing out the window as the visiting Agent's SUV pulled out of the parking lot.

"If everything is in order and you can get it to me tonight, I'll throw in a little something extra after the job is done."

"I'll get it taken care of," Phillipe said.

"Any idea where I can find that little problem?" Matt asked.

"As a matter of fact, I do."

"WHAT?" STEPHANIE ASKED WHEN MATEO HUNG UP.

"Your hero has returned to save you," Mateo slung his phone across the room onto the bed, angrily. "It's time to make yourself scarce. Think you can do that?"

"I've been scarce for the better part of the last … how many years?" Stephanie purred in his ear, running a rough nail along the curve of his tightened jaw. "Just leave it to me," she said. "I'll take care of everything. I just need one of those fancy portable phones and perhaps a trip to the salon?"

"You act like I'm made of money." He grabbed her abruptly, flipping her around into his lap, eliciting a startled yelp which turned into a giggle. She wrapped an arm over his shoulder and leaned in to kiss him.

"I know you're not made of money," she said. "But I am …"

"Uh huh…" His hand ran down her back and pulled her into him. "But until you have it in your hot little hand, no trips to the salon … no shopping trips … no champagne or caviar." He accentuated each item with a quick kiss; first her palm, then her elbow, and lastly, her neck.

Stephanie sat back and stuck out her lower lip. "Well you're no fun."

"When we find the money, we can have all the fun you want," he said.

"Are you sure we can't have just a little fun?" She held up two fingers spread only a few inches apart, as she batted her eyelashes and lowered her chin.

The inuendo was not lost on Santiago. He lifted a dark brow, considering her suggestion for a moment. "Well ... maybe just a little ... but only the free kind."

Stephanie smiled coyly at him, as she ran her finger down his chest, and twisted it into a curl of hair at the base of his throat. "Now, now. You know I don't do *free* or *cheap* ... but I do accept credit."

"Mmm..." his lips captured her's. "Credit huh?"

"Visa ..." She kissed him quickly as he had her. "Master card .... Or American Express..."

"Never leave home without it..."

IT WAS LATE IN THE AFTERNOON WHEN THEY ARRIVED AT THE hospital. It took nearly an hour before they got to the right person. Finally one of the nursing supervisors was able to tell them who the woman was and who had picked her up when she was finally dismissed.

Fortunately for Rowan, Miller's Spanish was flawless. "The woman told hospital staff her name was Olivia Harper. She was checked out by none other than Dr. DeLaFuentes," Miller explained. The hospital administrator pulled the files and sat behind a desk with them closed in front of her.

Miller asked to see the security tapes, and the administrator hesitated for a minute before offering a resigning gesture. With a motion for them to wait, she went and contacted the security department to pull the tapes. When she returned, she explained to Miller that they would have to go to the security office to get any more information.

The tapes confirmed what the administrator had told them. As soon as the couple left the hospital, the information was completely worthless. Where the two might go was the next mystery they would have to solve.

"She didn't look afraid to you when they left. Did she?" Rowan asked. "In the video?"

"He had his hand in the middle of her back, but she seemed to be going with him willingly," the federal agent agreed. "We need to retrace your steps, I think."

"My steps?"

"He approached you, Rowan. Of all the teams working at Chichén Itzá that week, it was you and your team that he gravitated to. I just can't see that being a coincidence."

"If the impostor killed the real Dr. DeLaFuentes, he could have found the man's itinerary in the car. It could have had my name on it." Rowan wasn't so sure it wasn't a coincidence.

"But why would he bother impersonating an archaeologist?" Miller queried.

Rowan thought about that for a minute. "Good question."

THEIR ROOMS WERE READY WHEN THEY ARRIVED AT THE Hotel Mérida, which was located closed to the Cathedral near the middle of the city. They would make for Chichén Itzá in the morning. Miller wanted Rowan to walk him through their previous expedition. Rowan wanted another look at the circle of stones.

That night, they walked through town to find dinner, discovering a raucous New Years' celebration. Dinner wasn't a problem, every street vendor in town was out. The perfume of grilled meat and tortillas had Rowan's mouth watering. Miller appeared from the crowd with a couple of margaritas in plastic cups. Rowan didn't hesitate to take one and drain it. They feasted and toasted out the New Year ahead of the midnight fireworks celebration. Miller insisted on staying, but Rowan was tired. He wanted nothing more than to go back to the inn and call Lauren. Since his experience the other night, all he wanted was to hear her voice.

As he walked back to the hotel, the margaritas were swirling in his veins. The music throbbed in his head. The surging crowds passing him added to the problem of simply trying to walk straight. He stopped at the steps of the inn, startled by the man leaning on the arched entry way.

"Hello, *mi amigo*." He grinned devilishly. "I didn't expect to see you so soon."

"You are *not* my friend," Rowan snarled. This time he really meant it too. "Where's Stephanie?"

"She's safe," he said. "You don't have to worry about her."

"I'd like to hear that from her." Rowan leaned on his knees, trying to stop the world from spinning.

Santiago considered him for a moment before he chuckled wickedly. "You have no idea what you've stumbled across. Have you?"

"I'd really like some answers about that," Rowan stated flatly.

"I'm sure you would," he said. "But this isn't the time nor the place."

Rowan swayed. The tequila hit him hard. "You're right," he said, reaching out to catch the lamp pole next to him. He tried to steady himself.

"Did you enjoy your margaritas?" Santiago grinned. "You know the good thing about lime and tequila? They hide the taste of any kind of drug you want to dissolve in them. Drugs like benzodiazepine. You've heard of that, right?"

Santiago's words seemed to swirl in the void around Rowan's head like echoes. "Date rape drug." The words slurred. Rowan dropped to one knee.

Santiago came to his side and lifted him to his feet. "That is a horrible name for it, considering this isn't a date and I certainly have no intent of anything so nefarious," he said. "I like it because it makes you do what I want you to do." Santiago led Rowan down the street, struggling to keep the bigger man on his feet and moving in the right direction. "It's also useless as a date rape drug on men... makes it hard to get a decent stiffy."

"That's not very nice," Rowan's words slurred as the drug began to take its full effect on him.

"Don't worry," Santiago said. "You'll forget all about it by morning."

"Oh, that's good. Where are you taking me?"

"I need your help," Santiago said. "I need you to help me find something."

"Oh," Rowan stumbled and lost his feet, taking Santiago down with him.

Santiago swore in Spanish as he wormed out from under Rowan's limp body. "You could stand to go on a diet, my friend. You're as solid as they come." Rowan made a decent attempt to get to his feet on his own, but Santiago got him up and all but drug him into a small house, before he passed out cold.

LAUREN SAT UP UNTIL AFTER TWO A.M., WAITING FOR ROWAN to call. She hadn't talked to him since he left, and she hadn't expected the new year to come in without at least a call from him. She'd tried to reach him other ways too and thought for sure she'd found him a few days before. The effects of her efforts had been surreal. She'd dreamt of making love to him in a way she hadn't been able to in a long time. His body had responded to her's. It had felt so real to her. She thought for sure he'd felt it too, but now... she wasn't so sure.

Tsul'Kalu had told her she could call to him when she needed him, but apparently that kind of need wasn't what he'd meant. She was prepared to try again, since he wasn't answering her phone calls.

She tossed the phone aside and lay down, closing her eyes, willing sleep to come. She was certain she could find Rowan in his dreams. He wasn't one to stay up late. So she was certain he must be asleep.

Distance and darkness were no obstacles, but Rowan's consciousness wasn't responding to her. She could feel herself pacing around him, but the room was dark, and as she reached for him, she found only a void. "Rowan," she called, but he wasn't there.

It had been so much easier before. He'd been willing and had accepted her presence even though it made no sense to him. That acceptance had allowed her to touch him, to feel his breath on her skin, and to love him the way he needed her to. His hunger had fueled her energy and given her authority over him. But once his need was sated, she couldn't hold on to him any longer.

Clearly, she'd done her job too well. He didn't need her, and she couldn't reach him without that energy. She woke up before dawn, aware of the futility of her efforts. It irritated her. What had been so easy before, hadn't worked a second time. She got up and went to the kitchen to make some breakfast. She was sitting at the table when the phone rang. She didn't recognize the number, but she answered anyway.

"Lauren, it's Miller," he said, his voice heavy.

"What's wrong?" She felt it in her core immediately.

"Have you talked to Rowan in the last twenty-four hours?"

"No, why?"

"He was headed back to the hotel last night to call you," he said. "He wasn't in his room when I went to meet him this morning. It doesn't look like he slept here last night. I have no idea where he is."

Lauren stood, the baby kicking as she did. "What?" She ran a hand through her hair. "You lost my husband?"

"Lauren, don't panic," he said. "I will find him. I just needed to know if he called you or not."

"Well he didn't," she said, brusquely.

"I'll call you as soon as I find him," Miller said, and the line went dead.

21

Lauren paced the living room. Her hands trembled. Worst-case scenarios played out in her head. Had he been *unavailable* to her because he'd been with another woman? That was the first thing that came to mind, but she promptly dismissed it. Female fans were always mooning over him, but she knew his heart. She knew he would never cheat on her. *Rowan Pierce loves me.* That was the truest sentence she knew.

Her second thought was that he was dead in a back alley somewhere. That thought chilled her heart and almost made it stop. She hurried to the bedroom, debating what to do first. She had to do something, but what?

She willed herself to calm down. She took a deep breath to slow her racing heart. Panic wouldn't help Rowan. But if she could help him, she had to try. Steeling herself, she closed her eyes, and reached for him in the darkness. "Rowan!" She called for him silently, but as forcefully as she could. The force of her effort made the room spin and she stumbled back on the edge of the bed. She managed to sit rather than fall. Safely positioned, she tried again. This time she mustered all the energy she could. "Rowan!"

～

ROWAN SAT UP A BIT TOO QUICKLY, LOOKING AROUND IN THE dark. Disoriented and sore, he moved in an attempt to improve his position. He found his hands and feet tightly bound. He realized he was moving, when the vehicle hit a pothole and he was tossed about, banging his elbow against something hard. A pained cry escaped his throat and the darkness threatened to envelope him again. A second pothole was his undoing, hurling him headfirst in the side of the truck.

THE FAINT HAD BEEN KIND ENOUGH. WHEN HE CAME TO A second time, he was no longer moving, and he had the distinct feeling that it was Lauren's voice that had called him from the void. He took comfort in knowing he wasn't alone. He didn't know where he was, or what had happened to him. He could feel she was close. That assured him that he'd be okay. He genuinely believed it.

A rattling at the door made him freeze. A lock was being opened and he debated the feasibility of lunging past whomever it was. He had to try to make an escape, but then with the bonds around his hands and ankles he knew it would be futile.

Daylight blinded him as the door swung open with a metallic groan. "Welcome back, Mr. Pierce." Santiago Mateo stood grinning at him. "I hope the ride wasn't too rough on you."

"I've had better." Rowan groaned as Mateo pulled a knife from his belt.

Rowan recoiled, throwing up his hands defensively. "Whoa, there's no need for violence..."

Mateo sniggered at him, and reached for the bonds around his feet, pulling him around so he could cut the ties.

"Don't get your panties in a twist, Rowan," he said. "You can't help me with your feet tied."

"What makes you think I'm going to help you?"

"You don't have any choice," he said. "I'd sure hate for your beautiful wife to have an accident, especially considering how close she is to delivering."

Mateo held up a picture of Lauren standing on the balcony of their townhouse, gazing off into the distance, looking concerned. "She's amazing." He muttered something that sounded salacious as he licked his lips. His gaze lingered over her image. He turned the picture back for Rowan to see. "I wouldn't mind having a piece of that! Man, she is hot!" Rowan did not like what the man was implying. "You didn't tell me your wife was so fine!"

"You can't hurt her if you're here." Rowan acknowledged, angrily.

"I have my connections," Mateo said. "You know the police here in Mexico are easily bought and paid for? I've made a lot of money over the past year or so, and I've made good use of my resources. I can get whatever I want. Fake ID, fake passport? No problem. Stephanie was more than happy to get back to the States when I suggested you might need some...persuasion. I just have to make a phone call. I'm sure you don't want me to do that."

"Stephanie? Why would she help you? You kidnapped her," Rowan demanded.

"I didn't kidnap her. She was in on the whole thing. She couldn't get her daddy's money without my help. Now, she's helping me."

Rowan's ire boiled in his bones, rage building in his veins. He could feel his face going red with hate. "If you hurt my wife, I will kill you with my bare hands."

"Yeah, yeah," Mateo waved him off. "Just get on your feet. You've got work to do."

∾

LAUREN FELT DRAINED, BUT SHE COULD FEEL THE CONNECTION with Rowan restored. He wasn't dead, at least that much she knew. He was still out there. She still couldn't tell where though. She debated what to do now. After long consideration, she decided she needed to take care of herself, and trust in Rowan's abilities. He would call her as soon as he could. She would be patient, no matter how much she wanted to go to the airport and get on a plane.

She showered and dressed, and was debating going to get something for dinner, but a knock on the door interrupted her thoughts. She looked through the peep hole, not recognizing the woman at the door. When she opened it, however, she knew immediately who it was.

"Hi, uh... I'm looking for Rowan Pierce," she said nervously. The woman was trembling and looked frightened. "Is this his place?"

"Stephanie ..." Lauren wasn't sure it was her at first. But she reached out and caught her hands, pulling the woman inside. "He's not here. I'm his wife."

"Lauren?" She looked at the piece of paper she carried as she asked.

"Yes. I'm Lauren," she said. "Are you by yourself?" She looked around before she closed the door behind her. "How did you get here?"

"I...it...I..." she stuttered, her voice trembling as much as her hands. Lauren led her to the table and sat her in a chair. "I had to get away..."

Lauren sat down across from her. She had a million questions. At the moment she didn't even know where to start. "How did you find me?" Lauren finally managed.

"I met your husband..." she started. Lauren detected a bit of an accent but found it hard to put her finger on it. If she'd been living in Mexico—ancient or modern—for the last decade or so, it wouldn't be unexpected. "I don't even know how to say this without sounding crazy..."

"He found you at the site of Chichén Itzá," Lauren said. "He told me."

"He came to see me at the hospital... the man that was with him..."

"Santiago Mateo," Lauren nodded.

"That wasn't the name he was using, but... yes, that's who it was."

"He's one of the men who took you hostage a long time ago."

"Yes," she swallowed hard. "He told my father he would kill me if he didn't pay the ransom. I believe they would have killed me too."

"But you escaped," Lauren said. "You jumped out of the airplane."

"How did you know?" Stephanie nodded, tears building in her eyes. "I didn't see any other way. It was the best chance I had of escape."

"Stephanie, we have to call the authorities," Lauren said.

"No!" She gasped. "No, please! No one can know I'm here! He'll come after me, I know he will."

"All the more reason to get the authorities involved," Lauren said. "They can protect you."

"No, you have to promise me," she said. She clung to Lauren's hand. Her grasp was so strong. Lauren's fingers went numb and it was all she could do not to pull them away from the frightened woman's clutches. "I'm the only one... the only one who knows where the money is."

"What money?" Lauren asked.

"The ransom," she said. "I grabbed the bag when I jumped out of the plane. That's why he's after me. He's still trying to find it."

"All the more reason to call the authorities." Lauren protested.

"Please!" Stephanie begged. "I just need a safe place to hide until this all blows over. Please. Can't I stay with you?"

Lauren sat back in her chair, her belly between her and the table. "I..." she started to say no but stopped short. It was against her better judgment, but she relinquished. "Okay, but the first sign of trouble, we're calling the police."

"Thank you," Stephanie all but climbed over the table and threw her arms around Lauren's neck.

"But we can't stay here," Lauren said. "If you found me, then chances are good, he could find me too. We'll have to go somewhere else."

"I have money," Stephanie said, pulling a wad of cash out of her backpack.

"Most hotels won't give you a room without a credit card," Lauren thought out loud.

"That's why I didn't go to one," Stephanie said. She wiped the tears from her reddened face.

"I could probably get something more... discrete," Lauren said, thinking about her old apartment on Ambrosia Lane. The landlord had been a nice old fellow, quiet, and kind. Maybe he had a rental property they could use until all this settled down. Her thoughts went back to Rowan. She fretted, but then realized, she hadn't even tried to call him on the sat phone. Lauren glanced at the woman across from her at the table and smiled, though it was forced. "Are you hungry? Can I get you anything?"

"No," she said. "I don't want to impose."

Lauren had to force her face to remain placid. She was already imposing. A turkey sandwich or a cup of coffee was no more of an imposition at that point. "Well, I'll go make some phone calls and see what I can find," Lauren stood. "Make yourself comfortable."

Her first call was to Rowan's satellite phone. It rang and rang. He didn't answer. She hadn't expected him too, but had hoped beyond hope that somehow, he would. Her second call was to Martin, her old landlord.

~

ROWAN THREW UP A HALF A DOZEN TIMES BEFORE THEY GOT UP the narrow jungle path to the site where the circle of stones stood. The heat, the drugs, and the lack of water, were working against him. By the time they got up the path to the clearing it was late afternoon, and the humidity was oppressive. He was furious at Mateo and he had a million questions he wanted to ask but doing so would force him to show his cards. Mateo didn't know Rowan knew about his ruse at the university, and if he asked about the artifacts, and the codex, he might lose the upper hand.

As they entered the clearing at the top of the trail, Rowan wasn't the only one to freeze in surprise when they discovered the clearing... was empty.

Where was the altar? Where were the pillars of stone? Those kinds of things didn't just disappear.

"What the hell?" Santiago sneered. He turned to look at Rowan as if he had absconded with the megalithic stone circle.

"Why are you asking me?" Rowan snapped back.

"This is the right place, isn't it?" Santiago darted frantically across the clearing, looking for his stones.

"You're the one who brought me here," Rowan said.

A long chain of expletives, all in Spanish, spilled from Santiago's mouth as he kicked dirt clods. He threw his hat down stomping it repeatedly. Rowan took a step back, but his eye went to the line of bent grass and bare earth where the altar had been, noting a subtle discoloration. He said nothing and let his captor have his tirade. He scanned the circle and noted similar patterns in the landscape where the other stones had been standing, but there was no sign of any trails where a

20T stone might have been drug away. With the mountainous terrain and dense cover of trees, there was no way a crane had been hauled in to take them out. Yet, they were gone.

"They were here! They were right here!" Santiago finally exhausted himself. He turned to Rowan looking wounded. "You saw them, right?"

Rowan's hand went to his fading multicolored forehead. "I have proof." The goose egg was still on his head; the bruises faded on his face.

"Exactly! Who stole my rocks?"

"How the hell would I know? I'm just a hostage here."

"Dammit!" Santiago stormed off, leaving Rowan standing alone in the circle.

It was just the opportunity he was waiting for. Rowan knelt. He inspected the ground, running a hand over the broken blades of grass that were yellowed. There was an obvious bare depression that told him there had once been something exceptionally heavy sitting there. He walked to the edge of the clearing. He stood and followed the circle, studying the most subtle of details. He was trying to figure out where the stones might have been taken, but he could find nothing to suggest they'd been removed manually—or so he thought, but then he saw something that made him pause.

Rowan knelt at the tree line, finding the trunk of one of the trees had been damaged. The wound to the bark looked fresh. That's also the moment he realized his sat phone was still in the leg pocket of his cargo pants.

He glanced around to see where Santiago had gone, but he was nowhere around. Rowan feigned the effort necessary to drop to one knee to tie his shoe. As he leaned into the tree line and then took a couple steps into the cover of the brush. He reached for his phone in his pocket and turned it on. The battery was almost dead, but he might be able to get a call out. He dialed the first number that came up.

"Rowan?" The voice on the other end came back.

"Don't talk, just listen. I'm okay but..."

Rowan froze, recognizing the sound of a pistol being cocked, just behind his ear. The phone slipped from his fingers and Santiago put it to his own ear. "I have your husband, Mrs. Pierce. He's going to help me find what's mine. Until he does, you won't be able to talk to him."

He barely finished before the phone went dead.

Rowan bit his lip, shaking his head as his hands raised.

"Nice try, my friend," Santiago said, taking Rowan's phone and lobbing it into the thick cover of trees.

"Let's get this straight once and for all. You are *not* my friend." Rowan turned, rolling his eyes as he raised his hands toward his head. He froze as his phone made an odd plunking sound deep below where they were standing. Santiago froze too.

"What the...?" Santiago started in that direction. Rowan followed, scrambling through the brush. Santiago skidded to a halt. Rowan nearly crashed into him. There, they stood on the edge of a hidden cenote.

Rowan leaned over to look down. Santiago grabbed his shirt, pulling him back, stumbling and falling backwards himself, bringing Rowan, who was nearly twice his size, down on top of him. A loose rock, kicked by Rowan's boot, tumbled off into the void, and both men had time to lean forward and find the edge. A few seconds later the plop of it hitting the water found its way back up to the surface.

"Christ!" Rowan gasped, moving so Santiago's boot wasn't in his back. "Look at that! That must be, what? A hundred-twenty-five meters deep?"

Santiago gave him a wicked grin, shaking his head. "You Americans..." His attention returned to the deep hole in front of them. "That could have been a fatal leap."

"Glad you saw it before I did," Rowan sat back on his rump in the dirt.

"Me too," Santiago said, holstering his gun. "I'm sorry I had to take you hostage."

"Yeah, me too," Rowan said.

Santiago got back up on his hands and knees and leaned over the edge to peer into the abyss. For a moment, Rowan considered placing his 12 1/2 boot right in the guy's backside and giving him the old heave-ho. He decided against it. He might come to regret it later, but killing a man, wasn't something Rowan was willing to do, even a slime ball like Santiago.

Patience was his friend now, Rowan decided. He would wait out his captor and find a way to either escape or subdue him. In either case, his first stop would be home to Lauren, no matter what.

Screw that! Rowan lunged.

22

Lauren sat up slowly. Her head throbbed. She felt sick to her stomach. The world was spinning. The last thing she remembered was walking into the apartment on Ambrosia Lane, with an overnight bag in one hand and her cell phone in the other.

The world around her came into view, but it was hard to focus. She fought to keep the bile from rising in the back of her throat. She managed to prop herself up against the wall. Her hand went to her stomach. She wrapped her arms around it. She was not sure what had happened to her. She prayed her baby was okay.

Tears ran down her face, and her head felt heavy. She struggled to keep herself vertical. Her stomach quivered and her breath caught. *Contraction?* She froze, and it did it again. Foot, not contraction.

A sigh of relief escaped her. A blurred face moved into view. "Hey, there you are," Stephanie knelt in front of her. "Don't worry. You're okay. So is your baby."

"What happened? What did you do to me?" Her hand went to the back of her head and the knot at the base of her skull told her everything she needed to know. There was drying blood matted in her hair, but the wound didn't seem to be deep.

Lauren simmered. "What the hell! You could have killed me... or my baby!"

"I could have, but I didn't," she snapped back. "You remember that. I don't want you or your baby dead. I just need you... out of the way for a while."

"Why?"

The woman considered Lauren for a long moment. "I don't think I want to tell you," she said, rising without effort. It was a move Lauren envied. "Hungry? I got moo shoo."

Lauren looked up at her with a sneer. She leaned over and puked all over Stephanie's shoe.

Stephanie jumped back startled. "Dammit!" She wrinkled her nose. "I guess I deserved that." She kicked off her shoe and carried it to the bathroom to clean up.

WHEN SHE COULD DO IT, LAUREN MANAGED TO GET TO HER feet, leaning heavily against the wall. The world was still spinning. Her legs felt like rubber. Dots danced in her eyes. She scooted over towards the windows. They were covered from the outside with paper. The landlord had been renovating. The exterior stucco was being painted. The painters had taped off the windows. Now she wished they were clear so she could at least see out, or someone could see in.

The entire block of apartments was currently vacant which meant the privacy they had been seeking was now her undoing. No one would know where to find her. No one would miss her for a few days, at least. *God! She was an idiot!*

Where had her phone gone? The memory of her last phone call flooded through her, and she felt sick all over again. She'd had it in her hand when she heard Rowan's voice telling her he was okay, then someone else had taken the phone just before it was dead. Her phone was probably in Stephanie's possession. As long as it stayed on, someone could find her. Rowan wouldn't be coming for her, but Jean-René and Bahati had been taking turns checking on her every few days.

How long had she been here? She was certain she had a concussion, but how serious it was, she couldn't be sure; it was bad though. It was daylight when they got to the apartment. It was daylight still. It could have been a few hours or a few days. Based on how stiff and sore she was, she was convinced it had been at least a day.

Lauren sunk into the corner of the room, across from the door feeling lethargic and numb. She wasn't afraid, but she felt like she should be. Rowan was in trouble in Mexico... she was in trouble in California. There had to be a bad country song about that, right?

Could she reach Rowan as she had the night he was in Mexico City? Had she reached him before Stephanie showed up? She couldn't be sure, but she had to try. If she couldn't reach Rowan, maybe she could reach someone else.

BAHATI HANDED JEAN-RENÉ A BEER AND SAT DOWN ON THE floor, leaning against the sofa. She reached over her shoulder to snag a handful of popcorn from the bowl nestled between his crossed legs. The beer was cold, the popcorn was hot, and the movie was just starting.

"Think we should have invited Lauren to come watch with us?" Bahati asked.

He glanced at the clock on the wall, taking a drink. "It's getting late," he said. "And she's supposed to stay in bed."

"Not like watching a movie is overly taxing," Bahati said, tossing back a handful of popcorn, munching happily.

Jean-René set the popcorn bowl on the coffee table in front of her and leaned down. "If she was here, I couldn't do this," he said, taking her lips in his, his hand finding hers, lifting her into his lap so she could wrap her arms around his neck. Bahati giggled, breaking the kiss. "What?" Jean-René grinned, his hand running down her side, brushing her breast through the fabric of her t-shirt.

"Are we fooling anybody?" She asked, her lips just inches from his. "Rowan and Lauren couldn't hide it. Are we?"

"Please," he scoffed. "You guys didn't even know I had been married until I told you. I don't wear my heart on my sleeve."

"Maybe not, but I can tell what you're thinking about right now," she purred. "It's written all over your face."

"And what does it say?"

"It says let's forget the movie and take it to the bedroom." She nipped at his lip with her teeth, just grazing him. His breath caught in his throat.

"I like how you think. Come here *Hottie Bahati*," he stood, unseating her, and lifting her at the same time. He bumped the bowl of popcorn and it spilled on the floor, crunching under foot.

"*Hottie Bahati?*" She wrapped her long legs around him, grasping his firm buttocks with her hands, as she kissed him feverishly. "I like that."

"Hottie is right." He carried her to his room and lay her on the bed, peeling out of his shirt before reaching for the hem of hers. He lifted it over her head.

Aside from his arms, his skin was pale. Her skin was smooth and deep brown. She smelled of something spicy and warm. He reached for a bare breast as it was exposed. He'd dated plenty, been married for a time, but he'd never had a woman like her. They came from two different worlds. He was French-Canadian. She was from South Africa. In any other time or place, they would never have come together.

It had been a slow journey—almost ten years of working together. He had always liked her, but she hadn't seemed interested. So he didn't pursue her. It wasn't until Lauren and Rowan's wedding that she glanced over and caught his eye, and a blush came to her dark cheeks.

Now her small breasts filled his large hands and she arched beneath him, encouraging him. The last eleven months had been a wild ride, and he was enjoying every moment of it.

"Your hands are cold." He pulled away from her touch.

"Sorry." The corners of her cheeks curled into a mischievous grin. "Let me warm them up for you..."

"Oh no you don't." He pinned her arms to her side.

"So do you think we'll get fired when everyone finds out?" She asked.

"I don't even care." He pulled her to him, kissing her jawline, running his hands along her slim waist and around her hips. "If I am to be damned, let me be damned."

She giggled heartily at him. "I don't think the bosses will care... but I do think they will be surprised."

"Are we going to talk all night, or did you want to enjoy this?" He arched a cocky eyebrow at her.

"Oh," she said, leaning over him. Her breath was hot on his skin. "I am enjoying it all right."

LAUREN LAY STILL, TRYING TO FOCUS. SHE HAD DONE IT ONCE, but since then, she hadn't been able to find Rowan in the dark. "Tsul'Kalu, help me."

"You need no help from me," came the deep answer a moment later.

"Use the force, Lauren." She muttered to herself. She took a deep breath. She tried to extend her mind outside her own body.

The damp smell of rain on green foliage reached her nose, and she opened her eyes. She found herself in the circle that had once been surrounded by stones. "Rowan?" She whispered but heard only the songs of night frogs and insects. She looked around, letting her eyes adjust to the darkness of the jungle.

She felt better than she had a few hours ago. She was no longer dizzy or queasy, but she knew she couldn't stay here long. She had to find Rowan. She felt like he was close.

"Rowan!" She called a little louder. She wasn't sure where Santiago was, but she also sensed he wasn't far away either. "Rowan!"

She was drawn to a break in the tree line behind the clearing where the altar had stood just a week or so before. She was oblivious to the missing stones. She focused solely on finding Rowan. The vegetation was dense as she walked. She noticed the broken branches that were glistening with dew. They sparkled in the moonlight, lighting her path to Rowan.

She stopped short of the crevice where the jungle dropped off. "Rowan!"

"Lauren?" A weak voice came back from below.

"Rowan? Are you hurt?" She peered out over the edge, relieved to see Rowan on a precipitous ledge less than ten feet down.

"Yeah, just a little." He had a gash over his eyebrow that had bled profusely. The blood had now dried. His eyelid was swollen shut. She could sense he'd broken a bone when he caught the ledge. It had saved him from a nasty fall. "What are you doing here?"

"I came to help you," she said. "Where's Santiago?"

"I'm not sure," he answered. "I tried to push him over the edge, but he dodged. I ended up going over. I knocked a large rock off when I fell. He probably thinks I hit bottom."

"I'll get help," Lauren said, not really sure how she would accomplish that. At the moment, she couldn't even help herself. "Just hold on."

"Lauren?" Rowan's voice sounded tentative.

"Yes?"

"Are you really here? Am I hallucinating?"

"No. Yes," she said, stuttering. She wasn't sure how to explain it but decided that it didn't matter now. "But I can help you. You just have to hold on."

"Okay," he said, wincing. "Just hurry."

"That's what all the men say." She reminded him of their first meeting, when it was she who was injured.

"I got you," she said.

"I know you do."

BAHATI. THAT WAS HER NEXT OBJECTIVE. SHE CAME BACK TO herself just long enough to make sure she was okay, and the baby was fine. It was still dark, and the apartment was quiet. Then, she reached out for her best friend.

"Bahati?" She leaned and whispered. She couldn't visualize her surroundings. Still, she found her friend in the darkness. "Rowan is in trouble. He needs your help."

Bahati rolled over, muttering something in her sleep. She tucked herself up against the form beside her. Lauren suddenly realized where she was—where Bahati was—and who she was with.

The bond broke immediately. Lauren sat up abruptly, blushing as she realized what was going on. She had not expected that—not one bit. She smiled to herself as she realized her two best friends had finally given up any pretense that had held them back. She didn't care. She just wanted them to be happy. But... that wasn't going to help Rowan at the moment. Maybe she could find Agent Miller. He was the last one with Rowan, he should still be close.

"Andrew... Agent Miller? I know you're there..." she whispered, as she closed her eyes.

He was harder to find, but the sun was coming up when she realized she was standing in the streets of Mérida. She'd been there before. Before Rowan had joined the team, they'd gone on the hunt for some jungle monster—or was it aliens? She couldn't remember.

Miller looked unkempt, disheveled, and unshaven. She'd never seen him like that. He was dead on his feet, and she knew he'd been looking for Rowan. She stood in the middle of the street, looking at him as a car passed. He paused, as if he saw her. She took a few steps toward the curb and his movements mirrored her's.

You're not supposed to be here, she could hear his thoughts.

Rowan's in trouble. He needs your help, she responded.

You know where he is?

There's a cenote behind the circle of stones not far from the El Castillo. He's there, and he needs medical attention. He doesn't have much time. She could feel him slipping away from her.

Help me find him, came the Agent's thoughts.

Go to El Castillo. I'll try to guide you.

23

On the drive from Mérida to Chichén Itzá Andrew convinced himself he was going crazy. That was the only explanation for this whole rigmarole. Early that morning, he'd woken up on a park bench in the town square. He had a pounding headache and a vile taste in his mouth. He had no memory of the night before. He considered for a moment he'd been drugged. *Free margaritas* indeed. At least his wallet was still in his jacket pocket with all his cash and credit cards, and other than his throbbing head, he was fine.

He was staggering towards the hotel when he saw Lauren. His heart froze. She wasn't supposed to be here. He was seeing ghosts. *Was that the right word? Lauren was still alive, right? So was that her ghost? Her phantasm? What'd you call that? Doppelgänger. That was it.*

He followed the illusion of her through the street until he lost her in the crowd. He had heard her warning, but then second-guessed himself. He still couldn't explain why but he decided to go back to the hotel. Maybe he was looking for Rowan. Maybe the TV show host woke up with the same fuzzy-headed heaviness in his skull on a park bench somewhere farther across the town square and had staggered home earlier. But Rowan wasn't there.

"Well, where the hell *is* he?" That's when he first decided he'd gone crazy. He was talking to himself.

He's in trouble. Go to the temple. Go now! Lauren was suddenly in his face, and he nearly lept out of his skin, falling back against the wall, tripping over Rowan's duffle bag.

"Okay! Okay," he gasped. "I'm going!" Now, as he drove, he was still trying to make sense of it, but also plotting what he would need to do once he got to the temple-site.

MILLER HAD ALWAYS THOUGHT LAUREN WAS A FASCINATING woman, to say the least. He had learned not to second guess her. She was something else. He wasn't sure what she'd done in Washington State. Her stories never really added up, at least not to him. She had signed the official report, which was a legal affidavit. He'd seen criminals sign untrue statements before. He had a higher opinion of her character. She wasn't a criminal, and he didn't think of her as a liar. Still, he was convinced there had to be more to her story, if he could just get her to tell it.

I'll tell you whatever you want to know. She was waiting for him when he got out of the Range Rover at the parking lot adjacent to the Maya temple. He was still cussing himself out for believing any of this was real, but he also knew to trust his senses when they started telling him something was wrong.

How are you doing this? he thought to himself. *Or am I going crazy?*

You're not crazy, Lauren answered.

Which way do I go? He pulled on his FBI ball-cap, his hand going to the weapon in the holster under his arm pit out of habit, more to check that it was still there than anything.

You're going to head west. Can you see me, in the tree line?

His eyes scanned the jungle across the clearing and saw something move. *I think so.*

Come to me.

He followed Lauren's directions, now certain that he had gone crazy. He went along with it; for now. She remained an elusive shadow in the trees. She was the rustle of the wind in the foliage, the parting of limbs as she passed, just beyond his reach.

He stopped in the middle of the clearing. Somehow, Lauren showed him what it had looked like when she last saw it—misty shadows of the pillars where the white stones once stood.

"*These were the pillars Rowan told me about. Where'd the stones go?*" Andrew asked.

The gods took them, she said, in the back of his mind. He turned, expecting to see her behind him, but she wasn't there. *You've heard how Prometheus stole fire from the gods to give to man?*

"Yes," Miller said out loud.

The trickster is always stealing what is not his to take. But there is justice in the universe and the gods return ill-will with just-desserts. As the trickster has hidden the treasure, the gods have taken the landmarks that were meant to lead him to his heart's desire.

"*Who put them there?*" Andrew queried.

They were placed there to distract those who came to witness the end of the world. To keep them from following the rabbit's trail into the jungle. The story of the Jaguar Queen was used to create an illusion, to place doubt in the minds of those seeking the truth. The trickster doesn't work alone, she came to find him here. Long ago, she loved a man, but her father did not approve.

Stephanie Wentworth, his thoughts went directly to her.

Yes. When they knew he would not give his blessing, the rascal convinced his friends to help him take what was not his, the woman, and her father's money. She went with him willingly. Lauren's haunting voice in his head gave him the chills.

"The plan didn't work though." Andrew walked through

the circle, the stones appearing as mist, the glyphs so real he could almost touch them.

No. No one expected them to have engine trouble over the jungle. They all agreed Stephanie would need to jump, to take the money and hide with it until they could make their way back to her in the jungle. They never expected to get caught.

Bad guys never do, Andrew thought, as much to himself as to her. *They didn't know it would take so long, did they?* He looked for the rustle of leaves in the jungle to ensure he was still on course. A flock of birds flew from the undergrowth and it was as if the jungle exploded. He followed the narrow gap the birds had abandoned in the tree line, the subtle markings of a path previously trodden.

No, and she rages because she fears he doesn't love her any more, and he will double-cross her and take the money and leave her.

Andrew stopped. *Would he do that?*

No, but... she might. Lauren answered. *And you should know, they've got the local police in their hip pocket.*

What? How do you know all this? Miller thought.

She told me.

The trees parted just past the clearing and he continued to follow. *Where is Stephanie?*

Watch your step! Lauren's voice came as an echo just behind him. He froze. *See him?*

Andrew dropped to his knees and looked down over the edge of the abyss. "Rowan?"

Rowan lay on the outcropping, with one arm dangling over the edge, limp, and still. "Rowan!"

Miller took out his satellite phone and called for backup. "Lauren? Are you still here?" He spoke out loud.

The wind found its way through the trees, caressing his cheek. "I've got him. I'll get him home."

Watch out! She shouted in his head, just as something charged him from the jungle.

Santiago tackled him, but he'd had just enough warning to

back away from the edge of the cenote, so his momentum carried them into the dense cover of the jungle, away from the ledge. It was a hard landing, but Andrew came up on top. Santiago already had his gun drawn. The agent couldn't get to his weapon fast enough. He stood, backing up. He held his hands over head. Santiago honed the pistol on him, and got to his feet, gingerly. "You the cops?"

"FBI, Andrew Miller," he said, hands still on his hat, as he caught his breath. "I'm a U.S. Federal Agent."

Santiago cackled uncontrollably, wincing as he did, then laughed some more. "I guess you're gonna try to keep me from getting what's mine too?"

"What's that?" Miller glanced out of the corner of his eye as something moved in the jungle. Lauren was still with him. He knew he needed to stall while waiting for back up.

"The money," he said. "It's here, you know?" Santiago grinned. "Thanks to my friend Rowan, I know where it is."

"Oh yeah?"

"There's a cave just beyond the cenote," he said, his eyes darting in the direction of the dense jungle. "Stephanie knew she hid it in a cave, but it had been so long. When she came back, she couldn't find it. The jungle had grown around it. But I found it," Santiago grinned brightly. "I thought I'd need the ground penetrating radar to find it, but all it took was a swift kick in the butt." Rowan had shoved him, but he'd rolled away from the cenote's edge. He landed near the mouth of the cave. There, he found the duffel bag. The money still inside.

Bad guys liked to brag, Lauren reminded him. *Keep him talking.*

Miller knew that. "Well ain't that something," his suppressed Texas drawl came out. "You've got it all figured out, now. Haven't you?"

"You could say that." Mateo drew back the hammer on the gun. "I don't need his help any more," he nodded his head over his shoulder towards the cenote. "And I sure as hell don't need you."

"So you and Stephanie gonna run off to South America and live off her daddy's money?"

Mateo chuckled. "I don't know about South America, but I'm sure we'll find some place to disappear. Just like I'm going to make *you* disappear." He raised his arm and Miller was certain he'd have pulled the trigger if a dark form hadn't leapt from the jungle. It pounced with a wicked roar, and a swipe of sharp claws.

The gun went off. The jaguar knocked the man from his feet and the two of them tumbled into one form, disappearing over the edge of the cenote. Miller rushed to check on Rowan, watching the flailing form disappear into the darkness with a sharp thud as he hit the water far, far below.

There was no sign of the jaguar... if there had ever been one.

IT TOOK NEARLY AN HOUR FOR THE RESCUE TEAM TO GET Rowan moved to the Stokes basket, and hoisted from the ledge by ropes. He'd been conscious for most of it. By the time they got him to the ambulance, he'd surrendered to the void. The pain couldn't reach him. Neither could Lauren.

He hadn't lied to his wife. He was hurt, badly. Besides bruised ribs, he also had a compound fracture of his left ulna and radius. The bones had snapped just above his watch band. He had managed to wrap it with a scrap torn from his shirt, but the bleeding had been bad. Far worse than the laceration on his scalp.

While the medics did their triage on Rowan, the rescue teams went back in to look for Santiago Mateo. It was so deep; they didn't have ropes long enough to reach the bottom. From the end of their repelling cables, they shined down their high-powered spotlights. There they discovered the water flowed like an underground river. If Mateo had survived the fall, he'd likely been swept away by its current as it disappeared, deep underground. There was no sign of the reported jaguar either.

∾

LAUREN FOUND ROWAN IN POST-OP. HE WAS STILL LOOPY ON medication. The euphoria actually made it easier to reach him. He didn't fight the illusion she was able to create, and she manifested in a vision. She was able to touch him. She ran her hand along his cheek.

"You saved me." He said with a dopey grin. His eye was still swollen shut. A line of butterfly bandages held the jagged flesh above his brow together, and his face was a rainbow of colors. His injured arm lay on the pillow beside his head. They were keeping it elevated. An ice pack was used to relieve the swelling. His arm was splinted to protect it from further injury.

"Saved you plenty," she said. He'd said the same to her once before. Now, they were even.

She put her hand on his chest. She could feel the rise and fall of his breath. His good hand went to hers, and she could feel his touch. "Thank you," he said, taking her hand and drawing her knuckles to his lips, kissing them. "I thought I was a goner there for a while."

"I will always come for you."

24

She slipped away just as quickly as she'd appeared. He found himself alone in recovery. He was hallucinating, he was sure of it. He'd seen a jaguar fly over him into the cenote. He'd seen Lauren at his bedside. He must have lost a lot more blood than he'd thought.

"Hey, cutie," a nurse with a thick Spanish accent appeared at his bedside. "You speak English, right?"

"Yeah." His voice cut out. His throat was sore and dry. "I'm Rowan."

"I'm Claudia. I've been taking care of you since you came in. How's your pain?"

"Eh." He winced. "Could I have some water?"

"Sure," she said. "One second."

She fetched a cup and raised the head of the bed, helping him move his injured arm onto a pillow in his lap. One of the leads attached to his chest pulled against the blue hospital gown and tugged on his chest hair. He grasped at the gown, and she helped him get comfortable. "Better?" She asked, holding the cup.

"Yeah," Rowan said. "Where am I? Is this Mérida?" He took the cup and drained it in one swallow.

"It is," she said. "What are you doing in Mexico?"

"Research," he said. "For a television show."

"I bet you're sorry the world didn't end last month." She leaned on the bed rail, watching the monitor over his shoulder.

"Not really." He sighed. "Kind of happy to be back in the land of the living."

"Tell me that again in an hour when the medication starts wearing off," she retorted. "We'll have you moved to a room by then."

"I have to stay?"

"Just for the night. The doctor wants to monitor you. You have a head injury, and they did surgery on your arm."

"Fair enough." He handed back the empty cup and leaned his head back on the pillow. "Do I get a phone call?"

"International?"

He grinned sheepishly. "Yeah. My wife?" He smiled his best and most charming grin, hoping the dimples would sell it. But she crossed her arms and shook her head. "Fair enough," he sighed. "I'll ask my friend when he comes back."

"Who? Andrew?"

"Oh, you know him?"

"He waited in the post-op waiting room until you got out of surgery. He had to go. He said he'd be back. He said something about filing a police report."

"I could live my whole life and never fill out a police report again." Rowan groaned.

The nurse had his chart and was tapping something into her tablet. "Rowan are you right or left-handed?"

"Right," he said, glancing at his bandaged left arm. "Lucky me."

"Lucky you indeed." She lay the tablet in his lap. "Police report for you to fill out... when you're feeling up to it."

"Suddenly my pain level just went up," he said, picking up

the tablet and groaning as he used his thumb to scroll up... and up... and up.

"Nauseated?"

"Suddenly, yeah. Now that you mention it."

"I can fix that," she said, taking the tablet out of his hand. She brought over a plastic cup with a pill in it. He asked no questions, but tossed it back, taking the cup of water she held to go with it. "That's for your nausea," she said. Going back over to the cabinet, coming back with a vial and a syringe, adding the medication to his IV. "This is for your pain."

"Thanks," he said, feeling a dull ache in his arm, as if on cue.

"It'll probably make you sleepy," she said.

It hit him just as quick.

BAHATI MOPED AROUND THE HOUSE ALL DAY. JEAN-RENÉ SAT on the sofa watching hockey. It was the only flaw she found in his character. He seemed oblivious to other sports, but hockey seemed to be his one obsession.

They were still banned from work, and short of the usual distractions there was little else to do. They'd been distracted plenty last night.

"Why don't you call Lauren?" Jean-René suggested. "Maybe you two can go shopping."

"I left a message for her," she said. "I'm waiting for her to call me back. She's probably taking a nap."

"When did you talk to her last?"

Bahati sat down on the edge of the sofa, thinking. "I saw her yesterday."

His brow twitched. "You were with me all day yesterday."

Bahati made a face. "You're right." she said. "I would have sworn I talked to her... that I saw her..." Bahati stood and paced a moment. "What about Rowan? Have you talked to him since he went to Mexico?"

"No," Jean-René said. "I wasn't expecting him to call though."

Bahati shook her head. "I... she... she told me Rowan had some... trouble."

"What? Did he get arrested and end up in a Mexican jail again?" Jean-René said it before he could stop himself. He clamped a hand over his mouth as Bahati's jaw dropped. "That was supposed to stay a secret."

"What? He got arrested in Mexico?" Bahati gasped.

"He said he'd kill me if Lauren found out," he said. "You can't say anything."

"I won't but I can't believe he got arrested. What happened?"

Jean-René told her everything. "He didn't do anything, except be his usual goofy self."

Bahati sat down beside him and he put his arm around her, thinking she might sit and watch the game with him, but she got up just as he was about to get comfortable. "Get your shoes."

"What?"

"I don't know," she said. "I've got a bad feeling. I want to go talk to Lauren. If she won't call me back, I'll go let myself in."

"You have a key?"

"No, but I know where to find one."

BAHATI DIDN'T NEED IT. THE FRONT DOOR WASN'T LOCKED, but Lauren wasn't home. Bahati walked out on to the balcony, over-looking the beach, thinking she might be able to see Lauren in her usual spot, stretched out in the sun in her bikini. She was nothing, if not predictable.

Unfortunately, she wasn't there. When she came back in the living room, Jean-René was holding her purse and her cell phone. "I never met a woman who went anywhere without her purse and her cell phone."

"I don't carry a purse," Bahati said.

"Oh," Jean-René closed his mouth quickly. "I meant ones who carry one..."

"Uh huh." She took Lauren's phone out of his hand and inspected it. She didn't have a security code on it, so Bahati pulled up her call log. No calls in the last twenty-four hours. The last number that had called was a Mexican number, so Bahati hit the recall button and waited.

"*Hola?*" A voice finally came from the other side.

"*Buenos días,*" Jean-René said as his brow narrowed. "*¿Quién es este?*"

"*Esta es la policía,*" the man answered. Jean-René looked sharply at Bahati. Her hand went to her mouth, and her eyes went wide. "*Mi nombre es Detective Pérez. ¿Puedo ayudarte?*"

"*Estoy buscando a mi amigo,* Rowan Pierce. *Este es su teléfono.*"

"*Sí, el Sr. Pierce estuvo involucrado en un incidente. Lo han llevado al hospital.*"

"Hospital?" Bahati was listening over Jean-René's shoulder. She didn't speak Spanish, but that word was readily apparent.

"*¿Puedes decirme su condición? Su esposa está preocupada por él y me pidió que llame.*" Jean-René explained that he was calling because his wife was worried about him, and that she didn't speak Spanish. He covered the speaker and whispered to Bahati. "Tell him you're Lauren. Otherwise, he can't release any information."

"I can't lie to the police."

"He probably doesn't even speak English," Jean-René said.

"My English is actually pretty good," the police officer said. "I'm sorry, but you are right, I can't release any information. I can give you the number of the hospital. You and *his wife* will have better luck there."

Bahati glowered at him and Jean-René just shook his head. "*Gracias*," Jean-René said, taking the information before he hung up.

"How did Rowan end up in the hospital?"

"I don't know," he said. "Let's see if we can talk to him."

JEAN-RENÉ HAD TO JUMP THROUGH MORE THAN A FEW HOOPS before someone came on the line who could actually help him. "Mr. Pierce was released into custody this morning," the man, who said he was the hospital's head administrator, said. "The file doesn't say what he was charged with. It only says that he was remanded into custody."

"What was his condition? What happened to him?" Jean-René asked in Spanish.

"I'm sorry, sir, but you have similar regulations in the States. We cannot release information without consent, which Mr. Pierce did not give."

"Can you at least give me the name of the officer that signed him out, so I can have his attorney contact the police?"

There was a pause. "One moment."

"Any luck?" Bahati was sitting across the table, impatiently waiting.

Jean-René shook his head *no*. "I'm sorry, what was that?"

"Officer Matt Iago," the administrator said. "I'm sorry I can't be more help."

"Thanks," Jean-René tapped the phone. "Matt Iago... ring any bells?"

"Matt? Is that who you talked to?" she asked.

"No, that's the officer who took Rowan into custody," Jean-René leaned on his elbows.

"Custody? Why didn't the police tell us he'd been arrested the first time we called?"

"No idea. The hospital couldn't tell me the charges. Nor would he tell me the extent of his injuries." Jean-René anticipated her questions.

"Well, he must not have been hurt very bad, if they discharged him from the hospital, right?"

Jean-René made a face. "Have you ever been to Mexico?"

"A couple of times," she said.

"Do you remember having to bribe the police because the rental car didn't have papers? Remember how much trouble we had just trying to get across the border back to San Diego? Even with our American passports?"

"Just because you had a French accent, and I—" She stopped short, suddenly remembering being groped by the Mexican border patrol agent under the guise of being frisked. "How do we know it was a police officer..." Bahati thought aloud. Suddenly, her eyes widened, and her jaw dropped as she drew in a breath and lifted her hand to cover her mouth. "Matt Iago...Santiago Matteo...Jean-René, we need to get Rowan some help. What about the FBI agent?"

"You mean Agent Miller?"

"Yeah, I never could remember his name." She shook her head. "Is there a way we can call him?"

Jean-René scrolled through contacts on Lauren's phone. "Nothing here."

"Dammit. Maybe Lauren will be home soon," Bahati said optimistically.

Jean-René sat back, looking around, shaking his head. "Something's not right here," he said, standing.

"Where are you going?"

"I'm going to take a walk and see if Lauren's down on the beach."

"I'll come with you," she said, standing too.

"No." He shook his head. "I need you to stay here in case she comes back. Call me if she does."

"There has to be something I can do," she said.

"Call the hospital and see if she came in, maybe she started having contractions again," he said, unable to think of any other reason she might have left home without her purse and phone.

LAUREN WAS AWARE OF HER EXTREMELY FULL BLADDER AND her throbbing head at the same moment. She sat up, and looked around, aware that she was still being held in her old apartment. She got to her feet and made her way to the adjacent bathroom. She couldn't do anything about her head, but her bladder was another thing.

The door opened as she finished washing her hands. Stephanie stood there. "Welcome back, sleeping beauty."

"What time is it?" Lauren grumbled.

"Almost seven," she said. "I ordered pizza."

Lauren's stomach grumbled and churned at the same time. She felt like crap, and she decided quickly she didn't need anything to eat, certainly not pizza. "I just need water."

Stephanie stepped aside and let her pass into the living room. She followed her into the kitchen. The pizza box was setting on the counter and there was a six pack of Coke; one can was missing. She opened the cupboard where she'd kept the glasses. She quickly realized the pantry was bare. No cups, no bowls, no snacks. She turned on the water in the sink and used her hand to make a cup. She drank greedily. Loose locks of her hair got wet in the process.

"How long are we going to be here?" Lauren leaned on the counter top, stretching out her sore back and neck. She was miserable, but she didn't want to let on.

"As long as we need to be," she said.

Lauren noticed the woman's eyes going to the phone on the edge of the pizza box. Lauren knew she was waiting for a phone call, presumably from Santiago. It was a call that wouldn't come. She had pushed Mateo into the cenote. It was a fall no one could survive. Even her link with Rowan had been broken when she went over the edge.

LAUREN KNEW IF HER SITUATION WERE GOING TO IMPROVE ANY time soon, she would have to make it happen. She also knew she was vulnerable. In her present condition, she'd have to work smarter, not harder.

"I've never killed a pregnant woman," Stephanie said, with a mouth full of pizza, her hand resting-on the gun tucked into her belt. "But I really don't have a problem with it. I don't know what you're thinking about, but if you think you can take me, you might think again."

"I'm just thinking about how stupid all this is."

"Yeah, well, I thought I loved him. I thought he loved me."

"And do you?"

"I loved what he could do for me," she said.

"Any man can do that," Lauren scoffed. Getting her to talk was going to help her get away. She'd let go of something she didn't want Lauren to know if she just made her comfortable enough. If she let her guard down, Lauren might get a lucky break.

"Yeah, well, not every man could get me away from my father while still getting me some of the money."

"When your father died, he was worth nearly ten times the amount you two got out with. Most of it went to charity. You know that, right?"

Stephanie froze. "My father died?"

"You didn't know?"

"Uh, no. When?" She didn't cry, but Lauren could see she was moved.

"Not very long ago," Lauren said. "After your mother left him, he committed suicide."

A gasp caught in her throat, but still she didn't cry. "How?"

"Jumped off the top of an offshore oil rig," she said. "They never found his body."

Stephanie tossed the pizza back onto the box, her face contorting as she processed the information. She picked up her phone, tucking it in her hip pocket as she walked away turning her back. She leaned on the wall, her hair shading her face from Lauren's view.

Lauren glanced at the door, working on her exit plan. If she could get out the door, there were three steps to the sloping sidewalk. The path lead to the parking lot and down to the street. She could take a hard left and get around the building and out of view. Conceal and cover—that's what she would need to do. She had no improvised weapons in the apartment. The landscaper's shed was adjacent to her building. If it weren't locked, she could find all kinds of lawn tools and equipment that could be used for a weapon, if she had too.

Lauren wondered if her car was still parked out in the lot. She didn't have the keys though. Stephanie's jacket lay on the floor by the door. Maybe they were in her pocket?

"To say I didn't have a good relationship with my father would be an understatement," Stephanie said coldly. "He was a jealous man. He didn't even want me to be close to my mother. He was afraid... I would tell her."

Lauren immediately forgot her escape plans. "Tell her what?"

Stephanie kept her back to the room, hanging her head. "How he liked to touch me... liked me to touch him..."

"Your father... molested you?" Lauren took two steps towards her but stopped short.

"He was always trying to make it up to me." She sniffed. "He'd stop for a while. Try to pretend he hadn't done it. But when he was drinking or when he had a bad day... I had a bad day too."

"Did you tell anyone?"

"No," she said. "Not until I met Santiago." She glanced up. Her face was red, but her eyes were dry.

"He promised to save me," she said. "He said he'd make my father pay for what he'd done to me. He told my father if he didn't pay the ransom money, he'd tell everyone what he had done to his little girl."

"That's why he went against the advice of the State Department," Lauren thought out loud. That part had always bothered her. "And why you didn't go home after you escaped..."

"I couldn't go home," she said. "He had to think I was dead."

"How did you survive in the jungle?"

Stephanie turned her back on Lauren. "I did what I had to," she said, but offered nothing else.

"I'm sorry you had to go through all that," Lauren said, wondering now if her visions might have been false. It hadn't occurred to her until then that Tsul'Kalu might allow her to see an untrue vision. *Had he been testing her?* She had seen Stephanie on the other side of the tear in time, had gone to her there, and spoken to her. But then again, she'd also been burning with fever. Had her own mind been playing tricks on her? "I can't imagine being all alone... for so long." Lauren tried to coax her into telling more, but Stephanie turned quickly. She glared at her but regained control of her face. "I wasn't alone... but I was... lost."

"I can't pretend to know what you've been through," Lauren said. "But he's never going to hurt you again." Lauren was just feet from the door. She debated whether she could make it out before Stephanie could react. "You don't have to do this. You can start over... you can move on." She managed to put a sympathetic hand on Stephanie's arm.

Snapping her arm away, she turned on Lauren. "I'm not a child! Don't patronize me!"

Lauren recoiled. "I wasn't." Her hand went to her stomach as it tightened.

Stephanie started to say something, but her phone rang. She fumbled with it as she got it out of her pocket. She cussed at as she tried to activate it. She finally got it. "Hello," she said, glancing up at Lauren. "Really? Well, get it over with and get out of there. Yeah, I got the delivery." Her eyes darted to Lauren. "What do you mean?" She stopped short. "I don't care. We don't have time for delays," she snapped. "Fine. I'll take care of things here and meet you at the rendezvous."

Lauren didn't have a good feeling. Her stomach lurched and she doubled over, as a sharp pain hit just under her breastbone. It knocked the wind out of her lungs, and she wanted to vomit. The knot in her stomach kept her from doing so. She dropped to one knee. She managed to catch her breath.

"Cut that crap out." She snapped. "We're leaving."

Lauren caught her arm as she came over to help her up. "I need... I need to go to... to the hospital .."

"I'll drop you off on my way." Stephanie shoved her, but Lauren grabbed her and nearly drug them both down as the spasm returned. Suddenly, she felt a flood down her leg. Her water had broken. "What the...!" Stephanie tried to break free of her grasp, but Lauren had a death grip. She felt like her body was being ripped apart. She closed her eyes. In her mind, she screamed, "Rowan!"

∽

ONE MINUTE, SHE WAS IN AGONY, THE NEXT SHE FELT AS IF SHE had been consumed by fire. There was a blinding flash of lightning at the same time. The world around her screamed as the pressure of the air shifted dramatically. Her ears popped. The burning smell of ozone assaulted her nostrils. Lightning bolts crackled over the surface of her skin.

Lauren's grip on Stephanie's arm couldn't be broken. When she came to herself, she straightened, and looked around, feeling disoriented. The room tilted and dots danced in her eyes. She shook her head, trying to clear her vision. Her grasp tightened as a wave of dizziness swept over her.

Rowan sat, tied to a chair. His splinted arm rested on his leg. He looked dazed. A startled Santiago Mateo stood at the bar in the kitchen holding up a document and a magnifying glass, looking completely stunned. Stephanie finally broke free and backed away from her. She looked at Lauren as if she had the plague. For nearly a full second, no one seemed to breathe, and the four of them looked at each other, stunned by the other's sudden presence.

Lauren managed a tentative step towards Rowan, but Stephanie had her weapon drawn. The hammer clicked as she locked it back. "What the hell?"

"Where did you come from?" Santiago demanded to know.

"How the hell do I know?" Stephanie snapped. "One minute, we were headed for the car, the next minute... we're here," she said, still stunned, breathless. She glared at Lauren, expecting answers. Lauren didn't have any.

She managed another tentative step closer to Rowan, holding her stomach with one hand, dropping to one knee as she reached him. "Lauren?" Rowan looked at her, puzzled. "What are you doing in Mexico?" She inspected him. His arm was in a cast, and he had bandages over his brow, his eye swollen shut.

"Mexico?" Lauren gasped, her face contorting with the next contraction.

"We have to get out of here," Stephanie said, gathering her wits. "Do you have the money?"

"No, but I know where it is," he said. "I found something else you just won't believe. It makes this codex practically worthless when you compare it to what I've found." He held up the document and tossed it aside. The plastic protecting the ancient tome crunched as it hit the floor. She didn't know what the document was, but the word codex piqued her interest, despite the contractions that washed through her. She noticed Rowan's eye had gone to the document as well.

"What?" Stephanie demanded.

"There's a cenote with an underwater river... there are artifacts... Maya gold... tons of it... more wealth than your father ever dreamed of." He lowered his voice, but Lauren was not completely unaware of what was going on around her. She *was* in pain, but she was exaggerating the severity. She hoped they would find a pregnant woman in labor more trouble than she was worth. While they were involved in their conversation, the gun had lowered in Stephanie's hand and wasn't pointed at her.

Lauren took a moment of distraction to find the edge of Rowan's ropes and start working them loose. She managed to give him a look with a silent caution about what she was doing. Neither of them was in any condition to fight, but the element of surprise could be in their favor. "What codex is he talking about?" she whispered.

"Grolier's." He rested his head on her shoulder, needing to touch her, just to make sure she was really there.

"What are we going to do with them?" Stephanie's voice interrupted their conversation.

Suddenly, Santiago and Stephanie were looking at them. Lauren dropped her head on Rowan's knee, doubled over, panting. The contraction subsided. "I'm in labor... I need a hospital ..."

"Just leave them here," Stephanie said. "Who cares?"

"They know too much." Santiago sneered. "We can't leave any loose ends. I've been in jail and on the run too long. I don't want to live my life that way."

Stephanie surrendered, handing him the gun. "Do what you need to do," she said. "I just want to get the hell out of here."

Santiago took the gun from her. Stephanie started for the door, pausing with her hand on the knob. She waited for him to finish the job. Santiago considered his captives both for a minute. He arched a brow at Lauren, as her hand went to Rowan's arm. "Damn Rowan, even pregnant, your woman is fine!"

"Leave her alone, Santiago!" Rowan snapped. His speech was slurred. Lauren couldn't tell if he'd been given pain medication, or if he'd been drugged to keep him compliant.

Santiago grabbed Lauren by the elbow and yanked her to her feet, she stumbled, purposefully. She nearly pulled him down with her as she landed on her side, protecting her abdomen by rolling away from him. "I said leave her alone!" Rowan leapt to his feet and his ropes fell away. He charged Santiago, knocking the gun out of his hand, sending it flying. Lauren scrambled towards it, as Stephanie made a lunge in the same direction.

Three things happened all within the span of a rapid heartbeat. First, a contraction gripped Lauren with such force, she collapsed just out of reach of the gun. Second, Rowan took down Santiago. The two landed hard, rolling into Lauren. Their momentum gave her the push she needed to get back on her knees, putting her at just the right angle to take out Stephanie's Achilles' tendon with a perfectly executed fist. Third, the front door burst open and half a dozen Mexican Federal Agents flooded in. One pissed-off FBI

Agent, followed. Everything came to a screeching halt except for the contraction that had Lauren gasping for air, trying not to scream.

Miller jumped for the gun, knocking it away from Stephanie's outstretched hand, just inches from where she had frozen. Two of the agents caught Santiago by the back of his jacket and yanked him to his feet before planting him face first in the carpet. They wrenched his arms behind his back and cuffed him. Rowan was lifted to his feet, but his knees wouldn't hold him. It was everything he could do to call Lauren's name. He reached for her. She raised a hand to him as the contraction passed. She managed to get to her feet and fell into his arms. The agents held them both up.

"She needs an ambulance," Rowan announced.

"So does he." She ran her hand over his injured face. Someone got a chair behind each of them. They sat in each other's arms, holding one another up. His splinted hand rested on her back where his fingers entwined in her disheveled braid.

"Lauren." Miller knelt at her elbow. "What are you doing here? You're supposed to be home in bed."

"Rowan was in trouble..." she said, taking a deep breath. "I had to..."

She sat up, inspecting Rowan, as he did the same.

"Lauren's in labor," Rowan slurred. "We have to get her to the hospital."

"Paramedics are on the way," Miller said. "How far apart are your contractions?"

As if on cue, another one came over her. "Minutes..." she gasped. Rowan's uninjured hand went to the side of her stomach. He could feel the muscles as they went tight under her shirt.

She pressed his hand under hers. Her grasp tightening as she leaned back. She held her breath and gritted her teeth. "Breathe, Lauren," his brow creased deeply. "Just breathe."

"Wait," Lauren gasped, turning her attention to where Mateo had been standing. "The codex?"

Miller followed her gaze and went over to the counter. The ancient document was sealed in a zippered bag with a piece of cardboard behind it. He picked it up and brought it over. The contraction passed and Lauren took the document, holding it where she and Rowan could both see it.

"What does it say?" Rowan asked.

"It's... Maya iconography... a calendar that charts the movement of the planet Venus."

"The missing calendar?" Rowan asked.

"No," the word hung in her throat as it turned into a groan. Another contraction gripped her.

"Give me that," Miller took the page and let the paramedics move in and take over. "You can study it later. We have to get you both to the hospital."

BY THE TIME THEY GOT HER TO THE MATERNITY WARD, LAUREN was in hard labor. The nurses took over from the paramedics. Miller pushed Rowan in a wheelchair and stayed close behind following her into a labor and delivery room. They stood in the doorway, helpless as the staff went to work getting her prepped and checked.

"We need a doctor that speaks English," Miller announced.

"She's in good hands," the nurse said. "If you are not the father, you may leave."

"I'm the father," Rowan grinned broadly. He used his foot to pull the chair toward the bed. He took Lauren's hand. It hit him at that moment. He was going to be a dad. His head swam and tears swelled in his eyes. His emotions overtook him.

"Don't sap out on me now, you bastard! You're the one

that did this to me. Man up and let's get this over with." Lauren snarled, just as the doctor came into the room and stopped at the sink to wash his hands.

"Mrs. Pierce, I'm Dr. Miranda," he said, as he scrubbed, glancing over his shoulder. Lauren unleashed a tirade in Spanish, and even Rowan pushed the chair back, though the doctor didn't seem fazed.

"She's fully effaced and dilated to a 10." The nurse informed him, in her thick accent.

"As if I couldn't tell," he said, smiling brightly at the nurse. He looked over to Lauren. "Are you ready to have a baby?"

"Get this thing out of me!" Lauren screamed, as a hard contraction hit her. She felt like she was about to come out of the bed. The nurse put her feet up in the stirrups as the doctor came over, drying his hands. Another nurse helped him into gloves.

"Okay, let's do this and then you can get back to your vacation," he grinned.

MILLER PACED UP AND DOWN THE HALLS, HEARING LAUREN'S voice peeling the paint off the walls of the hallway. Her screams pierced the closed door. He winced every time she did it. He couldn't believe they weren't giving her something for pain. He had never been around a woman in labor. He had no idea they let them scream like that. He decided it was time for him to make his way downstairs. Maybe he could find a cup of coffee or a soda.

Instead, he found the gift shop. When he came back upstairs, he had a bouquet for Lauren, and a box of cigars for Rowan. The doctor came out of her room, pulling off his scrub hat, smiling brightly. "Is the baby here? Is Lauren okay?"

He smiled and said. "Yes. Yes. Of course."

Rowan came out behind him, grinning radiantly, the ill effects of his recent ordeal seemed forgotten. "It's a boy!" He cheered.

"Congratulations!" Miller shoved the box of cigars into his hand. "I didn't know which to get, blue or pink, so I got the yellow ones."

"Thanks!" Rowan grinned. "You wanna see him?"

"May I?"

"Come on." Rowan motioned with his injured arm. He led the agent into the dimly lit room. The nurses were still busying themselves measuring the baby and getting his weight and footprints. The baby wasn't fussing. He seemed content to watch the goings on around him. One of the nurses put a blue hat on his head. He was small, but perfectly formed. He had dark blue eyes, and a button nose. He looked curious about everything going on around him.

"Six pounds even," the nurse said to Rowan. "His APGARs are 8 and 9. He's 21.5 inches long."

"He's going to be tall, like his father," Lauren said. The nurse bundled him up and laid him in Rowan's good arm, making sure he had the baby well-supported. She took the box of cigars and set them on the bedside table. Rowan glanced over at Lauren, grinning like a Cheshire Cat.

For having just delivered a baby, she looked remarkably beautiful. Rowan brought their son over and sat on the edge of the bed, so they could admire him together. "So, what are we going to name him?" Rowan asked. "We never really decided."

"I don't think there's ever been any doubt," Lauren said as Rowan gingerly passed the baby to his mother. "Henry Jones Pierce," she said, beaming as the baby looked up at her.

"You're going to name your son after Indiana Jones?" Miller wrinkled his nose.

"Can we call him Indy?" Rowan seemed to inflate.

"We can name the dog Indy," she chortled.

"We can get a dog too?"

"Someday." Lauren smiled dreamily. "A boy needs a dog."

"Henry, huh?" Rowan took her hand. His dimples cut so deep she was sure they had to hurt. "I like that."

"Me too," Lauren said. Rowan leaned in to kiss her.

"I know this isn't the best time, but... I have questions," Miller said, interrupting the intimate moment.

"You're right," Rowan said. "This is a bad time. Any questions you have, can wait."

"But... I have reports to file, paperwork has to be done ..." Miller protested as Rowan rose and put a hand in the middle of the Agent's chest. "I have deadlines."

"Make something up," Rowan said, pushing him backwards.

"What? Like what? I don't even know what the hell Lauren is doing in Mexico. Lauren, how did you get here? Most airlines won't let late-term pregnant women fly?"

"Later, Miller!" Lauren called back.

"You said you'd tell me everything..."

"Later," Rowan said. "I need to spend some time with my family. I'll call you."

He handed Rowan the bouquet he'd still been holding. Rowan tucked a cigar in his shirt pocket and patted it. "Thanks for everything." Rowan slugged his arm.

"Congratulations!" He called before the door closed.

Rowan turned back to Lauren, and his son. He set the flowers on the table. "Wanna go find some Maya gold after this?"

Lauren smiled. "Sure," she said. "Just let me feed the baby and I'll be ready to go."

EPILOGUE

"I guess no one can say we never find anything any more. Can they?" Lauren stood at the edge of the cenote Rowan had gone diving in the last time he'd been in Mexico. A crane hoisted up the giant stone circle. *This* was the new b'ak'tun—the missing Maya calendar.

Finally, a mystery they could talk about! They couldn't tell people everything. They were under a gag order to prevent them from talking about the case against Mateo and Wentworth while the local authorities investigated and prepared their case.

SLICK RICK HAD TOLD ROWAN THE GIANT STONE DISC WAS THE story of the jaguar queen, but that wasn't exactly true. Lauren's translation of the stone was completely different. It was a narrative of the gods will for the Maya tribes. It was a calendar first, but also a prayer for an end to war. A prayer for rain. A prayer for a world where no child would go hungry.

The Grolier Codex had been returned to the University, and the renewed interest had universities from all over begging for access to the document for further study. Lauren had Miller take pictures of it for her before they returned it. He had almost as many pictures of the codex as he did of Henry on his phone. He'd sent copies to Lauren, since she'd gotten to Mexico without her phone. She'd danced around the subject of how she got to Mexico each time he asked. She didn't have a good explanation. She still wasn't sure herself.

∾

ROWAN STOOD BESIDE HER, WATCHING AS THE WORKERS MOVED the disc to the back of a flatbed truck. He had the baby strapped in a carrier to his chest. "We really do need a new catch phrase. Don't we?" He beamed brightly.

"Jean-René!" Lauren called him over. "Make sure you get some good photos of the calendar. I will need them when I start writing my research papers and blog posts on it. I'll give you photo credit and we'll be published in every scientific journal in the world."

"We'll have funding flooding in from every possible source," Bahati said.

"We already have an extension to our contracts from the Network," Rowan said. "I can't wait to show you what we negotiated for you and Jean-René."

Bahati's expression could light up the jungle on the rainiest of days. The four of them had an agreement. Jean-René and Bahati trusted Rowan implicitly. He had their permission to negotiate any contract on their behalf. Because they were a team, they refused to be separated by contracts. If Rowan and Lauren did well, so did Bahati and Jean-René. Rowan made sure of it.

"So when do we start?"

"Slow down." Lauren insisted. "We still have to finish this episode, and then... we are taking at least six months off."

"That should give us plenty of time," Jean-René said, as

he came over and hooked his arm around Bahati's waist. "So where do you think you'd like to go on our honeymoon?" He pulled her into him, kissing her cheek.

Bahati's whole face dropped. Jean-René glanced at Rowan. He reached over and took the camera. Jean-René fished a hand into his pocket as he dropped to one knee. "I saved a little something from our last project," he said with a glint in his eye, as he opened the box. The diamond wasn't as big as Lauren's but, it was beautifully cut. He'd been planning this for some time. He'd been waiting for just the right moment. "Marry me?"

"Hell yeah!" Bahati screamed, her voice sending a flurry of birds swarming from the tops of the surrounding trees.

Henry startled, and his cry pierced the jungle. Bahati covered her mouth with her hand, looking startled. "Sorry!" She cringed.

Rowan grinned, patting the baby to calm him, as Lauren leaned against Rowan, grinning at him. Jean-René stood and kissed his fiancée. "Come on, let's wrap things up here. We've got a long drive back to Chichén Itzá. I want to check in with the team of archaeologists to see how they're doing documenting all the artifacts," Rowan said.

"Are you sure you're not too tired? We could find a hotel if you don't want to drive back today," Lauren said.

"Nyah," he insisted. "I'm good," he said. "I just hope Henry will sleep most of the way."

"He's a good little world traveler," Bahati said, running her hand over the baby's copper hair.

"Well, he better be. He's my kid." Rowan beamed proudly. "Come on, let's go."

～

THEY SPENT WEEKS FINISHING UP THE POST PRODUCTION OF the two-hour special episode of *The Veritas Codex*. Lauren and

Rowan had been lauded by the Mexican Government, the Maya Preservation Society, and the Historical Society of the Yucatán. The University of Mexico had taken over the archeological management of the cenote south of Chichén Itzá. Curators of the site at Chichén Itzá ultimately had control over the cavern where the treasures had been found. Those would most likely go to a museum once Lauren and Rowan and the site's team had completed the initial cataloging of artifacts and treasures.

The charges against Mateo were a laundry list of offenses ranging from murder, kidnapping, escape from custody, eluding capture, bribery of a government official, impersonating a police officer, and unlawful sale of antiquities. Charges had been brought against Stephanie as well. In the course of the trial it came out that Mateo and Wentworth had conspired to defraud her father.

Lauren's statement included Wentworth had claimed to be a victim of sexual assault at the hands of her father and that their plot had been a plan to get away from her abuser, and while that might have saved her from the most severe penalty of life in prison, it didn't keep the jury from convicting her, as well as Mateo. She was given 30 years, with a chance of parole, while Mateo faced the death penalty for the murder of the real Dr. DeLaFuentes ... and Ria Flores-Cortez, whose body was discovered only a few weeks before the trial began.

While their part in the discovery of the new Mayan calendar and the treasures that accompanied it was made know to the public, their role in the capture of a fugitive and his accomplice remained a secret they were sworn too. Lauren was happy about that. They were able to video record their statements and depositions, so they could bask in the limelight of their great accomplishment.

But the moment was bittersweet. The Network had bigger and better plans for television's top-rated travel-adventure power-couple. A new discovery awaited them with their brand new, family-themed travel show; one that would be produced between seasons of *The Veritas Codex*.

They had time before production of the pilot would begin, but they were also overdue to start their maternity/paternity leave. That was their first priority once they finished here.

"I've been thinking about your idea about finding a place outside California," Rowan said, as he packed up their equipment and Lauren sat feeding the baby.

She lifted her head, a euphoric look on her face. "What's that?"

"Well, buying a house is a serious commitment," he said. "I know we talked about putting down roots, and I still think we should, but since the market is so sketchy in San Diego, I thought maybe we could rent for a while."

"But our lease is almost up ..." Lauren started, but Rowan lifted a finger to silence her.

"You wanted to maybe find a house in Hawaii," Rowan began. "Why don't we rent a place and see if we like it."

"But Hawaii is so expensive," Lauren said.

"Can't possibly be any more expensive than San Diego," he shrugged. "Besides, if we're right there in San Diego, Jacob won't leave us alone long enough to enjoy our leave. You know that, right?" Lauren was quiet for a moment, but Rowan could see she was processing the idea. He expected her to protest, but he had a plan. "Never mind. It's a lousy idea. I don't know what I was thinking." Rowan suddenly switched speeds, making her think he thought she didn't like the idea.

"No," she said, abruptly. "It's not a lousy idea. I'm just trying to figure out the logistics."

"Look." Rowan came over and sat down beside her. "Logistics is my department. You let me work out the details."

Lauren gazed at him a moment, then nodded. "If you can make it work, I won't say no."

THE RENTED BUNGALOW OVERLOOKED THE WINDWARD SIDE OF the Big Island. It was the home she'd envisioned while searching the real estate websites all those months back in California. The exterior was painted a beautiful Caribbean blue, with white trim. There was a wrap-around *lanai*, which included a screened in room where she'd hung a cradle for Henry, next to his-and-hers rocking chairs. There was also a small breakfast table where they often enjoyed their morning coffee, grown just a few miles away. It was roasted fresh, and Rowan ground it himself. He quickly perfected an excellent cup of Kona's best.

Beautiful birds-of-paradise grew in clumps around the raised porch, along with plumeria bushes, which perfumed the air. There were tall yellow hibiscus trees, known as *Ma'o Hau Hele*, in the native tongue and the bright red berry producing *Ohelo Kau La'au* shrubs surrounding the property. Of course, the landlord had to point out each of the plants and explain their origins. Lauren was an attentive pupil. The retired schoolteacher seemed happy to impart his knowledge each time he stopped by to check on them.

LAUREN STOOD IN THE KITCHEN WITH THE WINDOWS THROWN open wide, watching the late-afternoon rain coming in off the ocean. She could hear the thud of Rowan's boots on the deck as he came up the stairs and entered with Henry in the pack on his chest. They'd made it home just before the daily deluge. They were just in time for supper.

The sun often started setting around seven, and Lauren found her circadian rhythms resetting to the daily routines of caring for her son. While Henry had arrived early and had been considered small at birth, it hadn't taken him any time to gain healthy round cheeks, and dimples much like his father. His hair was a thin mist of copper, but the wise gaze in his dark blue eyes were proof that he was also his mother's son, despite the fact that he looked remarkably like a smaller version of his father.

"How was your hike?" Lauren asked, coming over to help Rowan get the pack off his shoulders without upending Henry. The baby had been nodding off, but he brightened when he saw his momma. "Hi," Lauren grinned at him. He grinned back.

"We had fun," Rowan said. "We picked mangoes and got chased by a rooster." He produced the mangoes from the pocket on his hoodie.

"Ooh." She, took Henry and lifting him to her shoulder before she took the mango and sniffed the perfectly ripened fruit. "That smells delicious."

"We can have them in our fruit salad for dessert," he said. "What's for dinner?"

"What do you think?" Lauren asked.

"Moco loco?" He lifted a brow. "Third time this week."

"Well." She lifted a shoulder unapologetically. "When in Rome..."

"Smells delicious," he said. "Want me to hold him while you eat?"

"No," Lauren said. "Go ahead and make yourself a plate, I'll feed him and put him to bed before I eat."

AFTER HENRY WAS SAFELY TUCKED INTO HIS BASSINET, LAUREN sat at the counter while Rowan warmed a plate up for her in the microwave. When it was done, she ate. He stood across from her, cutting up the mangoes, along with some pineapple, and papayas. He'd already opened a coconut and had the sweet white flesh cut into long, thick curls in the bowl.

"We'll have to start thinking about going back to work

soon," Lauren sighed, as she ate. The cool breeze off the sea tossed her hair back. "I'm going to miss this place."

"You won't have too," Rowan said. "While I was out this morning, I made a stop at the rental office."

Lauren's brow lifted. "You did?"

"The rental agent was able to contact the owner to see if he was interested in selling," Rowan said, popping a chunk of coconut flesh into his mouth. He grinned as he chewed. "He was. So, the place is all ours if we want it."

"What?" Lauren's face lit up. "Are you serious?"

"Serious as a shark attack."

"Rowan, can we afford to buy a house here? We won't be able to stay here that often anyway. We are planning on going back to work when Henry's older." She had a list of arguments and could have kept going.

Rowan caught her hand and silenced her.

A twinkle sparked in his eye. "Actually, we can afford it," he said. "I negotiated a fair price and I've already talked to the bank. Besides, we can always rent it out when we're off on business. Tourists will pay good money through home-sharing apps, and no one will ever know it's our house. The extra income isn't needed, but it could make the house payment considering how much we travel."

"You've really given this a lot of thought, haven't you?" She softened.

"I have," he said. "Besides, what's travel without a home to come to. And if there's anything more precious than our time, and where we spend it, it's who we spend it with. I can't think of anywhere else I'd rather be, and no one else I'd rather make a home with."

"Oh, Rowan," Lauren jumped to her feet and threw her arms around his neck. "Thank you. We have a home."

"Now, about that dog..."

ABOUT THE AUTHOR

Betsey Kulakowski has thirty years of experience as an occupational safety professional and recently completed her degree in Emergency Management. She lives with her husband and two teenage children in Oklahoma. Betsey has been writing since she could, and created her first book at the age of six—cardboard cover, string binding and all.

ALSO BY BETSEY KULAKOWSKI

The Veritas Codex (Book 1 of The Veritas Codex Series)

ABOUT THE PUBLISHER

Babylon Books is a division of Bernhardt Books, a family-owned publishing house founded in 1999 that showcases emerging authors and compelling fiction.

Editor-in-Chief: Alice Bernhardt
  Chief Financial Officer: W. Harrison Bernhardt
  Marketing Director: Ralph Bernhardt

Learn more at: www.babylonbooks.net